SMALL WONDERS

SMALL WONDERS

COURTNEY LUX

interlude press • new york

ISBN 13: 978-1-941530-45-0 (trade)
ISBN 13: 978-1-941530-46-7 (ebook)
Published by Interlude Press, New York
http://interludepress.com

Book design by Lex Huffman
Cover Design by Buckeyegrrl Designs
Cover and Interior Illustrations by Elizabeth Vest

Epigraph quotation, Written by Joseph Fink and Jeffrey Cranor. Narrated by Cecil Baldwin. "The Candidate," *Welcome to Night Vale.* Episode 12. December 1, 2012. http://commonplacebooks.com/

10 9 8 7 6 5 4 3 2 1

For Janice Lux.

If you were still with us today, and I told you I wrote a book,
I know exactly what you'd say:
"Of course you did. You're the best writer I know."
Despite never having read a word I wrote.
Thank you for always believing in me.

Sleep heavily and know that I am here with you.
The past is gone, and cannot harm you anymore.

And while the future is fast coming for you,
It always flinches first,
And settles in as the gentle present.

This now, this us, we can cope with that.
We can do this together, you and I.

—Welcome to Night Vale

At first, people called me a miracle. Well, some people did anyway.

My mama didn't even know she was pregnant until one fine Sunday morning as she was walking to her car. You'd think after having had five babies already, a woman would know a thing or two about what a pregnancy feels like, wouldn't you? I'm not sure if her having no idea says more about my mama or more about me.

Story goes that my mama and a pack of my brothers were walking to the car with some groceries when it happened. The twins were hollering about a shared bottle of Coca-Cola and Gid was crying over a sore ear, so my mama turned to tell him she'd leave both his ears hurting if he didn't stop his crying. As she turned, she caught a toe on the sidewalk, tripped and then, just like that, her water broke right out front of Christ Fellowship Baptist Church.

I came so fast, she had me right there in front of that church with a whole crowd watching and Pastor Jimmy Welk in charge of delivery. Pastor Welk was pretty damn proud of himself, and I think he felt sort of responsible for me after that because he was one of the only people who stayed real nice to me during that time between when things were *kind* of bad until right before they got *really* bad.

Anyway, I was born out there in front of the church and the pastor called me a miracle, but my mama took one look at me and had only one thing to say.

"There's something the matter with his eyes."

You ever seen a newborn baby? I think they all kinda look the same, if I'm being real honest. Especially their eyes—how the hell can anyone tell when a baby's got blue eyes or brown ones or gray ones when they're that new? I sure can't.

I guess I was special or something, or maybe other people really are just better than I am at telling new-baby eye colors apart because apparently people talked about nothing else in that fucking town for weeks except that Mallory-Beth Morgan had a baby on the steps of the Baptist church, and he's got two different-colored eyes.

For the record, there's nothing wrong with my eyes. I mean they move normal and work normal and neither of them is twitching or lazy or nothing. One's just green and the other's brown, that's all. Good fucking luck trying to shrug that off in Bekket, Alabama, though.

I came into my life in that little town with a reputation before I could so much as crawl. That reputation stuck so hard that when someone made the teasing suggestion that my mama and my daddy ought to call me Trip on account of how my mama's water broke and all that, that's exactly what they did, and no one's called me anything different for as long as I can remember.

It's not my official name—there's a birth certificate somewhere with the name Trevor James Morgan printed on it. And

I suppose if I'd ever gotten my driver's license, it'd be on there, too, but Trevor James Morgan is a boy I don't know, and I'm not sure anyone else does either, so, as far as I'm concerned, that name has never been mine.

I am Trip Morgan, the would-be miracle who's got something the matter with his eyes, and I am meant for greater things.

ONE.

Today is a good day until the rain. In the early morning hours, Trip plays Springsteen and Dylan and old country songs he remembers hearing on staticky radio stations in his younger years.

People like Trip, with his plastic sunglasses and wicked smile and nice voice, the same way they like the sunshine and the park and the shopping bags on their arms. He's an aesthetic, a piece of the park, a wind-up music man. Drop some loose change in the cleaned-out coffee can at his feet and watch him go.

He doesn't take requests, but he's perfected the art of knowing what people will respond to. He trails after pretty NYU undergrads through Washington Square Park and sings the Beatles and Billie Holiday songs until, baffled and charmed, they fish a few coins from their bags and offer them up. He provides pretty boys with the same treatment with mixed results.

Tourists are the best, and Trip Morgan can spot a tourist five miles away with his eyes closed. He grins at them and pushes his sunglasses up on his head to meet their eyes. He sings them

Sinatra and Broadway tunes and any New York song he knows. The tourists are the ones who offer cash, pleased that they've funded some interesting-looking park musician.

Southern tourists are even better. Now that he's old enough to not have to worry about someone recognizing him from a PennySaver flier, Trip makes sure to talk to the southern ones. He turns up his accent to match theirs and nods enthusiastically when they tell him their hometowns as if he has any fucking clue where this or that little spit of a Mississippi town is. The southern tourists dish out fives and tens and the occasional twenty. Once, some old codger from Atlanta offered him a hundred-dollar bill and a keycard to his hotel room. Trip put both to good use and got another fifty and a few good meals out of the deal.

Today, he has encountered no southerners and only a few tourists from elsewhere, and he'd be okay with that if it weren't for the rain. It comes fast. One minute it's sunny and lovely and easy pickings, and the next the sky's gone black and people are running from the park with street-vendor umbrellas popping open over their heads or shopping bags held up as makeshift shields. Trip switches to catchy pop numbers and more recent music, but it's no use.

Some days this works. People take pity on a not-quite-twenty-something singing in the rain. Older women especially seem to take in the auburn hair stuck to his forehead and his relatively petite stature and read hungry young desperation in him. They offer him sympathetic smiles and a few soggy dollars.

Other times, playing in the rain has the opposite of his intended effect—strange boy with strange eyes playing his guitar as if he doesn't know the rain is there. Those people see the darkness in him: a boy with a chip on his shoulder that makes them nervous. Those people give him wary looks and a wide berth. Trip's not sure he blames them.

He's a little put out and a lot cold, so he sells his umbrella for a few dollars before shouldering his guitar and closing the lid on his coffee can to set to work at his other favorite occupation.

He'd been a decent pickpocket in his younger years, but now, after a lot of practice, he's a better thief and a good runner when he needs to be. Not that he steals anything of particular worth. He finds value in treasures scrounged from the bottoms of pockets.

Loose change, hair binders, halves of Vicodin, broken cigarettes, crumpled matchbooks. All of it has a purpose, a certain sense of importance. He envies women and their big purses. They've got whole bags of riches waiting to be exhumed. Though, more likely than not, those little trinkets will remain forgotten and neglected in the bottoms of Marc Jacobs clutches and Target sale hobo bags.

Other people don't see it—the value in these things. Maybe that's why he steals from them. Nothing they'd miss: a worn dollar here, a business card there. He keeps it all close and works out a life he could have if he could ever let someone keep him long enough for him to build up a treasure trove of small wonders all his own.

For now, he will live with worn shopping lists, broken crayons and ticket stubs he lifts off of others. He keeps them in a beaten-up bag that is more duct tape than canvas and lets them build up stardust. Then, in those lonely hours of the night, he scatters them across the floor and works them into constellations to which he assigns stories. Some he writes down; others, he forgets before the next day. It's not a financially savvy task, but it's his favorite, and it passes the time as well as anything else.

The rain makes his project easier. No one stops to check their pockets when they're trying to get out of the rain. Hell, no one stops to give him a second glance. People are not particularly interesting today. He acquires a heart-shaped keychain, a racy note from someone's secretary and, his most fascinating discovery, the shell of a bullet. He drops his finds into his bag and has to run after more than a couple individuals when he winds up with a credit card or a wallet. They're always all so grateful, wide-eyed and alarmed by their own clumsiness when he claims they dropped it. He's guilty of lifting a dollar or two before he hands them back. A guy has to eat, after all.

When the rain proves to be too much and the park is nearly clear, he retreats with everyone else under the arch. He sits down out of the way with his guitar on his lap, his bag at his knees. Amused by their disgust for the weather, he watches the crowd of disgruntled park-goers.

When he tires of listening to angry mutterings and he's sure no one here is going to offer him money for his services, he occupies himself with his bag. He's had to get smart about what he keeps and what he tosses. He doesn't have the space to keep it all and he's not sure his poor bag will last through much more. It's not all that hard to make a decision about what stays and what goes. Some things just aren't worth keeping: empty matchbooks, gum wrappers, dried-out pens. He disposes of those items as soon as he's given them a careful once-over to make sure there's no value in them. In a zipper pocket lined with plastic on the inside of the bag, he keeps his most important find.

He unzips it now and pulls out a few things to get to what he's looking for only after he's dried his hands as best he can on a napkin. (See? Valuable.) It's not as though he needs to look at this thing to know it. He's carried it the longest and he knows it the same way he knows the colors of his eyes and the feel of his guitar.

This item is not monetarily valuable, nor is it any more or less mysterious than some of his other finds. It's important because it's the reason he thought to start his collection of small wonders. He did not steal this particular treasure. Rather, he found it on the floor of a bus depot in Virginia back when he was barely sixteen. It's a photograph. Old, worn, handled too much.

It's not a particularly interesting picture. Three children on a white painted porch with trees reflected in the glare of the window behind them. The oldest is a boy. His hair is dirty-blond and not much shorter than Trip's, a few inches off of his shoulders. He's somewhere in his early puberty years. His legs are long and he holds himself as if he's not quite sure what to do with all his newfound height. The second child is a little girl, smaller than her brothers. She has a frizzy blond ponytail and, scowling, she stands on tiptoe to see over the rail. The third child is the middle one. He's caught in a laugh, bright and big enough to reveal a few missing teeth, and with his eyes directed at his brother. All three of them have bruised knees and summer tans and wild hair.

The back of the photo tells him nothing except for a small note in the top left corner: *The Kids—Summer 1996.* He doesn't know to whom the picture once belonged or where it was taken, but he knew the moment he lifted it off the ground that the photograph, almost as battered as he was at the time, mattered somehow. So he pocketed it and used the last of his cash for a ticket to New York City. The past few years haven't been particularly kind to his photograph. It's beaten at the edges, worn thin where he's touched it too often. The ink on the back is all but gone.

He's wary of what the rain will do to the picture, so he leaves it safe and dry in a Ziploc inside the zipper pocket and pulls out a book of poems instead. He flips through the pages and ponders idly over the annotations scribbled in the margins as he has so many times before. He's hungry and tired and soaked to the bone, but the puzzle of the book is a decent distraction.

"I've been looking for you for a thousand years, you asshole."

He doesn't look up. He focuses on replacing his things in his bag. "I saw you two days ago."

"And rent was due yesterday. Ms. Melnyk is losing her shit. The only words I know in Ukrainian are 'money,' 'late' and 'get out,' and she used all of them. Even Dev got his share in on time, and you're out here playing like it's no big deal!"

Trip does look up then. "What the fuck did you do to your hair?"

Liam touches a hand to his bleached curls. "I needed a change."

"Uh-huh." Trip offers no further comment.

"Do you have rent money or not?" Liam taps a foot against the pavement.

"Sorry, what?" Trip squints at Liam's hair. "I'm distracted."

"Fuck you." Liam kicks him in the shin. "I don't need your shit, Morgan."

"Just being honest."

"Honesty doesn't pay the rent." Liam flaps a hand at Trip's bag. "You make enough playing today to pay it?"

"That peroxide go to your head?" Trip shakes his coffee can of cash. "How much do you think I make out here?"

"Trip." He speaks through gritted teeth.

"Settle down, Marilyn. Jesus." Trip pushes himself upright, grimaces when his knees pop. "I've got more back at the apartment. Come on."

Liam opens his mouth to retaliate, but in the end just sighs. "Honestly, you are such a fucking piece of work."

"You picked me out of the crowd, pal, not the other way around."

"And I've regretted the decision every day since." Liam pops open a pink umbrella that's bowing at one side. He shifts it farther over so they can both walk beneath it.

Together, under the drooping pink umbrella, they attract more than their fair share of attention as they cut back through the park. Up close and personal, Trip is usually the more alarming figure, but, at a distance, Liam Forrester is always the one people notice first because, really, he's almost impossible *not* to notice.

For the most part, Liam's features are nothing particularly remarkable: dark eyes; dark complexion; dark, curly hair. He's handsome in a generic way, with graceful hands and eyelashes so long they nearly touch the lenses of his thick-framed glasses. It's his height that makes him stand out. At nearly six-foot-nine, Liam towers above most anyone who comes near him. He's not tall in an athletic sort of way either. Liam is all long, thin limbs that look as if they ought to creak and groan like the staircase of an old house when he walks. Trip has always been reminded of the big daddy longlegs that used to skitter across the side of the trailer back in Alabama. And, as if his height didn't already make him the most notable figure in any space, Liam has an affinity for doing all kinds of bizarre things to his hair, although something about his current bleached curls is particularly alarming.

Trip tips his head back to study Liam's hair again, but it is just as off-putting as the first time he saw it. "You really going to keep it like that?"

"I don't have a problem not sharing this umbrella if you're going to keep acting like a prick." Liam sniffles. He peers at Trip. "What the hell have you been doing all this time, anyway?"

Trip yawns. "More of a 'who have I been doing' sort of thing."

"Based on your usual brand of customer, I'm sticking with 'what.'"

Trip snorts. "Nothing and no one particularly fascinating, and no one who fed me much more than a little vodka. I'm fucking starving."

"That's your problem to sort out. I don't have money to feed you." Liam shrugs.

Trip digs in his bag until he comes up with a cigarette. "You gotta light, at least?"

"You've got everything imaginable in that stupid bag and you don't have a lighter?"

Trip shakes an empty brown lighter at Liam. "Not one with any fluid in it."

"Go find yourself a new one then, magic man. I've given up smoking." Liam catches the cynical look Trip throws him and pauses to glare back. "I have! It's too expensive."

"So is all that hair dye." Trip nods at Liam's curls. He steps closer, sneaks a hand toward Liam's hip. "Not to mention the canvas and acrylics and brushes you literally burned last week."

"The paint- and canvas-burning was a symbolic gesture to cleanse my artistic palate. And at least the hair dye won't kill me." Despite Liam's irritation, he isn't oblivious to Trip's fingers. He slaps at his wrist. "Fuck you! Get your hand out of my pocket!"

Trip retracts his hand and makes a show of rubbing his wrist, although Liam's done no real damage. Trip's not used to getting caught, but since the previous spring Liam's managed to call him out nearly every time he's tried to get a look in his pockets. "You're getting too good at that."

"I've had three years of practice with your sticky fingers, you obnoxious hillbilly. Go find a mark dumber than me."

"Don't call me that." Trip tucks the cigarette back into his bag. "You're the hillbilly, not me. Look at a map, you fuckin' hick."

“I’m not a hick. I think I was a Tibetan monk in a past life, or maybe one of those big rainforest butterflies.” Liam cocks his head to the side, thoughtful. He casts a look at Trip. “You’re still channeling some residual sewer rat or something.”

“Only life I’ve ever known is this one, and I call a spade a spade, Forrester; you’re one of the hill people.” Trip knocks the umbrella from Liam’s grip. “And I’m third- or fourth-generation white trash. Ain’t no butterflies or monks for us.”

“You prick!” Liam reaches for the toppled umbrella with one hand and clamps the other over his hair.

Trip moves away fast, wary of the punch Liam will most likely direct toward his arm after he’s got the umbrella back overhead. Liam’s usually good to him, but even Trip knows when not to push his luck. He’s late on rent, he’s gone missing for a few days and now he may or may not have ruined Liam’s hair.

Trip and Liam have known each other a long time. They first met on the bus from Virginia to New York when Liam—apparently oblivious to the way Trip had curled himself safe and small beside a window trying to be less visible—had dropped down in the open seat beside Trip and asked to draw him. Trip had refused, shocked and angered by the request. Liam had looked from Trip’s split lip to his hands curled around the neck of his guitar and nodded as if his refusal made sense.

He’d kept the seat, though, and spoken in hushed tones about his recently drafted artistic mission statement, which included moving to a place that pushed him to his creative edge. Trip had no idea what he was talking about, but when Liam suggested they stick close for a while once they arrived in the city, he’d had no reason to refuse.

They fight almost constantly. Trip is too crass and too rough for Liam’s tastes; Liam is too sensitive and whimsical for Trip’s. But that shared first few hours of their relationship on a hot bus barreling toward the unknown largeness of the city had bonded them in some unspoken way that neither has been able to shake.

The umbrella is back over Liam's head. The drooping side is even worse from its fall, but he doesn't seem to mind. He's frowning; his gaze on Trip doubles back the way they've just come. "Where the hell are you going?"

"Not far," Trip calls over his shoulder. "Just have to see about that light."

"I'm not waiting for you."

"Never asked you to," Trip calls back.

"Trip, goddamn it, we need you to—"

"—Pay rent, I know. I'll be back soon." Trip twists to look back at Liam. "Scout's Honor."

"Boy, you are the fucking anti-Boy Scout." Liam twists the umbrella so the drooping side is behind him and he can keep an eye on Trip.

Trip presses his palms together in front of his chest. "Swear to God, then?"

Liam rolls his eyes. "You've got two hours to get your sorry ass back to the apartment, Morgan, or *I* swear to God, I'll kick your ass."

"I'd love to see you try, Forrester."

Liam turns and shouts over his shoulder. "Two hours, Trip. I mean it."

Trip watches Liam go until he's just a spot of pink floating above a sea of black umbrellas.

When he finally turns his attention back to finding a lighter, the rain is coming down even harder and almost everyone who'd been in the park has found shelter elsewhere. With a sudden lack of marks and fingers that are too shaky with hunger and cold to be trusted with quick work, Trip opts to look for a light the old-fashioned way: He asks.

People aren't particularly friendly. An older woman meets his eyes and immediately makes a wide arc around him. Another woman at least shakes her head in response before moving away from him. He tries a couple more people. Some have the decency to answer him; most take one look at him and walk a little faster.

Trip's ready to give up on the whole damn thing when someone clips his shoulder. Startled by the sudden contact, he shoves the stranger and snarls, "Hey, watch where the fuck you're going!"

It shouldn't make him as angry as it does, but he has little patience just now for anyone trying to shake him down, and his temper has never had a particularly long fuse. Besides that, he wants his cigarette for the heat of it on his fingers and some smoke in his lungs to curb the ache in his gut.

The man turns. Judging by the surprise in his brown eyes, he'd had no intention of running into Trip. He shakes his head; his gaze flits around the park as if he's not entirely sure how he got here. "Sorry. I'm distracted, I wasn't—sorry."

Trip could normally fire off some sort of smart remark or maybe push this guy enough for a fight, but in this particular moment, he's speechless.

The guy turns to walk again, and Trip acts fast before the opportunity disappears along with this stranger into some other recess of the city. The guy doesn't notice Trip's fingers touching him, nor the sudden lightness in his back pocket.

Trip stands in the rain and works fast to fish the driver's license out of the wallet he's just lifted from his discombobulated stranger.

His name is Nathaniel Clark Mackey. He's originally from Minnesota. He's twenty-six, six-foot-one, one hundred eighty-five pounds. And Trip is sure the way he is sure the sky is blue and he is never going back to Alabama that this man is the happy, bruised-kneed little boy from his photograph.

He stuffs the card back in the wallet, sets off at a jog. "Hey!"

Nathaniel doesn't slow down, doesn't turn.

"Hey!" Trip sticks two fingers in his mouth and manages one sharp, whistled note. He is not about to lose Nathaniel Mackey without at least exchanging a few words.

Nathaniel finally turns to look.

Trip slows to a walk, holds the wallet up and spins it idly between his fingers.

Nathaniel doesn't seem to see it. He's staring at Trip with so much surprise that, for a moment, Trip thinks maybe Nathaniel recognizes him, too.

"You have incredible eyes." It's spoken in a quick rush. The accent decidedly less Minnesota than Trip had expected, but definitely Midwest.

"Incredible" is not usually the word of choice for his eyes. Odd, disturbing; has-to-be-contacts, crazy-looking, yes, but "incredible" is a new one. Trip regards him. "It's been said."

Nathaniel has the decency to blush; his gaze drops. "I just—I mean—"

Trip almost laughs, amused with this bumbling, nervous person. He lifts the wallet higher. "Missing anything?"

Nathaniel studies the wallet in Trip's hand with something akin to alarm while he pats his back pockets. "Oh. Yeah, I guess I am. Thanks."

Trip is still watching him as he hands off the wallet. "You're welcome, Nathaniel."

Nathaniel meets his gaze again. He frowns. "Do we know each other?"

Trip cocks his head to the side with a smirk. "Not just yet."

TWO.

Nate doesn't think Trip is funny. Nate doesn't seem to think much is funny—not their meeting, not Trip's wet clothes or the found wallet or anything about this situation. He is as solemn and gray as his three-piece suit and the weather around them. His gaze darts from Trip's left eye to his right, as if unsure where to focus.

Trip offers his hand, empty this time. "Trip Morgan."

Nate looks at Trip's wet fingers before actually accepting the handshake. His palm is dry and warm; his grip is solid in the way Trip is sure people must learn during college or those lost high school years he never experienced. "Nate Mackey."

Trip holds onto Nate's hand for a moment longer before releasing him. "Now we know each other, don't we?"

"I guess so." Nate looks Trip over and makes little effort to hide his disdain for Trip's wet clothes. "You look cold."

"And wet," Trip agrees. He waits and he's not sure exactly for what. Maybe Trip's waiting for Nate to mumble another thank-you for the returned wallet and be on his way, or perhaps mention a hotel or apartment nearby. Anything. Something.

Nate's fingers drift toward his jacket near where he's tucked his wallet safely in the inside breast pocket. He meets Trip's gaze. "Could I buy you a cup of coffee?"

They stare at one another in mutual surprise. It's the most unexpected thing Nate could have said, but Trip recovers first. He cocks his head to the side. "Sure."

"Yeah?" Nate's cheeks are pink, his eyes wide. Like this, Trip can see that child in him more readily. There's a familiarity in the way Nate is tousled and flustered by his own floundering mouth. Trip nods to confirm that, yes, Nate's boldness has paid off. He can buy him a cup of coffee.

Nate seems to find his center again. He stands straighter, steps a few inches closer so that Trip is suddenly shielded from the rain. Trip looks up at the black dome of the umbrella and scratches his wet collar. "A little late for that."

"Better late than never." Nate looks Trip's outfit over a second time, and Trip considers how he must appear to this well-dressed stranger.

His shirt is not all that bad. It's a gray V-neck T-shirt commandeered from the floor of someone's hotel room, but the rest of him is not nearly so well kept. His jeans have a hole near the knee; his once white Converse are muddied and missing much of their plastic siding. The left one's lace is broken and tied off two eyelets too low. His hair is getting long enough that he can secure much of it back in a short ponytail. His knuckles are still bruised from a confrontation he doesn't entirely remember, and his bag and guitar are as battered as he is. Men in nicer suits than Nate's have taken Trip home when he's been in greater disrepair, so he maintains his air of easy confidence.

"Unless you plan to start walking sometime tonight, I'm gonna step right back out into the rain." Trip takes a step to emphasize his point, but Nate remains by his side with the umbrella still held carefully above their heads.

Nate knows a place nearby, so Trip follows him out of the park and down a few blocks, whistling as they go and keeping an eye on the people who pass them.

At the coffee shop, Trip stands sentinel at Nate's side in line and watches the other patrons with their glasses of wine and mugs of coffee painted pretty with designs in the foam. He feels Nate watching him and he allows the continued look for a few moments before turning to meet his gaze. "It's not polite to stare, Nathaniel."

Nate's gaze jerks to his feet as he mumbles, "People call me Nate."

Trip nods, but he has no intention of calling this specter from his bag of little treasures "Nate." Nate is too unique a found presence to be called something so incredibly dull.

They order black coffees, and after following Trip's gaze to a display case of pastries, Nate adds a croissant. They tuck themselves into a front corner table where Nate takes one of the open chairs and Trip takes up residence on the bench lining the wall opposite Nate, knocking his knees in the process.

Warmer and settled in, Trip takes inventory of his things. His bag seems mostly all right, protected by too many layers of duct tape, but his guitar is dripping and sloshing with every movement. Trip tips it over on the floor beside him. Water sloshes out of the sound hole and forms a puddle beside the one at his feet.

Nate pushes a few napkins toward him, frowning as though he disapproves of this whole process. "That can't be good for it."

Trip lays his guitar across his lap and accepts the napkins. He pats the body dry, shakes his head. "She's fine."

"Doesn't all that water warp the wood or something?" Nate glances around the table as if he's hoping he might discover a few more napkins.

Trip looks over the guitar. It's on the small side; the body is all dark mahogany with a pretty decal around the sound hole. It's seen better days, though. The black plastic of the pickguard is chipping, the strings look too worn, one of the tuning pegs does not match the others and the whole thing is pretty banged up. He can think of no one in the world he has more in common with than that damn guitar. He pats its neck affectionately. "We've seen worse than a little rain."

He puts the guitar down gently on the open space of the bench beside him and reaches for his coffee, unable to resist the smell of it any longer. The mug burns his hands straight through the ceramic.

"It's hot," Nate warns. His hands are wrapped around his mug, but his coffee remains untouched.

Trip takes a drink anyway, but Nate's right. It scalds his tongue and the back of his throat. "Very hot."

He wants the damn coffee in a bad way, so, hoping he's burned his tongue as badly as he can, Trip tries for another drink. He cringes when it burns his tongue a second time, and Nate sighs audibly. "You could wait a second for it to cool down."

"I could," Trip agrees. He considers trying one last time, fairly certain he's running out of layers of skin on his tongue to burn through. When he lifts the mug, soft fingers on his wrist stay his hand barely an inch from the table. He meets Nate's eyes and raises his eyebrows in silent question.

Nate releases him, then pushes the plate with the croissant toward Trip. When Trip just stares at it, not sure what permission is being granted, Nate motions. "Eat it. You're driving me crazy with the coffee. My mouth hurts for you."

Trip doesn't need to be told twice. The croissant flakes brown crust onto the plate and melts butter-soft on his tongue. Trip moans because it's so damn good.

Nate glances around before looking down when Trip pushes the plate back his way. Nate shakes his head. "All yours."

Trip sits up straighter and pulls the plate close. "Nathaniel Mackey, you are a gift straight from God."

Nate doesn't respond. He sits with his hands wrapped around his mug and casts his gaze from his coffee to the plate to Trip's still-dripping hair. He looks vaguely uncomfortable, as if maybe he wants to say something but isn't entirely sure what.

Trip doesn't mind. He's done stranger things with stranger people, and having coffee with someone he's met barely twenty minutes ago is a nice change. He jiggles a foot under the table and studies the frown line between Nate's eyebrows. "So, Nathaniel, why the look?"

"It's Nate." Nate looks from the plate to Trip's face. He's quiet, no doubt waiting for more elaboration on the question. When Trip gives none, the frown line grows. "What look?"

"More storm clouds on your face than there are out there." Trip nods toward the rain beating against the window.

"Oh." Nate twists to look toward the window and then turns his gaze back to Trip, resigned. "Rough day, I guess."

"Boss man give it to you good?" Trip looks over Nate's suit. He doesn't know much about designers or fabrics or cuts, but he knows a good suit, and Nate's isn't cheap. He must do something Wall Street-based, probably finance.

"No, not really." Nate straightens a coffee spoon beside his mug, then clears his throat. "I got dumped."

Trip talks around another bite of the croissant. "You work with this person or what? He do it in the office?"

"No, um, he called me." Nate takes a drink of his coffee, puts his mug down. "At work."

"You got dumped over the phone while you were at work," Trip echoes. He's momentarily lost interest in eating in favor of watching Nate. "What the fuck did you do?"

"What was I supposed to do?" Nate shrugs. "Leave work and beg him to change his mind?"

Trip tilts his head. "I meant what the hell did you do to the guy that he thought dumping you over the phone on a Tuesday was a fine idea?"

Nate's eyebrows shoot up and he sneers at Trip. "Who says I did anything?"

"You got your ass dumped, didn't you?" Trip sips his coffee that's finally cooled to a more drinkable temperature. "Don't tell me he didn't give you a reason."

Nate sits up straighter, adjusts his tie and looks Trip over as though he's not entirely sure how he wound up having coffee with this person. "This is kind of none of your business."

"It's not?" Trip settles his mug down on the table. He's fully aware this is not appropriate, but he doesn't care much for appropriate and he kind of likes Nate's reproachful scowl.

Nate stares at him as if he's considering the possibility that Trip may be right and this may be a perfectly reasonable way to speak with a stranger. The expression passes quickly and he's shaking his head. "We don't even know each other."

"On the contrary, I know a thing or two about you, Nathaniel Mackey." Trip leans his elbows on the table and glances around before his gaze falls back on Nate. "What if I told you I'm clairvoyant?"

Nate looks at Trip in a way he recognizes; he's considering the possibility that Trip might be completely insane. He's seen this look before, from people in the park and the men who invite him to their hotel rooms. The look doesn't bother him; he's not entirely sure he's not a bit crazy.

"Um... cool?" Nate looks between Trip's eyes again, guarded.

Trip doesn't want Nate to get up and go, so he tries to make his expression more teasing. "I knew your name, didn't I?" Nate nods but says nothing, so Trip tries a new technique. "Let's make a deal."

Nate looks as though he isn't entirely sure he wants to make a deal with the crazy kid from the park who doesn't own an umbrella or have the sense to seek shelter when it rains. He drums a finger on the tabletop. "What kind of deal?"

"I tell you three things I know about you." Trip holds up three fingers. "And you tell me why you got dumped."

Nate eyes him, clearly wary of whatever trick this might be. "You're not gonna tell me I've got brown eyes or I'm drinking coffee or some bullshit like that, are you?"

"Please." Trip tries to match Nate's reproachful frown with one of his own. "I'm better than that."

Nate sighs, apparently resigned to indulging Trip's game. "Fine."

Trip sticks out a hand. "Gotta shake on a deal or it's no good, Nathaniel."

Nate reaches for Trip's hand. His grip is as firm as it had been in the park; his palm is warmed from his coffee mug. "All right, go ahead and read my mind then, I guess."

Trip props his elbows on the table and leans close; his gaze flits over Nate's face. He knits his brow and hums a note under his breath. "Give me a second."

"Fine." Nate lets out a surprised laugh, and the sound of it shakes some of the grayness from his body.

"You should laugh more. You've got a nice laugh." Trip's eyes come up to meet Nate's. "You used to—laugh more, I mean. You were a happy kid."

Nate snorts and rolls his eyes. "That's hardly reading my mind."

"Just getting warmed up, pal." Trip studies him before speaking again. "You've got a younger sister."

Nate shifts in his seat. At first he looks surprised, but then he's clearly decided it could be a good guess, nothing more. Trip holds his gaze and keeps equally quiet, hoping for some extra detail Nate might provide—where his sister lives or what she does or if she still scowls the way she did as a child. Nate simply responds, "Nora."

Trip drums his fingers on the tabletop and makes a show of looking deep in thought. "You're not from here."

"Neither are you." Nate lifts his coffee mug to his lips. "I'm not a mind-reader, and I can still figure that out. Where are you from?"

"South of here." Trip's not interested in sharing pieces of himself; he just wants some extra piece of Nate, some added piece for the puzzle of the photograph in his bag. "And you're from Minnesota. Do you have a white porch? I'm seeing one of them big ol' white porches with the green floorboards."

Nate coughs around his coffee. His knee knocks Trip's in his sudden surprise. "How do you know that?"

"I'm right, yeah?" Trip laughs. He is near-giddy to have this particular detail confirmed.

Nate's expression softens. "You ought to laugh more, too."

Trip's always found his laugh odd. It's loud and hoarse and happier than he feels most of the time, but Nate is not the first one to compliment it. "I laugh when things are funny."

"So do I." Nate nudges his toes underneath the table. "You still have one more."

Trip is still reeling over the thrill of having the detail of the porch confirmed, so he forgets to maintain the showman aura when he offers his final fact. "You're a middle child. You got that baby sister and an older brother, yeah?"

Nate looks suddenly even drearier than he had out in the rain. He shakes his head.

Trip is oddly panicked that he has made a mistake and he does not know the person across from him after all. "No?"

"I..." Nate meets Trip's eyes. He opens his mouth, closes it. He looks down at the tabletop. "I do, kind of."

Trip is soothed slightly, but he watches Nate, intent on reading the words that he had decided not to say. He can't find them.

"He said I lacked passion." Nate speaks suddenly, his gaze still on the tabletop.

Trip blinks, frowns. "Huh?"

"You named three things and a deal's a deal." Nate looks less miserable discussing this particular subject, although not much. "My boyfriend dumped me because he said I lacked passion... or we lacked passion. Something about passion."

Trip wants to know about that older brother, but, for now, he can let it be. He studies Nate's drooped shoulders and perfectly kept dirty-blond hair. "I guess I can kind of get that."

"Thanks a lot," Nate mumbles.

A shiver works its way up Trip's spine even in the relative warmth of the café. He wraps his hands around his coffee mug. "What's the ex-boyfriend's name?"

Nate sips his coffee before responding. "Lovett."

Trip laughs. "Really?"

"Yeah." Nate looks at him, reproachful. "I thought you only laughed when something was funny."

"Hell, if that's how the guy introduces himself, that is goddamn funny." Trip takes a drink of his coffee, still grinning at Nate over the rim of his mug. "That's his honest-to-God name?"

"It's not that weird. It's just waspy. Like yours."

"I can promise you, Nathaniel, my name ain't the product of Park Avenue parents." Trip gives Nate a once-over. "A full-grown man, you'd think he'd change it or something... Unless he's not a grown-up. You're not one of those creepy kiddie-fuckers, are you?"

Nate looks at him sharply, but then relaxes. "He's twenty-four."

Trip shakes his head in a continued show of disgust. The name doesn't actually bother him, but it's fun to get Nate riled up.

"How old are you?" Nate looks Trip over. "You go to college around here?"

"How old do you think I am?"

Judging by Nate's expression, he can't quite make up his mind. "Christ, you're not like some high school kid or something, are you?"

Trip cocks his head to the side. "Why? You have plans for me, Nathaniel?"

Nate blushes scarlet. "It would just—that'd be weird, ya know? I mean, like, I'm—"

"Twenty-six."

Nate is apparently too flustered to ask how Trip knows another detail about him. He fiddles with his coffee mug. "So you're how old then?"

"Does it matter?" Trip nudges the handle of the coffee spoon beside Nate's mug.

Nate reaches out to straighten the spoon. "You know how old I am."

Trip waves him off. Nate seems like a good guy, but nineteen might seem too young to him, and Trip's not ready to cut him loose just yet. "Hush, I wanna hear more about this Lovett thing. How long were you with him?"

Nate shifts in his seat as though unsettled at being put off, but he responds all the same. "Four and a half months."

"Where'd you find him?" Trip asks.

Nate hesitates for a beat. "Um, eHarmony?"

Trip laughs again. It's been a long time since he laughed so much. "Not even Grindr? You met this guy through eHarmony?"

"You're a dick." Nate folds his arms and his posture grows stiff.

"You're absolutely right, I am," Trip agrees. "So you met Lovett—the boyfriend of four and a half months—on eHarmony, went on some lovely coffee-shop and museum-touring dates, and then this guy dumped you over the phone at work because you're as dry as day-old toast. Am I following this right?"

Nate's shoulders droop. He turns Trip's empty plate in a slow circle on the tabletop. "That pretty much sums it up."

"Jesus." Trip pushes his hair off of his forehead and out of his eyes. "Sugar, you need a shot of whiskey, not a cup of coffee."

Nate looks up, clearly charmed, but by what, Trip's not entirely sure. "He called me when he was about to get on the subway."

Trip is pleased and surprised Nate has offered this small piece of information without prompting. "Of course he did. Do you think he's fucking somebody else?"

"Maybe. I don't know." Nate keeps spinning the plate in slow circles.

Trip's never been in any sort of relationship, but he's fairly certain that people are supposed to seem more upset when they get abruptly dumped, especially when the dumping happens over the phone in the middle of a Tuesday. He reaches across the table to close a hand around Nate's arm. "Nathaniel, calm down. Try to put a cap on all that boiling jealousy and rage."

Nate stares down at Trip's hand until he tucks it back into his lap. "I wasn't in love with the guy or, like, planning on marrying him or anything."

"If you're not jealous, maybe you should be pissed that he was such a dick about the whole thing. Seek revenge or something, ya know?" Trip flaps his hands. "Go put laxatives in his coffee or fuck up his place or tell all his people he's got herpes or something."

"I'm a little old for revenge plots." Nate rubs at a water spot on the handle of his spoon with one of the napkins from the table. "It just kind of 'is what it is' at this point. It's fine."

"'Fine' is what people say when they don't wanna say what they're actually feeling." Trip lifts his cup and is disappointed to find it nearly empty. He finishes off what little there is.

Nate looks into Trip's mug and then his own. He fidgets with the handle, talks down toward his empty cup. "You want another cup of coffee?"

Trip wants five more cups of coffee, ten more cups of coffee, twenty more cups of coffee, and whatever time that buys him in this corner of a café with Nathaniel. He shakes his head. He has rent to pay and Liam waiting at home to tear him apart for being late. Normally these things would not bother him. What makes him uncomfortable is how much he wants that second cup of coffee. "Can't. Places to be."

"All right." Nate looks vaguely disappointed, but he pushes himself upright and waits at the edge of the table while Trip gathers his things.

They walk outside together to discover the rain has abated but has not gone entirely. Nate pops open his umbrella and holds it over both of their heads.

Nate shows no signs of leaving, so Trip rifles through his bag before coming up with a slightly soggy cigarette. "You got a light?"

Nate reaches into his pocket and offers a silver Zippo.

Trip accepts the lighter. "Good man."

Nate glances out toward the rain. "You taking the train home?"

The lighter flares orange and warms Trip's face with its small flame as he lights his cigarette. He inhales deeply, then blows smoke toward the street as he offers back the lighter. "Nah, I'm gonna walk."

Nate accepts the lighter and returns it to his pocket. "You live around here?"

Trip blows a stream of smoke in Nate's direction. "Why? You looking to come home with me?"

"I'm just asking a question," Nate snaps.

Trip lowers the cigarette. "Yeah, I live around here. You Upper West or Upper East?"

"Who said I was either?"

Trip takes another drag on his cigarette and doesn't say anything. He knows Nate's type. If it's not the Upper East Side or the Upper West Side, it's Gramercy Park.

"Fine." Nate speaks after a brief silence. "Upper East."

Trip flicks ash toward his shoes. "Doorman and that whole bit?"

Nate shrugs. "It's got a decent lobby."

Trip hums a thoughtful note. "Sounds nice."

If Nate wants to take him home, this will be when he decides to do it. It wouldn't be hard even for someone as bumbling as Nathaniel Mackey, and it wouldn't be totally unexpected. Nate's having a bad day, he's just been dumped and he has the lonely, put-out look of an abandoned puppy. Trip might even like going home with Nate. He's handsome, broad-shouldered and tall. His eyes are a warm honey brown and his nose is just a little crooked. Besides that, Nate does not seem like the type to send Trip home with injuries that won't heal themselves within a day or two.

Nate looks at him as if he's considering the same thing. His eyes drift from Trip's slim hips to the wiry muscles of his arms to his hair and then back down to his wet T-shirt. He holds out his umbrella toward Trip's unoccupied hand. "Here."

Trip assesses the umbrella in Nate's hand, confused about what it is Nate wants from him.

"Take it. I've got another at home and I'm taking a cab anyway." Nate tucks the umbrella into Trip's hand. "Consider it a thank-you for getting my wallet back to me."

Trip startles at the contact, but he holds on to the umbrella. He stretches his arm so they can both stay underneath. It's not an easy task. Nate's a good half-foot taller than him. "I thought that's what the coffee was for."

Nate shakes his head when Trip offers his cigarette. "Coffee's just coffee."

Trip studies him, perturbed. Nate apparently doesn't want to take him home, nor does he want so much as a drag from his cigarette. It's strange and amusing all at once, so Trip offers him a smile. "Thank you, Nathaniel."

"Nate." There's a cab with its light on coming down the street. Nate steps toward the curb and sticks out a hand. "Nobody calls me Nathaniel."

The cab pulls over. Nate and Trip stare at one another.

"Thanks again for the coffee." Trip spins the umbrella. "And this."

"Not a problem." Nate nods. "So, um..." He looks at Trip, as if waiting for him to fill in the silence.

The cab driver opens his window. "Buddy, you wanna ride somewhere or what?"

"Yeah, sorry." Nate looks from Trip to the cab driver and back to Trip. "Maybe I could give you my—"

Trip steps forward before he can think about what it is he's going to do. He lifts the umbrella higher, pushes himself up onto his toes.

The kiss is so sudden and so brief, Trip's not sure either he or Nate fully register that it's happening. It's not passionate; it doesn't taste like coffee or spring or fate or whatever the hell it is people think kisses taste like. It's quick and light, and Nate smells like cologne, something woodsy. Trip has barely had the thought before he's stepping back and away from Nathaniel and his cab.

Nate appears slightly stunned but not altogether unhappy.

Trip watches him from beneath the shelter of the umbrella. "Goodbye, Nathaniel."

Nate pulls open the cab door, hesitates. "So maybe I'll see you around?"

"Maybe," Trip agrees.

It's not too late for Trip to just get in the cab. Nate could reach for him and pull him in for a better kiss. Trip could change his mind about that second cup of coffee. Nate could suggest they make plans for drinks and a meal better than a day-old croissant. The next few moments could play out in a million possible ways.

Trip takes another step back.

Nate slips into his cab and waves an awkward goodbye through the window.

Trip winks and waves back. He walks south. The cab takes Nate north.

Trip spins his umbrella as he walks and ponders what might have come of one more cup of coffee.

ii.

I NEVER SAW A BABY being born before last week, and it just so happens that baby and me now share a birthday.

Funny things, babies. People always think they're so fragile, but after seeing the way they force themselves into the world, I'm not sure we give them enough credit. June Noelle came a few weeks early and scared the hell out of all of us. Well, scared the hell out of me anyhow.

Scarlett had been waiting tables at night since she wasn't exactly the best material for the strip club with the whole pregnant thing. Drove Liam half-crazy that she was on her feet all day, then kept it up at night. He kept saying if she thought she needed the extra income, she ought to get a job manning a hotel lobby or something like that where she could at least sit at a desk and answer phones. Jobs like that are hard to come by, and since working was gonna have to be put off after the baby showed up and she'd still need to be able to pay rent, Scarlett switched her waitressing job from day shifts to nights and—since Liam's always Mr. Fuckin' Optimist and insisted—she gave the hotel thing a shot. Didn't get the front desk gig, but they needed an extra set of hands making beds and folding towels for people a hell of a lot fancier than us for a solid nine bucks an hour.

I don't worry about Scarlett. She's a tough girl and she can hold her own, but Jesus did she scare us when she came home from the diner looking as if she could just about drop dead she was hurting so bad. She didn't want to go to the hospital, something about fake contractions that come early and unnecessary hospital bills and that sort of thing, so she paced the apartment back and forth in that ugly green polo with her nametag still on, sweating up a storm. Hell, she brought me home a damn piece of cake from the diner and just that once made jokes about liking the cold weather. Girls and babies, man, I'm telling you. They're made of tougher stuff than what we give them credit for.

Things just got crazier from there. Jude was doing his method-acting thing and wouldn't stop with his goddamn southern accent that he's been modeling after mine; Scarlett was just about taking a knee the baby was hurting her so bad; Liam was driving us all crazy trying to capture the moment with his art or something. I just about knocked his lights out when he asked Scarlett to hold still for a second so he could paint her. Not that I was any more help than he was. I sat and watched and waited with Li and Devon and Jude. Bunch of useless boys, the whole lot of us; we all knew that damn baby was coming and all we could do was sit and stare and hope it changed its mind and stayed in Scarlett's belly.

Scarlett can usually smack us all into some sort of action when she needs to, but mostly she just kept looking out the window toward the blizzard outside and shouted at all of us to stop looking at her. I think the storm made her nervous and us watching her just made it worse.

I thought about being a good distraction and telling her about how I came to be on that same day nineteen years earlier. I could have told her about the church and Pastor Welk and my mama and all my brothers. I like to talk. I can talk for hours, but not about me. Not about Bekket or Mama or Daddy or the boys or the business or any of it, and I wasn't ready to start gabbing about it then just because it was the coldest fuckin' December we'd ever had and Scarlett was in labor and I wanted to feel like I was doing something more useful than shivering on the couch and watching her pace.

When Jude finally broke character long enough to tell her she was being stupid and we had to go to the hospital, she wasn't having any of it. Told him we had to wait. Had to be patient and just fuckin' wait one more minute. I don't know what we were supposed to be waiting for. The storm sure as hell wasn't about to let up and none of us know who June Noelle's daddy is. Scarlett doesn't believe in wasting time on bad men, so she drops boyfriends just about as quick as she picks them up and she doesn't bring many of them around. My money's on the doorman from Harlem... Jose or Jorge or something like that. Whoever it is, Scarlett's not interested in him being in the picture, so Lord knows we weren't waiting on him. The more I think about it and the more nights I hear Scarlett out in the main room walking with the baby or checking to make sure she's breathing or feeding her or just talking to her, the more I think maybe she just wanted one more minute to herself, one more minute before she had to give herself over to this other little person. I could be wrong about that, but whatever her reason was, we let her be.

Scarlett just about wore a hole in the floor with all her walking until finally her minute was up and her water broke all over Liam's salvage art project that's been taking up the left side of the family room for months now. I'd have just about died laughing if Scarlett hadn't looked so damn scared. Scarlett never looks scared. So instead of laughing, I punched Liam in the gut for hollering about his stupid fuckin' statue, then me and Devon hauled Scarlett off to the hospital. Not sure why I agreed to go. I hate hospitals and I can still smell that place like it worked its way up my nose and just decided to stay there.

Not only did I pony up and take that girl to the hospital, but somehow I managed to get saddled with holding Scarlett's hand in the delivery room while a nurse kept telling me to tell Scarlett to breathe. I had no business being in that goddamn room, but there I was, getting a talking-to from an irritated nurse about helping out my girlfriend and being "emotionally supportive." We didn't bother correcting her or mentioning we were doing the best we could with the whole breathing thing. We breathed and breathed and breathed. I dripped snow all over the place. Scarlett just about broke my hand into a thousand pieces when the nurse said to push, and then all of a sudden we had June Noelle Holliday.

Let me tell you, babies are not all that cute-looking when they come out. They holler their tiny heads off and they're a bloody, wet mess, but hell, was she an amazing sight. I think if I still believed in miracles, I'd have believed in them then because I still can't wrap my head around how incredible it was that I'd just seen a whole other person come into the world.

Scarlett says she named the baby after her dead mama. I still think it's because we're all so sick of winter already that we're just about willing to make a crossroads deal for some sunshine. That and seeing Scarlett look at that little girl for the first time, you'd think someone had put summer right there in her arms for real, she was so happy.

I keep thinking about that. About the way Scarlett looks at Junie like she's summer and sun and everything good in the world. Maybe some ladies are just meant to be mamas and others aren't, or maybe some babies are just easier to love; something in their chemistry makes them something a mama wants to hold onto. I don't know. I don't know a whole lot of babies or a whole lot of mamas, so I don't have much in the way of experience with either of them, but that question's dug its way into me just like the smell of the hospital, and I can't shake it.

Whether Scarlett got a good baby or June got a good mama, I'm not sure. They both seem pretty damn good to me, and I'm grateful for it, for June's sake at least. I don't know where you run away to when you're already in New York City.

THREE.

Trip is tired and starving. He's always so goddamn hungry. He doesn't have anything in the way of groceries, and he's not particularly interested in getting out from under the covers, so he stays where he is, listening to the noise of the apartment.

It's always loud here. Trip loves the noise. He's never lived someplace quiet, and it might make him crazy to listen to all that silence. This morning, though, the noise grates on his nerves. He's got a headache and his joints ache in a way they probably shouldn't when he hasn't even hit twenty yet. Still, he stays where he is and listens. There's the usual constant hum of the washing machines from the laundromat downstairs; Liam is hammering away at something out in the main room; Jude's running lines in the shower; and Scarlett's shouting over the baby's cries. Devon's violin is missing from the usual hum of activity, but he might not be at home. Trip blinks in the dark and wonders absently what time it is.

His room is not a real bedroom, not exactly. His bed is an egg crate folded in half on the floor of the walk-in closet, a couple blankets thrown over the top that scratch at his skin and a pillow that smells like too much Downy. There are a couple rickety shelves, three abandoned wire hangers he's never bothered to hang anything from and a pull-cord light above him with a fresh bulb that cost him a whole $2.79. He chose this space because it stays dark in the mornings and warmer in the winter than the drafty bedroom it's attached to. It gets horrendously hot in the summer, but the first few days of September have been unseasonably cool and have dropped the temperature at night enough that Trip can close the door again when he wants to. He'd almost be grateful for a little July heat. He's used to sweating, but he's never fully adjusted to the cold.

Suddenly, the sound of the door grating open against the floor is loud in Trip's ears and he's bathed in light. He groans. "What's your fucking problem?"

Scarlett settles down on the floor and lowers a mug beside his shoulder. Even with the baby wailing in her arms, her voice is clear and calm. "I made coffee and saved you some. You're welcome."

Trip peeks out from under his pillow. "What's the catch?"

"Why do you always think everything has a catch?" She bounces the baby on her lap until she settles down.

"Because there always *is* a catch." Trip shifts the pillow back under his cheek so he can see her more fully.

During the daytime hours, Scarlett doesn't usually bother with makeup and throws all of her dark curls into a ponytail, but today, mascaraed lashes frame her brown eyes, her cheeks are dusted a soft pink and her hair's washed and dried and flowing around her shoulders. She's dressed in her gray jacket and the jeans without the hole in the knee and a pair of black pumps that are more Sharpie fill-in for the nicks than actual black material. "You have a job interview."

"Smart little mind-reader." Scarlett nudges the coffee mug closer. "Drink that before it gets even colder."

"Still waiting for you to tell me what it is you want." Trip fixes her with a look.

She hesitates. "I need you to take the baby for the day."

Trip huffs out an irritated breath. "It's not my turn."

She groans and nudges him with her foot. "Come on, I'm begging you."

"No way. Nope. Nuh-uh."

Scarlett's expression goes immediately dark. She's always been good at that. Scarlett's sweet and funny and good for a dirty joke, but when she means business, she can switch from sweet as sugar to cold as ice in under a second and she's proven on more than one occasion she can kick ass when there's a need for it.

None of that fazes Trip. He returns the look. "Goddammit, Scarlett, get someone else to do it. I've got things to do."

"No, *I* have things to do. You just want the option to disappear for an afternoon for a quick fuck and a free meal," she snaps back.

He reaches for his jeans crumpled in the corner of the closet and drawls, "What're *you* out doing every night then, honey?"

It's not a fair thing to say, and he knows it. First off, Scarlett's a stripper, not a prostitute—he's the one willing to get on his knees if it means a quick twenty or a free meal. And second, the tips are damn good—a hell of a lot better than what the waitressing job paid her before they fired her on account of being overstaffed (or that's the reason they gave her, anyway). And third, it's not as if she has the option of just looking out for herself with what she can scrape together from a few odd jobs. Scarlett knows all of this and knows Trip knows it, too. She asks for no apology, just stares at Trip cold and flat, waiting.

He groans as he wriggles into his jeans. He takes the coffee cup in his right hand, holds out his left toward the baby. "Give it here."

Scarlett's expression goes from stormy to beatific immediately as she tucks the baby onto Trip's lap. She kisses June and tugs a lock of Trip's hair. "I love you."

"We're slightly resentful of you." Trip grumbles back. He sips at his coffee. It's watery and cold and he's endlessly grateful for it.

"Don't say that." She squeezes June's fisted little hand against her palm. "You think she might be?"

He grits his teeth against saying something nasty. "You weren't nearly such a sap before the baby."

"They change things." Scarlett runs a hand through her baby's hair, her expression caught somewhere between exhaustion and affection. "Babies change absolutely everything."

"Wow, glad I won't be having any to fuck with my schedule then." Trip scowls at her.

"I took in a baby when I didn't have to once, you know." She fixes him with a look. She's barely four years older than him, yet even before the more recent days of formula and Pampers and obligatory sleepless nights soothing a fussing infant, Scarlett had chosen to play mother to Trip when she could. She'd taken both him and Liam in, fed them occasional bowls of ramen and generic macaroni and cheese if tips were good, and spotted Trip on more than one occasion when he was short on rent. Scarlett's kind to all of them, but she's always been especially nice to Trip. She says she's not sure if she's got a soft spot for him because he's the baby of the apartment by a couple years, or if it's more to do with the accent and his funny stray-dog mismatched eyes.

"Jesus, woman, cut the guilt trip." Trip rolls his eyes. "I took her, didn't I?"

She pinches Trip's cheek. "Yes, you did. Thanks."

Trip slaps her hand away. "What's the job?"

"Barista near Wall Street." She pushes herself to her feet, leans in the doorway. "I figure if I don't get it, I can at least pick up an investment banker boyfriend or something."

"Dream big, sugar." Trip yawns.

Scarlett crouches to give the baby one last kiss and to shoot Trip a look. She pushes the cell phone toward him. "You know the rules."

"No smoking, no calls except for emergencies and no taking the baby along if I meet someone." Trip pockets the phone. "Yes, ma'am, I know the goddamn rules. It'd be a real shame if I broke one and wasn't allowed to get saddled with the kid anymore, huh?"

Scarlett leans out the door. Her eyes dart around the family room before she looks back at Trip. She drops her voice lower. "And no leaving her with Dev."

"What's the matter with Dev?" Trip frowns at her. "He sick?"

"Keep your voice down." Scarlett glances back out the open door. "You know as well as I do something's going on with him."

"He's fine," Trip says. Devon loves Junie. He was the fourth person to hold her after the nurse and Scarlett and Trip. He's fed her, held her and played lullabies for her on his violin her entire life. As far as Trip's concerned, there's no reason for that to change now.

"I don't trust him with the baby, all right?" Scarlett's expression goes anxious. "Please, Trip. Just promise me."

Trip shifts the baby from one leg to the other when she crabs at him. "Fine, whatever. I'll sock him if he gets close to her."

"Don't make it sound like I'm being crazy." She tugs his hair before standing again.

"Wouldn't dream of it." Trip scratches his cheek against his shoulder. "When you gonna be back?"

"Sometime this afternoon." Scarlett drags a hand through her hair and twists it into a ponytail. Trip recognizes it as her go-to stressed out move; the higher the ponytail, the higher the stress level. Right now, it's at the nape of her neck. "If it doesn't go well, I might try some other places and see what I can find."

"Could just sell Junie to some sad infertile rich people on the West Side." Trip lets June off his lap to crawl around the little space of his room. "You'd like that, wouldn't you, sugar? Some nice, rich Republicans to dress you up and make them feel accepting of semi-diverse babies? They'll probably rename you Georgia or India or somethin', but that's a worthwhile trade for the silver spoon as far as I'm concerned."

"You're not funny, Morgan."

"I'm hilarious and you're gonna be late. Get out of here before I change my mind and June's going with you."

"Fuck, you're right." Scarlett stands and disappears. She's always doing that—taking her sweet time and then all of the sudden she's a hurricane of activity. The door scrapes against the floor. "Bye, darlings! I'll see you later. Thank you, Trip!"

June notes her disappearance and crawls toward the door, already wailing.

Trip grimaces and pulls the baby back onto his lap. "Aw, come on, you know I hate that."

She struggles in his arms and howls even louder.

"Good Lord." Trip releases her just long enough to drag his bag closer. "Hey now, come on and look here, what do we have?"

June goes quieter when Trip unzips the bag, quieter still when he rifles through its contents. He doesn't have much in the way of baby-safe items. He's stolen a rattle or two off strollers over the course of the year, but those things only stay in his bag until he can get them home to June. In the end, he finds nothing he isn't nervous might choke an infant, so he zips his bag back up and just shoves the whole thing toward June. "Have at it, cricket."

June is content to pick at the duct tape and teethe on the handles of the bag, so Trip sits back against the wall to nurse his cold coffee. Not for the first time, he longs for a cup as earthy and strong and hot as the one Nate bought him earlier in the week.

He's thought about Nate at random intervals since that day, bemused by the sullen, serious stranger. Nate was all storm clouds and frustration with the only traces of his smiling, sun-tanned youth showing when he'd laughed. Trip had liked his laugh and even liked his nervous babbling. He's not sure why he let him just leave, why he didn't request an address or a phone number, or, more to his usual style, just decided to get in the cab without asking.

He could blame it on needing to get back to the apartment before Liam decided to skin him alive, but that would be a lie. Liam could never beat him in a fight, and it's not as if his sulking has ever bothered Trip all that much. He's fairly certain it's the umbrella's fault. Nate had so willingly and suddenly handed off that small treasure, it struck Trip dumb and made him forget himself. Despite Nate's willingly offered gift, Trip hadn't been able to resist his usual temptation.

Nate's pockets hadn't proven all that interesting, so all Trip has from him is a business card. It's a nice card as far as Trip can tell. It's eggshell-white, matte. There's a logo for Ashbury-Whiteman Investment Banking in the corner, a phone number, an address, "Nate Mackey" printed in all caps in the center, a smaller blurb of italicized text below his name informing Trip that Nate's a financial analyst. Trip keeps it in the Ziploc with the photo.

He can't make sense of this mirthful, vibrant little boy and this dreary twenty-something Wall Street drone. Sure, things happen, people grow up—Trip knows that better than anyone—but there's something disconnected, something stormier in Nate. That's a feeling Trip knows even better. He'd kissed Nate partly just to see what he'd do, and partly because he just couldn't stand how lonely he'd looked standing there in front of an open cab door.

June's lost interest in his bag and crawled from the closet out to the bedroom, so, with a heavy sigh and popping knees, Trip stands to follow her, empty mug in hand.

Their apartment is small, and it's seen better days. For as long as Trip has lived here, the walls have been smudged with fingerprints and cracks; the baseboards are perpetually dirty with years of grime that not even the best cleaning will remove. The wood floors are nicked and gapping in places. The far end of the family room is packed tight with a floral patterned couch commandeered from a distant relative of Jude's and a coffee table that Devon picked up on a street corner. The table doesn't sit straight and they have replaced one particularly rickety leg with a cinderblock and a stack of old magazines. Most of the room is taken up by Liam's art projects: a jumble of statues, installations and half-finished canvases. Liam practices every art form he can, and every project accrues in the far-left corner near the door leading to Liam, Devon and Jude's bedroom and spreads out like ivy over the family room.

The projects are bright and strange and they make the space feel alive and interesting, if a little claustrophobic. Liam's art has moved to the walls, too. The space around the window is colored with smudged blue sky and clouds, the doorframe leading to the hall is etched with Sharpie sketches of the city, and the space above June's playpen has been made bright and happy with a field of painted sunflowers.

The kitchen and bathroom occupy the other side of the apartment. The bathroom isn't much—a sink, a toilet, a bathtub with water pressure that varies from a drip to a beating hard enough to turn skin slightly pink. The kitchen is equally Spartan. The fridge is held shut with a carabiner and a bungee cord rigged on the side, and a card table takes up most of the floor space. Liam painted the room an alarming shade of yellow that nobody likes, but no one has bothered to change.

The apartment is as mismatched as its inhabitants. The single unifying factor is the smell of laundry detergent, chemical and clean, that permeates everything from the couch cushions to the shower curtain.

Trip follows June as far as the family room. "Wanna make me some good money at the park today, June bug?"

June Noelle Holliday is a happy baby most of the time. Her skin is the same deep tan as her mother's, her hair is dark, her eyes are big and amber-colored, and she has a strawberry-colored birthmark that covers much of her left ear and part of her cheek. She hasn't shown any interest in walking, which has Scarlett nervous, but Trip thinks she seems just fine and he's fairly certain that babies don't walk this early anyway. Besides, no walking makes his life easier when he gets bullied into a babysitting gig. Scarlett doesn't pay him, but she's usually good for a pack of cigarettes or spotting him a few dollars on the shared cellphone bill. Besides, he's owed her for a long time, and Trip Morgan has a thing about debts.

Trip scoops June up in one arm, ignoring her angry protests until he's reached the kitchen and he can put her back on the floor.

Jude's still running lines in the shower and Devon is in one of the rickety folding chairs with a water glass cradled in his hands and the paper open on the table in front of him.

Trip nods a hello while he rinses his mug in the sink. "No work today?"

Devon scratches at his neck and then his wrist, shakes his head. "Nah, man. Keep cutting back my shifts."

Devon works at a corner market in Nolita unpacking deliveries and loading them onto the shelves. The pay isn't great, but he gets to bring home the food that's about to expire. They all survive on a regular diet of bruised fruit and stale cereal.

"Tough break, bud." Trip glances at him and tries not to stare for too long.

Devon Foley's a decent guy. He's good about paying the bills and keeps his things in order and he's a regular prodigy on the violin, or at least he was all of those things. Lately Devon's been off. He has dark circles under his gray eyes, and he's testy and shifty enough to put Trip on edge. They're all small things, but, Scarlett's right: There's something up with Devon lately, and Trip knows what it is. Devon's using, or maybe just using more heavily, and it's most likely meth.

Trip knows addicts—the look, the signs, the energy. He spent a lot of hours in his formative years around them, Devon included. Devon Foley is eight years Trip's senior, and he grew up in one of the houses closer to town back in Bekket. Devon had never been that bad when he was in high school; he spent a decent amount of time around Trip's brother, Jeremiah, which meant he did a lot of drinking and smoking, and though Trip didn't spend enough time with them to know for sure, most likely a decent amount of meth. The age difference meant they never spoke more than a passing word to one another until a chance meeting in New York nearly two and a half years ago when Devon had recognized Trip playing on a street corner.

Even after their reunion in the city, Devon and Trip never spoke much of why either of them had left Bekket. All Trip knows of Devon's time in Bekket is that his parents were decent people, he did okay in school and he disappeared from Alabama three months after finishing high school. People talked about it plenty, but no one knew where Devon went or why. Trip's best guess is that Devon dreamed of something grander for his life, most likely involving playing his violin, and apparently not involving his accent, based on his near-total suppression of it.

Whatever his reasons for leaving, Devon does not hate Bekket. As his one extravagance, he has the paper delivered all the way from Bekket to their New York apartment every week. It usually shows up a few days late, but once it arrives, Devon pores over each page as though if he looks at the words hard enough, he can be back there. He offers the pages to Trip for further inspection, often with an enticing comment about one of his brothers being arrested, but no matter how the offer is made, Trip declines. He and Devon have little in common, but even if Trip doesn't want to read the weekly news of Bekket, it's nice that someone in the city knows where he came from.

"You get saddled with the kid?" Devon's attention shifts to June pulling open all of the floor-level cabinet doors. He rests his elbows on his knees to put her more at eye-level.

"Yeah, Scarlett's got a job thing. I'm gonna tote June along to the park while I play to try to take in some extra cash." Trip replaces the coffee mug in an overhead cabinet and sets to work dumping saltine crackers into a plastic bag for June to eat later on.

"Weather's nice. Should be good crowds out." Devon dips his fingers into his glass and flicks water toward Trip. "Who wouldn't want to drop a few bucks for a cute June bug and a pretty little Lark?"

"Don't call me that." Trip wipes the moisture from his cheek and flicks it back at Devon.

No one calls him "Lark" but Devon. He'd christened him with the nickname the first time he'd caught Trip singing in the shower nearly two years ago and refused to let it go. He'd taken to pinching Trip's cheeks, cooing the name at him when he's in a particularly foul mood.

"Aw, come on, Lark. A cute songbird like you shouldn't get your panties all in a twist over something so small."

"I got a name that suits me just fine." Trip stares into the fridge. He grunts out an irritated note before slamming the door and filling a sippy cup with water from the sink.

"You hungry, kid?" Devon pulls June onto his lap, but his gaze stays on Trip. "I have a bowl of leftover pasta in the fridge you can have. I can hold onto June, too, if you want to shower or something before you head out."

"Nah, man, I'm fine." Trip reaches for June and hikes her up on his hip. He feels more than a little guilty about the whole thing. Devon's still Devon, even if he does seem sketchy lately. "You wanna come?"

"What? Out to the park?"

"Yeah." Trip moves back toward the bedroom for his things, raises his voice. "If you bring your violin, you 'n' me 'n' June could make a fortune. Buy one of them rotisserie chickens from Food Emporium and a six-pack and still have cash left over for bills by the time we're done."

Devon doesn't answer, so Trip slings his guitar over his back and lifts his bag in his free hand before going back to the kitchen. Devon's still in his folding chair, picking at a fingernail.

"Hey, you hear me?" Trip drops his things and settles June down, too. He scuffs a hand through Devon's hair as he passes him to pull the stroller out of the hall closet. "Music, a trip to the park; a decent meal? Any of that interesting to you?"

"No can do, Lark." Devon sniffles and scrubs at his nose.

"What? You got better shit going on?" Trip leans hard on the handles of the stroller, but it won't unfold. He sits down on the floor to try prying it open by the wheels.

Devon pushes himself up and out of his chair. "Nah, man." He pulls the stroller out of Trip's hands. "Sold my violin."

"What the fuck?" Trip moves back a few inches when Devon kicks the stroller hard on its crossbars. "You love that thing."

"Needed the cash, brother." Devon kicks the stroller again.

"I'm gonna say it again: What the fuck, man?" Trip pulls June into his lap when she gets too close to Devon and the stroller. "You made rent fine, and we don't have electric due for another week."

"Expenses." Devon slams the stroller against the floor with a grunt. "When the fuck's Scar gonna get the kid a better fuckin' stroller, huh?"

"When she's got a violin to sell, I guess. Don't break the damn thing. Christ. Treat it like you treat a girl you wanna fuck, huh? Take it slow, see how she's feeling. Ease into it."

"This funny to you?" Devon scowls at him. "You wanna carry the fuckin' kid all day?"

"Easy, buddy. Christ." Trip raises both hands, palms out. "You mad because you can't get the stroller open or you pissed because you have a tough time getting girls to fuck you?"

"What would you know about fucking girls, Morgan?"

"Only what Scarlett tells me about her preferences." Trip yawns to cover his surprise. Devon's rarely so surly.

"Yeah, well, these days, Scarlett doesn't say shit to me, so I guess it's a good thing I got you to relay it to me, huh?" Devon grips the handles of the stroller, leans his weight into it and gives the crossbars under the stroller one final kick. It snaps open with a pop.

Trip claps June's hands together for her. "Our hero."

Devon steps back and rolls his shoulders. He frowns at the stroller. "Good fuckin' luck getting that folded back up."

Trip pushes himself upright and shifts June to his hip. "So the violin..."

"Jesus, Morgan, since when do you give a shit?"

"Since I'm out a duet partner." Trip slings his guitar back over his shoulder and drops his bag into June's stroller.

"Yeah, well, you'll figure out a new gig. You always do." Devon digs in his pocket and fishes out a pack of Marlboros. He holds out the box.

Trip's fingers twitch at his side. "Got the kid. Scarlett'll skin me alive if she thinks I was smoking with her, and you know it."

"Since when do you turn down a free cigarette?" Devon shakes the pack so it rattles with a musical little rhythm; he's suddenly much more the Devon that Trip's always known. "Smoke it later, asshole."

"Thanks." Trip pulls one out and tucks it behind his ear. "What're you gonna do with your day then?"

"People to see, shit to do." Devon pulls out a cigarette for himself before pocketing the pack and trading it for his lighter. "You gonna get gone sometime today or you just gonna keep wandering your bum white-trash ass around this apartment talking shit?"

"What the fuck's it look like I'm doing?" Trip tugs the stroller toward the front door, "And I'm not talking nothing, but speaking of big talkin' pieces of shit, where the hell's Liam?"

"Something about gallery spaces." Devon stands with the paper tucked under his arm and moves from the kitchen to the family room. He pushes open the window and holds his cigarette out it. "I'm s'posed to ask you to keep an eye out for mannequin legs."

"What's in it for me?" Trip tugs the front door open with his free hand. He hates trying to drag his guitar and bag down the stairs when he has the baby and the stroller with him.

"Didn't say." Devon blows smoke out the open window. "Just asked me to ask you. Li's always good for spotting some cash on the bills or you could ask him to buy you that six-pack, kiddo."

"Not a fucking kid." Trip pushes the stroller out onto the landing. "And how the hell am I supposed to get the damn things home when I've got all this shit?"

"Much like your duet situation, I'm sure you'll figure it out." Devon points his cigarette at Trip. "When it's a matter of a few more bucks or a free drink, you always manage to turn some kind of trick, crafty little Lark that you are."

Trip raises his voice as he steps out the door and turns his attention to the baby. "Junie, can you say 'fuck you'?"

After Trip has made it outside, having the baby doesn't seem quite so bad. She goes into the stroller, his bag goes over his shoulder and then everything is easier. Trip's mood improves when they make it to the park and find it teeming with people.

He parks June not far from the Washington Arch, puts his bag by his feet, sticks the coffee can in front of the stroller, hands a second one with a slotted lid to June and then they're good to go. It's been a while since he got saddled with babysitting duty, and, though he'd never admit it to Scarlett, he'd forgotten what a good gig it could be.

People stop to listen and coo over June, and they're all too happy to tuck some cash into both the coffee can at her feet and the one in her hands. Without counting, Trip knows it's the best he's done in weeks.

They take a break when June throws a tantrum over being strapped into her stroller for too long and Trip's forced to follow her in slow circles around the park and pull wrappers and cigarette butts from her sticky hands. She throws a second tantrum when he won't let her in the fountain, but is quickly mollified when he purchases a squeeze package of applesauce for her from a nearby store and lets her make a smeary mess out of the applesauce and the crackers he'd packed. After that, she promptly passed out in her stroller. Trip takes the opportunity to get out of the park and study the trash outside a few storefronts. He doesn't find any mannequin legs or any other body parts, so he goes back to the park to keep playing while the crowds are still good.

He keeps out of people's pockets because babies draw attention and June's stroller won't allow him to run, but even that doesn't bother Trip today. He's had to dump both cans of cash and change into his bag to make more room by the time the sun starts to sink in the sky. He's sitting on a bench with June parked at his side and studying his fingertips, which are bloodied from a few too many hours of playing, when a familiar voice calls out.

"How'd I know I'd find you two here?"

"If I'm gonna get stuck with your kid, I might as well take advantage." Trip gives Scarlett a once-over. She's flushed and happy-looking. "How'd the interview go?"

"Oh, there's no way in hell I got it." She stoops to unbuckle June from her stroller. "Hello, my angel! How are you, hmmm? Trip, did you feed her?"

"No, I let the kid fuckin' starve." Trip sighs when Scarlett looks at him darkly. "Yeah, she made art with some crackers and we stopped in a bodega for one of them squeeze things. Do you have any idea how fuckin' expensive those are?"

"Well aware." Scarlett kisses June's cheek and snuggles her close. "I'll reimburse you, I promise. Oh, look at you, pretty baby, did you have a good day? Tell Mommy all about your day. Trip, you can put your bag in the stroller. I'll carry her home. Mommy's not ready to put her baby down, is she?"

"You're awful fuckin' happy for someone who just got shafted from a job." Trip drops his bag into the stroller and shifts his guitar to his back as he pushes himself to his feet. "You get somethin' else?"

"Didn't even try." Scarlett tears her attention from the baby to look at Trip. "I met someone."

Trip pulls his cigarette from his pocket, thrilled to finally be able to smoke it. "You telling me I got saddled with mandatory celibacy and a day with your drool monster so you could get a good fuck in?"

"I'm not you, Morgan. For me, meeting someone doesn't mean a three-hour romp in the sheets and then going on my way."

"I appreciate your opinion of my endurance." Trip digs a book of matches out from the mess of things in his bag.

"Stay away from us if you're going to be smoking that." Scarlett takes a few steps away from Trip as they make their way out of the park. "He bought me coffee."

"Well, ain't you special?" Trip takes a long drag on his cigarette. It makes him dizzy. "And for all you know, I've gone to coffee with people before."

"Sure you have." She rolls her eyes, but then she's casting a dreamy look toward the leaves above them. "We talked for forever."

Trip makes a show of gagging. "Jesus, woman, you going soft on me or somethin'?"

Scarlett doesn't acknowledge the jab. She takes a step in closer to Trip despite the cigarette. "He was just so good, ya know? There aren't a lot of good guys out there."

"You live with one." Trip takes a step to the side to put the distance back between them.

"I'm still a little convinced those eyes of yours are a sign you've got one foot here and one foot somewhere else entirely."

"Heaven?" Trip casts an innocent smile her way, but then laughs at how incredulous she looks. "I was talking about Liam, but, wow, cool. Good to know where we stand."

She shoves Trip a few inches away. "He wants to take me to dinner tomorrow."

"Who, Liam?"

Scarlett pushes him again, irritated this time.

"Take a joke, would you? And congrats, I guess." Trip blows smoke toward the street away from June and Scarlett. "D' you manage to mention in all them hours of talking that you have a kid you handed off to your roommate for the day?"

"Well, no, it seemed too soon." She rubs June's back. "Like 'Hi, my name's Scarlett, I'm a single mother.' Fuck, should I have?"

"You really wanna ask me about what's considered okay when it comes to lying to a stranger?" Trip quirks an eyebrow at her.

"Fair point." She drums her fingers on June's back. "I don't think he'd mind."

They're nearing their door, so Trip slows to finish the last of his cigarette. "And if he does?"

"Then he's not as good of a guy as I thought and he can kiss my ass." Scarlett hikes June higher up on her hip.

Trip holds the front door of their building open. “What about the whole I-rub-up-on-poles-in-a-thong-for-cash thing? He know about that?”

“Is there a reason you have to shit on everything, or are you just being a moody teenager?”

“My, oh my, look at you, all bent outta shape.” Trip follows as the stroller bangs on the edge of every step. “You know I don’t care what the hell you do to make your money, but I’ll take that attitude as a very solid, ‘No, I didn’t tell him.’”

“Would you mind folding that up instead of making all that noise?” Scarlett fishes out her keys when they reach their floor. “You’re gonna piss off Ms. Melnyk and scare the baby.”

“No way in hell am I folding this back up. We just about killed ourselves this morning trying to get it open,” Trip snaps right back. “By the way, you’re fuckin’ welcome for takin’ your baby all day so you could go play house with your coffee guy.”

Scarlett lowers the baby to the floor when she gets the door open and turns a softer look toward Trip. “Thank you.”

Trip shoves the stroller into the corner and shoulders his bag to take back to his room. He doesn’t care much whether he receives anything in the way of gratitude, but he’s antsy and tired of this conversation. “Uh huh.”

Scarlett stops him with a hand on his elbow and touches a kiss to his cheek. She rubs the lipstick off of his skin gently. “I mean it, Trip. Thank you.”

He’s embarrassed under the softness of the contact and has to hide a blush. None of them are particularly prone to shows of affection. “Yeah, whatever.”

Scarlett doesn’t let go of Trip’s arm. “Wanna make a deal?”

He can’t help but be at least mildly intrigued. Trip loves the opportunity for a good deal, and this seems more natural than talking about Scarlett’s Prince Charming. “What kind of deal?”

"Give me five bucks and take June for like ten more minutes—"

"Fuck you." Trip cuts her off, angry already.

"Jesus, you and that fucking temper. Would you mind settling down and listening for a second?" Scarlett pauses before speaking again. "Watch June, give me the cash and I'll go buy us a case of beer and a couple slices of pizza."

Trip tries to look indifferent while he considers it.

She pinches the back of his arm. "Don't even try to pretend you're not totally on board with this. You never say no to a drink, especially when I'm offering to pay for most of the beer."

Trip unzips his bag to pull out the cash. "Fine. Deal."

Scarlett pockets the money and the cell phone when Trip offers that, too. She raises her voice to be heard by anyone else who might be home. "Boys, Trip and I are going in on a case and some pizza, does anyone wanna get in on it?"

"Hey, yeah, I could go for pizza!" Jude calls from the kitchen; his voice is nasal and sharp with a fake Jersey accent.

"You keep up that fuckin' accent, man, and all you'll be getting is my fist in your face," Trip shouts back.

"Watch the violence talk, remember?" Scarlett points at June as she moves toward the kitchen. She's shockingly tolerant of cursing, but she gets sensitive about any mention of fighting.

"Right, because that's our biggest concern with a baby in this apartment." Trip watches while June tries to pry a piece off of one of Liam's sculptures.

Scarlett returns from the kitchen, pushing more money into her pocket as she goes. "If you wanna insult my parenting, Morgan, you better be prepared to do it to my face."

"You say you're making a beer run?" Devon appears from the second bedroom, cash in hand.

Scarlett stares at him for a moment before responding. "Yeah, do you want in?"

"Nah, but pretty sure I owe you a few bucks." Expression grim, he offers the crumpled dollar bills.

Scarlett stares at the money. "Thanks."

He nods a quiet acknowledgement.

Scarlett turns her attention to Trip. "If you want, I could take June with me."

"Get gone." Trip waves her off and scoops June up with one arm. "Another half-hour with her won't kill me, and you're not gonna have enough hands. I got her. Really."

"I'm headed out." Devon moves toward the door. He pauses with his hand on the knob. "If that makes you feel any better."

Before anyone can respond, the door opens and closes and Devon is gone.

Scarlett stares at the closed door and twists her hair into a ponytail at the crown of her head before letting it down with a sigh. "I won't be long."

Trip waves goodbye before settling down on the floor with June. He fills one of his empty coffee cans with odds and ends from his bag and puts the lid back on it before offering it to June.

She shakes it so hard she nearly topples herself and shrieks with delight at the sound it makes. Jude shouts something, apparently irritated by the noise, but Trip makes no move to take the can away. June's busy and it gives him time to count out the cash he's made today.

It's good money and it'll cover his portion of their bills for the month. He should feel good, or at least less stressed, but he's uneasy. He wishes he could have one of those promised beers now. The weather is turning cold far too soon for Trip's taste, and, come winter, he knows he won't be making even half of what he does now when he goes to play in the park. Rent split between five people is hard enough, not to mention electric and the cellphone and food and whatever else they need. Trip can't afford to be out a roommate. He counts his cash and convinces himself he's worried about the rent, and not about losing the only person in New York who knows where he came from.

FOUR.

Trip wakes to the sound of slamming washing machine doors and the dull rumble of dryers. He's sore and disoriented and vaguely aware that the apartment is quiet. He pushes himself upright and shoves his hair out of his eyes. He needs a haircut. He also needs Advil and a cup of coffee.

He flexes his fingers around his calves, feels the pull of it in the muscles of his back and thighs. Last night had been too much cheap alcohol on an empty stomach. Last night had been a guy Trip should have known better than to follow home. Last night had been a mistake. He pushes himself into action by tugging himself to his feet with one hand on the doorknob.

The light is already fading in the bedroom, and the sun glows pink on the unmade bed. The chemical aroma of paint wafts over the usual overpowering smell of laundry detergent and fabric softener. Trip follows it to the family room, struggling into a pair of jeans as he goes.

June burbles a happy hello and reaches sticky hands his way from her Pack 'n Play shoved up beside the couch.

Liam's hunched over a canvas lying flat on the floor, his legs folded under him. He doesn't look up, but he waves a magenta-saturated brush toward the kitchen. "There's some coffee left. It's cold and probably pretty burned. Basically, no one remembered to clean the pot out this morning."

"Just the way I like it." Trip squeezes one of June's chubby wrists before going to the kitchen for a mug. There's not much left of the coffee and it leaves Trip's cup half-empty, but he'll take anything he can get. He microwaves the cup for thirty seconds before returning to the family room. He drops down to the floor, grimacing as he leans back against June's playpen.

Liam smears his paintbrush on a color-stained palette. He still doesn't bother turning his gaze Trip's way. "Didn't hear you get in last night."

Trip nurses his coffee. It's bitter. "Didn't get in until late... or early, I guess. What time is it?"

"Like six." Liam finally does look at Trip. There's a spot of blue paint in his hair. "You slept all day."

Trip tugs a couch cushion onto the floor and shifts it under himself. "I've got all night to make myself productive. Say, is that paint in your hair an accident or a new look?"

"Hilarious as always, Morgan." Liam turns his gaze back to his canvas. "Call it a highlight of inspiration, I guess."

"You think these fumes are okay for the kid?" Trip does nothing to stop June when she reaches over the side of the playpen to tug his hair.

"Window's open and I put the fan in it." Liam motions toward where the window's propped open with a wooden dowel. "You can take her for a walk if you want."

"Mmm." Trip's not feeling entirely up to a lot of movement. He sips some more coffee. "Where's everyone?"

"Working." Liam chews the end of his paintbrush. "And so am I right now, so hush."

"Even Jude?" Trip glances toward the second bedroom. Jude's always getting prepared for roles that never seem to actually happen. When he's not keeping them all up with his incessant line-running, Jude picks up occasional shifts as a bar back, but that's usually only a late-night ordeal.

"Might be doing 'role research' somewhere, but I think he might have actually had something to get to." Liam sets to work on a new stroke against his canvas with one hand braced on the floor while he works. "Who knows with him?"

"He still doing the Jersey thing?" Trip finishes off his coffee and abandons his mug on the coffee table. "I swear to God, if he doesn't move on to something new, I'm gonna off him."

"I remember asking you to please shut up so I can focus on my work, like, barely a minute ago." Liam frowns at Trip over his shoulder before turning his attention back to his painting.

June starts crying, mumbling a sad "mamamama" on repeat. It's too early for a bottle and too late for a nap, but her schedule has been more than a bit off for the past couple weeks. Scarlett thinks she's cutting new teeth.

"So get a studio where I can't bug you." Trip lifts June up over the side of the playpen so she can sit in his lap. "Scarlett get a day shift somewhere?"

"Laundry at the Radisson or the Hyatt or wherever it is she was working when she was pregnant," Liam mumbles, caught up in his work for the moment. "Someone called in sick, so she picked up the shift."

"Hmmm, good, more laundry in our lives is exactly what we need." Trip shifts the baby until she's lying with her head on his shoulder. She keeps crying, but he ignores her and pats her back. Even if it is too late for a nap, Trip doesn't mind. He's got baby duty tonight and he doesn't usually sleep that well anyway, so the notion of waking up with June at odd hours isn't all that bothersome. "She coming back before her shift tonight?"

"No, she's going straight there from her—shit!" Liam sits back suddenly. "I totally forgot."

"Paint goes on the brush, then onto the canvas." June's stopped crying, but she's still sniffling. Trip keeps on patting her back. "I'm no artist, but that's generally how I think it goes. I can write it down for you if your memory's really shoddy."

"Very cute." Liam's apparently forgotten his paint-stained hands because he drags one through his white-blond hair and leaves a trail of pink in its wake. "I got wrangled into some ridiculous double-date thing with a friend of Scarlett's boyfriend."

"Guy or girl?" Trip hums under his breath. He bounces his leg despite the ache that the movement causes in his thighs and back.

"Guy." Liam stares at his canvas, forlorn. "I don't even know why I said yes to it in the first place. I don't want a romantic partner in my life right now."

"Who said anything about romance?" Trip keeps jiggling his leg even after June's gone quiet and loose-limbed against him. "Free meal, couple drinks, maybe a quick fuck. It could be fun."

Liam cranes his neck to try to get a look at the clock on the microwave. "Why is everything about food, alcohol and sex for you?"

"Hierarchy of needs and all that. Come on, what's the matter with any of that?"

"I'm married to my art right now." Liam waves a hand at the canvas. "That should be the only thing consuming my soul until this series is finished."

"What're you gonna do? Rub up on those mannequin legs I brought home to get off?" Trip stumbles to his feet, teeth clenched, so he can lower a now-sleeping June back into her playpen. "You still owe me for that, by the way."

"I told you, I'll help you out with electric." His face screwed up in thought, Liam drums the edge of his paintbrush against his thigh. After a moment, he lowers the brush. "What if I just paid your share on electric next month?"

"What do you want?" Trip watches to make sure June stays asleep before making a trip back to his room to fetch his bag. He's almost positive he remembers dropping an ibuprofen in there earlier in the week.

"I'll take Junie off your hands tonight and I'll pay that bill if you take my place on the date tonight," Liam says, leaning back on his hands to keep an eye on Trip from his place in the family room, "*and* I'll buy you a six-pack."

Trip drops his bag in front of his couch cushion before lowering himself beside it. He busies himself rummaging through his things to make a show of considering the offer. It's not a bad deal. Not having to pay his share of the electric bill saves him a decent amount of cash, and free beer is never a bad thing. He's reached the prescription bottle he keeps his found meds in. He pulls it out and palms the few pills in the bottle. "Throw in five more bucks for the MetroCard and you've got a deal."

"Done." Liam reaches for a shredded scrap of T-shirt to wipe his hands.

"Don't bother." Trip dry swallows what may or may not be an ibuprofen and shifts the rest of the pills back into the bottle. He spits in his emptied palm and sticks out his hand toward Liam.

Liam pulls a face, his gaze fixed on Trip's wet hand. "Why do you only ever do that when you make deals with me?"

"Dev would kick the shit out of me, Scarlett would take off my hand, and I don't ever need anything from Jude." Trip waves his hand at Liam. "Come on then, Li, do it for your art."

Liam sighs and spits in his palm before reaching for Trip's hand. "Deal."

"Fuckin' disgusting." Trip wipes his hand on his jeans and leaves a streak of green on the denim. "So where exactly am I going?"

Liam unfolds his legs to go to the kitchen to wash his hands. "Some place in the east thirties. I wrote it down somewhere. The boys are meeting you straight from work, so you might want to clean up a bit."

"Shower, got it." Trip pulls himself upright. This time, it hurts slightly less. "What time am I supposed to be there?"

"Six-thirty, meaning you need to get your ass moving." Liam points toward his bare wrist. For someone who believes in being in the spirit of each moment, Liam can be a real stickler for other people having to keep to a schedule, especially if he's the one who devised it.

"I'll be fashionably late." Trip pulls his shirt off and tosses it into the bedroom on his way to the bathroom. He raises his voice over the groaning of the pipes when he cranks on the shower. "This guy got a name?"

"Who? Scarlett's man or yours?"

"Either." Trip leaves the door open while he strips out of the rest of his clothes. He's not one for modesty when it comes to his body, and he's not interested in shouting through a closed door. "Do these blind dates come with résumés? Like names and bed sizes and sex kinks?"

"God help us if you ever discover dating apps." Liam throws a towel at Trip before returning to his place in the family room.

"All I know is, he's some sort of Wall Street baby, he's handsome and he's intense-ish."

"Intense-ish?" Trip echoes. He climbs into the shower and cringes when he's met with a wall of icy water, but he doesn't have the time to wait for it to get hot.

"All I know," Liam calls back. "And his name's Mick or Martin or something like that. Definitely an 'M' name."

Liam's terrible with names, but Trip's not worried. He can play games with a stranger for a couple hours if it means a good deal and a free meal. He's never been one for dating, at least not in the traditional sense. He'd gone out with his fair share of older men when he'd first come to the city, and they'd usually liked to spoil him with decent meals or at least decent room service, but he's getting too old-looking for the taste of most of them, and he's never been a fan of playing someone's pet for an evening.

He's well aware he's going to be more than a little late, but he doesn't mind. If he's lucky, his date will assume he's been stood up and leave before Trip makes it to the restaurant. If Trip stays out to prowl the streets, it means he'll still get his electric paid, and that promised beer, and if his date leaves before Trip can make it to the restaurant, Trip will be off the hook for trying to behave himself enough to keep Scarlett from killing him.

It's past six-thirty by the time he gets out of the shower, nearly seven by the time Liam scrapes together the promised subway fare and some extra for what Trip calls interest. His expression is pinched as he hands over the dollar bills. "Scarlett's probably going to kill me for this."

"Scarlett loves me." Trip tucks the money in his pocket. "She'll be thrilled."

"Uh-huh." Liam peers into the playpen at June. "Just try to at least pretend to be halfway civilized."

"If there was a way you imagined this evening going, you should have gone on the date yourself, bud." Trip swats Liam's hand away when he reaches to smooth Trip's hair. "Let me be."

Liam looks him over, frowning. "You going to come home tonight?"

"Depends on how well my date goes, doesn't it?" Trip pockets his keys but leaves his bag and guitar in his room. He'll make it home sometime before he has to go play.

Liam settles himself over his art, but his gaze stays on Trip. "Let Scarlett know if you follow the guy home, all right?"

Trip pauses in the open door. He leans into the frame. "What's it to you whether or not I go home with the guy?"

Liam waves his paintbrush in Trip's direction. "Believe it or not, Morgan, some of us actually get concerned when you disappear."

"Well, ain't you the sweetest thing." Trip clasps a hand over his heart before shoving off the doorframe and stepping into the hall. "Don't worry, Forrester, you can always sell all my shit and rent out the closet to one of them sad-looking kids over by St. Marks to make sure all the bills get paid if I ever manage to get myself tossed in the East River."

"Hilarious. I suppose if I remind you to use protection if you sleep with him, you'll have a smart remark for that, too."

Trip salutes him. "Rubber glove it. Will do. Thanks for the concern, Mom."

"Get bent, Morgan."

"I'll be getting something." Trip kicks the door with his heel as he moves toward the stairs and calls over his shoulder. "Don't kill the kid with those paint fumes or you'll be answering to Scarlett."

By the time he's outside, Trip's fingers are itchy and a familiar ache is starting at the base of his skull, so he opts to use the money Liam's given him paired with some from his pockets to purchase a new pack of cigarettes. He's not opposed to hopping the turnstile to catch the train.

He doesn't have a watch, but by the time he's made it to the restaurant, he's more than a little late. Still, he takes his time making his way through the doors. He'd be lying if he didn't say he was curious about Scarlett's new guy. She's been practically floating since that first day she met him at the coffee shop, so he must be doing something right.

The hostess eyes Trip warily when he informs her he's meeting a group that should already be seated, but she allows him to pass by her stand and explore the maze of tables nonetheless.

Trip glances over the crowd. Most of them are in suits, with their ties loosened and jackets cast over the backs of chairs. Trip's never owned a suit, and the idea of ties makes him claustrophobic. Still, the aesthetic isn't lost on him. He's contemplating just picking one of the cute suits at the bar to start a conversation with when his world freezes.

There, seated near the middle of the room, his hair neat, his tie still pulled tight and jacket on, is a solemn someone Trip knows. He stands and watches for a minute while Nate Mackey cuts his food and sips from a highball glass, and then he cannot help but laugh aloud because there, seated beside Nate, is Scarlett.

"Small wonders." Trip murmurs under his breath. He shakes his head and finally makes his way toward the table.

Scarlett sees him first and she looks immediately unhappy. Trip can't blame her; he doesn't have a good track record for behaving in these types of environments. He can't quite bring himself to care, though, because Nate has spotted him and the look of total befuddlement is priceless.

Trip takes his chair and leans his elbows on the table to get closer. "Hello, Nathaniel."

Nate's cheeks shade red beneath his five o' clock shadow. "What're you doing here?"

"I could ask the same thing." Scarlett aims a sharp kick at Trip's shin under the table. "Where's Liam?"

"Occupied at the moment." Trip turns his expression grave. "A stroke of inspiration. I think he might be getting intimate with that decomposed beauty installation taking up half of our family room."

"I don't think we've met," a voice chimes from Trip's right. Trip tears his gaze from Nate to study its owner.

The guy has dark hair and equally dark eyes. His narrow shoulders are held loose and easy; his elbows are propped on the table, and his sleeves are rolled. He regards Trip with a bright openness that Trip likes.

"I know for a fact we haven't." Trip could say something crude or cruel or ridiculous, but Scarlett would kill him and she deserves better than his games. He offers a hand. "Trip Morgan."

"Kellan Kipley." Kellan turns to face Trip more fully. "Christ, you have some interesting eyes. Are those contacts?"

"Just me." Trip raises and drops his eyebrows. "If I could afford a pair of contacts, I'd make sure they matched, trust me. Nathaniel likes them, though, don't you, sugar?"

Nate's been watching them silently from his side of the table, but his eyes go wide.

When Nate doesn't come up with a response, Trip winks. "I thought so."

Scarlett sighs, but then she's perking up and going into her entertainer mode. She's always such a damn good sport. "Trip, if I didn't know any better, I'd swear you and Nate have met."

"Nathaniel and I have history," Trip informs the table. He turns his gaze back toward Nate. "Don't we?"

Nate blushes even darker and then he's mumbling to his plate. "We had coffee once a few weeks back."

"And I never heard about it; how typical." Kellan takes a sip of his drink. "Nate and I were roommates all through college, and we've been working three cubicles away from each other since graduation, but he never tells me anything except to turn down drinks and stress over his paperwork."

"No cubicle or roommate experience with him, but that sounds about right." Trip likes Kellan Kipley even if he does have a stupid name and asks stupid questions. He keeps his attention on Nate. "I have your umbrella."

Nate's expression becomes more composed. "I told you that you could keep it."

"Oh, I remember." Trip reaches across the table and pulls a stalk of asparagus from Nate's plate. He takes a bite out of it, chewing and swallowing before going on. "Just wondering what you might have for me tonight."

"Trip, honestly." Scarlett turns her attention to the rest of their company. "Ignore him. He's all bark and no bite."

Trip points his spear of asparagus at her. "Now I wouldn't say that."

"How about a drink?"

They all look at Nate.

His cheeks are still red, but he's holding Trip's gaze. "What do you want?"

Trip masks his surprise at Nate's sudden boldness by looking him over. He's not as well shaven as he'd been before, but his dirty-blond hair is just as carefully kept. He's dressed in a blue suit shirt and navy jacket. A gold tie clip flashes bright against the soft yellow of his tie. Trip cannot deny that he's handsome in a suave, serious way. "That's a very big question with a whole lot of answers, sweetheart."

"To drink—what do you want *to drink?*" Nate pushes a narrow black menu toward Trip. "Are you even old enough to drink?"

"Still fixated on the age thing." Trip clicks his tongue while he studies the menu. He wonders why anyone would need eighteen varieties of whiskey.

"He'll be twenty in a few months." Scarlett pulls the menu from Trip's hands. "And you don't have to get him a thing if you don't want to, Nate."

"Why are you spoiling all of our fun?" Trip finishes off what's left of his commandeered stalk of asparagus. He doesn't like asparagus, and it's left a bad taste in his mouth.

"Why are you here at all?" Scarlett takes the piece of bread from the side of her plate and offers it to Trip.

"I told you, Liam and I had an understanding." Trip accepts the bread. "And I'm here to entertain Nathaniel. Speaking of which, finish your drink."

Nate looks at his glass and then back at Trip. "Why?"

Trip leans across the table for Nate's glass and takes a sip before offering it back. "There, I've helped you out. Now bottoms up."

Nate's got a frown line between his eyebrows. "I'm gonna ask you again: why?"

"I've been sent to entertain you, I'm too late for dinner, and Mama Scarlett isn't gonna let me get a drink here, so we gotta get gone." Trip takes a bite of his bread. He waits to speak until after he's swallowed. "Before I got here, you were contemplating leaving behind most of your dinner anyway. "

That makes Nate smile, big and genuine enough to show off a few perfect teeth. "You reading my mind again?"

"Little bit." Trip's still not entirely sure what he wants out of this night, but getting Nathaniel to smile a few more times is as good an endeavor as any.

Kellan throws his napkin at Nate when he pulls his wallet from his pocket. "Don't even think about it, loser. You kids go have fun."

Nate drops a twenty on the table. "Let me tip at least, would you?"

Kellan flaps a hand at him. "Yeah, fine. Get out of here. When are you going in tomorrow?"

"Early." Nate looks at his watch as he stands. "You?"

"Depends on where the night takes me, I guess." Kellan glances toward Scarlett. Trip does not miss the subtle move of Scarlett's hand from her lap to Kellan's knee.

Trip catches Scarlett's eye and pretends to make himself throw up.

She pulls her hand back into her lap and pushes herself to her feet. "Trip? Sweetheart, can I borrow you for a moment?"

"Not carrying any condoms at the moment, sorry, darlin'." Trip sticks his hands in his pockets as if checking them.

"Good thing I always carry my own." Scarlett grabs Trip's elbow and hauls him to his feet. "I'm going to the bathroom. I'll be right back."

Kellan squeezes Scarlett's wrist softly and kisses the back of her hand. "Yeah, yeah. Take your time."

Scarlett drags Trip toward the bathroom doors.

"I know ladies like to do the whole go-to-the-bathroom-in-packs thing, but, believe it or not, I'm a guy, so—"

"I have absolutely no problem beating you to death in the middle of a nice restaurant, Morgan." Scarlett rests a hand on her hip.

Trip raises both hands in a quick show of surrender. "Fine. Talk fast, then. Your date's waiting. I like him, by the way. You could carry him home in your pocket if you wanted."

"Could say the same about you." Scarlett glances toward the table and then back at Trip. "How do you know Nate?"

"We ran into each other a couple weeks ago. He bought me coffee. I wowed him with my clairvoyance. We had a nice time."

"You stole his wallet." Scarlett frowns, unimpressed.

"I gave it back." Trip steps out of the way of a group of women emerging from the bathroom. He resists the urge to reach into any of their purses.

Scarlett stares at him before speaking again. "Am I asking too much if I ask you to try and be at least kind of nice to him?"

"I am being nice to him." Trip stands on tiptoe to catch a glimpse of Kellan and Nate still standing beside the table. They're deep in a conversation that has Kellan punching Nate in the arm and Nate looking exasperated. "If he loosens up, I'll be very, very nice to him."

"Does anyone actually think all your sleazy lines are charming?"

"Some people must since they keep taking me home." Trip bats his eyelashes at her before giving her ankle a nudge with the edge of his shoe. "You gonna go home with Kipper?"

"Kellan," she mutters. She watches him from across the room. "I have to go to work."

"So invite him along and promise a private show afterward."

"You're disgusting."

"Just trying to help you out." Trip leans against the wall. "He know what you do yet?"

Scarlett raises a hand to pull her hair into a ponytail at the nape of her neck. She lets it go when she shakes her head. "He knows about June, though."

"Yeah?" Trip quirks an eyebrow. "And what? He looking to be Junie's new daddy?"

She directs a dark look toward Trip. "He didn't seem totally freaked out, but I'm not ready to let him meet her yet."

"Huh." Trip looks back at the table. Nate appears less disgruntled. He's nodding along to something Kellan is saying. "How 'bout that. I thought for sure that would have sent him packing."

"Not yet." Scarlett reaches for her hair, but seems to think better of it. Her hand drops to her side.

Trip looks her over. Scarlett has never been one for big shows of affection for anyone except June, but Trip can see the softness in her eyes when she looks back toward their table. He considers making a nasty joke, but he opts for nudging her arm instead. "You better take that bathroom break and powder your nose. Your john is gonna think you fell in or something."

"He's not a john."

"He's somethin." Trip pushes himself back off the wall. "Am I free to go now or what?"

"Fine." Scarlett pushes the door to the bathroom part way open. "If you don't go to Nate's apartment tonight, come home, would you?"

"What's with everyone these days?" Trip groans. "You and Liam are acting like my goddamn parents."

"If we were acting like your parents, I think we'd care a whole lot less about whether or not you came back home." Scarlett reaches out to pinch Trip's arm. "Behave yourself."

"Won't do anything you wouldn't do, baby."

Scarlett doesn't turn away quite fast enough to hide her amusement.

Trip makes his way back to the table and snags Nate's sleeve. "Off we go then, Nathaniel. Kellan, it was nice to meet you. I'd threaten to kick your ass if you do anything to hurt Scarlett, but I'm pretty sure she can do that herself, so have a nice rest of your night."

Kellan waves. "You, too, man. And Mac?"

Nate looks toward Kellan with an expression somewhere between alarmed and irritated. "What?"

"Have some fun, man." Kellan takes a drink of his beer. "Buy you and your new friend a drink or something. Show him those cute dance moves you acquire when you put some gin in your system."

"Yeah, make sure to show Scarlett yours, too." Nate claps Kellan on the shoulder before turning toward the door.

"I like him." Trip follows after Nate with a final glance over his shoulder to see Scarlett returning to the table. "Smart man."

"He's something like that." Nate looks over at him and his expression has gone suddenly anxious. "So, um, what do you want to do?"

"Well, now, I wanna buy some gin."

"Something that doesn't involve that."

Trip's stir crazy from the restaurant, too many people in too quiet a space. He needs to move. "Take a walk with me, Nathaniel."

Nate follows him obediently down the sidewalk.

Trip digs in his pocket for his new pack of cigarettes. He smacks it against his palm with his gaze still on Nate. Running into this grown-up stranger from his photograph should feel stranger than it does, as if some small magic exists around the fact that they've come together again. Mostly it just feels normal.

Nate clears his throat. "So, um, how have you been?"

"Peachy." Trip pulls open his pack of cigarettes and fishes one out before trading the pack for the lighter he lifted in the park just yesterday. "What about you? Still heartsick over Lois?"

Nate watches while Trip tries to light his cigarette. He lifts a hand to help shield the lighter from the breeze. "Lovett."

"Lovett." The glow of his lighter makes shadows dance across Nate's palm. Trip steps away from him when the tip of his cigarette finally flares orange. "You been writing him every day? Sending flowers? Leaving flaming bags of dog shit on his doorstep?"

Nate tucks his hand in his pocket. "None of the above."

"You're so dull, Nathaniel." Trip blows smoke out his nose. "Where's your sense of fun?"

Nate stares at the white glow of smoke hanging in the air in front of them. "Missing, I guess."

"Apparently." Trip takes another long drag on the cigarette before offering it to Nate.

Nate shakes his head. "I don't smoke."

"You carry a lighter, though." Trip turns to walk backward so he can keep an eye on Nate. Their height difference makes it hard to monitor his expression when they're side by side.

Nate pulls the lighter from his pocket, shakes it. "People ask for one a lot."

"So you carry it in case someone else needs it," Trip says. "You always done that?"

Nate inspects the lighter for a moment before pocketing it. "My brother used to. It was just a habit I picked up. I don't know."

Trip turns toward Bryant Park. "Call it a fuzzy spot in my mindreading abilities, but I can't quite figure out this thing with your brother. Did you two have a falling out?"

"That really any of your business?" Nate follows Trip into the park; his eyes flit from Trip to the trees above them.

"We're on a date, aren't we?" Trip's unfettered by Nate's sudden brusqueness. "I'm getting to know you."

Nate meets his eyes again. He reaches out and pushes Trip's shoulder so he turns to face forward again. "Thought you could read my mind."

"Like I said, it's a fuzzy spot." Trip tucks his cigarette between his lips and waits.

Nate pauses as if he's considering how to respond. "He's dead."

"Oh." Trip pulls the cigarette from his mouth. "Sorry."

They walk in silence for a while, this newly revealed information floating heavy between them. Trip can make a joke of a lot of things, but dead brothers don't seem particularly funny.

"So, um," Nate clears his throat, apparently ready to move past their awkward moment. "What do you do?"

"What do I do?" Trip echoes.

"Last time I saw you, you said you're not a student, but you're only like nineteen, so what do you do for, like, work?"

"This and that." Trip tosses his cigarette.

"What kind of this and that?" Nate prompts. His gaze follows the arc of the cigarette before moving back to Trip.

"Dog-walking, dishwashing, guitar-playing, mindreading," Trip says. "That kind of this and that."

"You get paid to read people's minds?" Nate's walking slows for a beat.

Trip matches his pace. "Sometimes. When there's a lot of tourists around; otherwise, I mostly just play in the park."

"Like what you did to me last time." Nate casts a cynical frown toward Trip, still caught up on the mindreading thing. "People pay you to do that."

Trip rolls his shoulders. He feels less out of sorts after walking, but now he's sore again. He drops onto an empty park bench. "People come to New York to fall in love and be amazed and all that sappy bullshit—find magic or whatever. For five bucks a pop, I help them out, or at least give them something funny to tell their friends when they get home."

Nate sits down beside him. "Why'd you come to New York?"

For the sex. For the cash. To be famous. Trip considers a thousand false responses, but Nate's watching him so intently, he offers the most surprising thing he can think of: the truth. "It's the place people run away to, I guess."

Nate nods. "Me, too, I think."

"You're a runaway?" Trip cocks his head to the side. "You don't strike me as the type to have spent a lot of time milling around the village with a cardboard sign and a hungry-looking dog, Nathaniel."

"Not that kind of runaway," Nate replies. "Were you?"

Trip nods.

"Huh." Nate studies him for a moment before turning his gaze back to the sidewalk. "Why'd you run away?"

"Same reason anybody runs away." Trip folds his legs up under himself. "Didn't want to stay where I was."

"Not for the magic or love or whatever?" Nate doesn't look back toward Trip.

"We know better than that, don't we?" Trip nudges Nate's leg with a toe.

"Guess we do." Nate turns his gaze toward Trip again.

Trip's not quite sure how to read his expression, so he just stares back. "You look tired, Nathaniel."

"So do you."

Trip wonders if it's the liquor in his system that's made him bolder or if it's something in the quiet of the park. Trip stretches his hands high above his head. A few of the vertebrae in his spine click. "On the contrary, I'm feeling pretty damn awake."

Nate kicks a heel against the pavement before speaking. "So how do you do it?"

"Do what?" Trip shakes a second cigarette out of the pack.

"The mindreading thing." Nate waves a hand at him. "You must get it pretty close to right if people keep paying you to do it."

Trip slips a hand closer to Nate, careful to keep the movement subtle. "I'm magic."

"Thought you didn't believe in magic." Nate's attention is on Trip's cigarette.

"Serendipity, fate, love, everything-happens-for-a-reason type magic, no, I don't." Trip steals a glance at Nate's wrist. "My own magic is a different story."

Nate hums, cynical. "A pessimistic magic man?"

"Something like that." Trip stands and nudges Nate's arm to follow. "I did a good job reading your mind, didn't I? And free of charge, I might add."

"Wow, thanks." Nate casts another dubious look at Trip. "Really, though, how's it work?"

Trip tucks his hands into his pockets. "I'll tell you in a few minutes. Could you check the time for me?"

"Why does it matter what—oh." Nate stares at his empty wrist.

"Missing something, Nathaniel?" Trip turns to watch while Nate spins in a slightly frantic circle with his eyes on the sidewalk.

"My watch. I had it on earlier." Nate looks at Trip.

"Check your pocket." Trip rocks back onto his heels and forward again.

Nate reaches into his pocket and fishes out his watch. "I didn't—"

"A lighter, breath mints, a condom and business cards." Trip pulls the items from his own pocket. "You're just about ready for anything, aren't you?"

Nate stares wide-eyed at his things in Trip's hands. Even as he stares at them, he pats down his pockets as if to make sure they're actually missing. "How did you do that?"

"Magic fingers." Trip offers Nate's things back to him. "Standard lubricated, huh? More of a bare-skin sensations, guy, myself, but to each their own, I suppose."

"Do you make a habit of stealing from people?" Nate puts his watch on his right wrist this time.

Trip grins at him. "Ain't stealing if I give it all back, is it?"

Nate keeps a hand hovering over his pocket closest to Trip. "Still doesn't explain how you do the mindreading thing."

"I pull gum and some cigarettes from your pocket and tell you that you like bubble gum and Marlboro Reds and you carry a lucky one with a woman's lipstick on it." Trip holds up his pack of cigarettes as an example. "Then I throw something in like 'I'd make sure to take a walk around the reservoir' or 'Huh, seems like you ought to take a trip to the Natural History Museum.'"

Nate's gaze is fixed on Trip's hands swinging loose at his sides. "And they buy it?"

"Yeah," Trip replies. "Usually offer me another buck or two if I can give them directions."

"Incredible." Nate looks disappointed. "So it's all a big scam."

"People like to believe in something larger than themselves, like higher powers and fate and all that romantic bullshit. Like I said, I'm just providing a service." Trip tucks a hand around Nate's elbow just to get him to stop staring. "You bought it, didn't you?"

Nate bends his arm as if by instinct and it makes Trip step closer. "I don't carry anything that would tell you I've got a sister or a porch or whatever."

Trip tips his head up to better see Nate's face. "Huh. Guess I really am a little magic then or something."

"Or something." Nate's arm shifts against Trip's hand. "So you're a pickpocket."

"That's not a very nice word." Trip's anxious this close to Nate—shoulders bumping, his hand caught up in Nate's arm—it's too quiet, too intimate. He doesn't pull away. "I prefer 'collector of forgotten antiquities.'"

"I feel like that's something you need a four-year degree for."

"I've got at least four years of education under my belt." Trip shifts his hand from Nate's arm, then twists to face him while they walk. "I'm guessing you've got a couple more years than I do."

"A few." Nate lowers his arm, apparently not overly perturbed at the lost contact. "I went to NYU when I was your age."

"'When you were my age,'" Trip says. "Jesus, Grandpa, you gonna start telling me about Vietnam next?"

"I remember when the subway cost two bucks a ride," Nate retorts.

"You and me both, pal." Trip sighs. "This city is gonna fuckin' kill me if it gets any more expensive."

Nate looks at Trip in the glow of a streetlamp. "It's been a while since a ride cost that. How long have you been in New York?"

"Three years or so." Trip pauses to watch Nate screw up his face as he tries to make sense of this new information. "Come on, Nathaniel, you can do it. Nineteen minus three equals what?"

"You came here when you were sixteen." Nate looks back up at him, that frown line back between his eyebrows. "By yourself?"

"You did the same when you were only a couple years older." Trip shoves his hands back down in his pockets. He wants another cigarette, but he needs to ration them at least a little bit.

"That was for college and that was legal." Nate's stopped walking. The streetlight halos him in soft yellow. "Didn't your parents come looking for you or something?"

Trip pauses just outside the glow of the light. He rocks on his heels. “If you’re gonna be asking about all my secrets, don’t you think we ought to be somewhere a little more intimate, honey?”

Nate’s eyes go wide and then he’s frowning all over again, and it’s kind of cute, that pouty, nervous downturn of his mouth. “I, um, I have to work in the morning.”

“Me, too.” Trip steps a few inches into the glow of the lamp with Nate.

“Early.” Nate’s eyes scan Trip fast before landing back on his face. “I have to, um, finish some stuff up and…” His gaze flits to the side, then back to Trip. “Let the dog out.”

Trip steps another few inches closer, hooks a finger in one of Nate’s belt loops. “You don’t have a dog.”

Nate doesn’t step out of the contact. “Really. I have an early morning and I wanted to get a run in. I just don’t think tonight is a good idea. Tonight’s not the best for, um, anything, and we just met, ya know?”

Trip keeps his expression controlled in a calm smirk while he walks backward a few paces, tugging Nate along with him. “We didn’t just meet.”

“Well, I mean, yeah.” Nate’s throat bobs in a quick swallow, but he keeps moving when Trip pulls him another couple inches his way. “I mean it’s just not a good night for this.”

“For this?” Trip echoes. He’s back in the dark outside the little circle of light. “You’re gonna have to spell things out for me here, sugar.”

“Like going home together.” Nate follows Trip another inch forward. “I mean, you’re a good guy and everything, but—”

“—But you’re not attracted to me?” Trip raises his eyebrows in mock surprise. “Or you just don’t want to fuck me?”

"No, you are, I mean I really am—attracted to you, I mean." Nate freezes. He reaches for Trip's wrist and unhooks his finger. "This is too fast. This is a lot."

Trip pauses to study Nate and his nervous hands and nervous eyes. He smooths the line of Nate's tie. He wraps the end of it around his hand and tips his head back to meet Nate's eyes. "I wonder, Nathaniel, have you ever considered doing something outside what you think you ought to do?"

Nate flounders for a response, but he doesn't seem to find one.

Trip rises up on his tiptoes, touches a kiss to Nate's mouth. It's just as quick as the first one. Trip's not a fan of kissing, but it seems to be just about the only type of physical contact that doesn't get Nate bent out of shape.

Nate blinks dreamily at nothing. He licks his lips, then refocuses on Trip.

Trip backs away with his hands in his pockets. "I'll let you get home then, Nathaniel. Big morning and all that."

"Wait." Nate raises one hand a few inches and steps forward.

Trip pauses, intrigued by this sudden change of heart. He hadn't thought Nate would take him home, but he's not opposed to the idea.

Nate looks as if he might say something, but then his hand drops and his expression goes back to its default flat and serious. "Do you want me to walk you to the subway at least?"

Trip's shoulders go loose, and he's not sure why they'd been so tense in the first place. "Nah. I think I'll walk."

Nate stares out toward the edge of the park. "That's a long walk back to the Village."

"Not that long." Trip keeps walking backwards. "Besides, the night's young. Plenty of possibilities before I make it home."

Nate looks back at him. "Are we gonna see each other again?"

"I think so." He says. *I hope so,* he thinks.

"You don't know for sure?" Nate hasn't moved out from under the streetlamp.

"Apparently our fates are intertwined, Nathaniel. I'm not too worried about it."

"Thought you didn't believe in fate." Nate steps forward a few inches, but stops.

Trip wants to go back into that little circle of light. He takes another step back. "I don't, but I don't know enough math or science or whatever to explain why you and I keep running into each other."

"Twice hardly counts as constantly running into one another." Nate has his hands in his pockets now in a mirror of Trip's posture. "Just kind of coincidence, really."

"You're the one with the fancy college degree, so I'll trust you to know the statistics better than me." Trip takes another step back, smaller this time. "Maybe you're right. Maybe this is it."

"My friend is dating your friend. I'm sure we could figure out how to get ahold of each other again if we wanted to."

"Now where's the fun in that?" Trip turns. He needs to go before that light pulls him in again. He calls over his shoulder, "See ya around, Nathaniel."

Nate's voice calls back, farther away than it really ought to be. "See you around, Trip."

Hey, Trip, you wanna do something?

Those words out of my brothers' mouths turned me into the world's biggest idiot. The answer was always yes. See, as the youngest of six boys, I had my work cut out for me. None of them liked me, and I wanted to hate them back, but dammit, I wanted to be a part of their pack, too. It wasn't like I had any good reason to like any of them. Michael's so much older we might as well be strangers, Jeremiah's meaner and stupider than spit, the twins don't care for anyone but each other, and I think if Gideon knew he could get away with it, he'd have drowned me or tied me to the tracks outside town or something. Still, being in a place where I didn't fit in anywhere else, the idea of having my brothers accept me in even some small way was sort of nice. I didn't need them to like me, even; I just needed to feel like I was a part of something. So, like I said, no matter how many times I got suspended by a teacher or beaten bloody by our daddy or broke a finger or three, the answer to that goddamn question was always, without hesitation, yes.

My brothers are in the meth business. Levi can barely add two and two, but the man can cook with the best of them. He snorts a lot of his cook, but with Paul's and our daddy's help, he got a nice gig going and, voilà, we have a family business. Levi and Paul cook, my daddy secures the clientele, Mike, Jeremiah and Gid do the dealing. Sweet, ain't it? Anyway, when I was about nine, Michael looked me dead in the eye and said those magic words. "Hey, Trip, you wanna do something?" So then I was in on the business, too.

I've always been on the small side; I won't deny it. Skinny and short and there's not much to me, but I am a Morgan and I come with a reputation and a baseball bat. That bat was the only gift I'd ever get from my old man, and damn, did I love it. I carried that stupid thing everywhere.

It was smart, if you think about it. No one thinks much of a kid wandering around town with his baseball bat, but, for my purposes, if someone thought they could give me the slip on a payment, all I had to do was wind up and crack them a good one and then they were quick to pay up. The boys loved it when they'd hear I'd taken someone out. They'd muss up my hair and shove me around (in the good way) and offer me a beer and a cigarette. Those were nice days. Even if it took breaking a kneecap or a wrist or something, I was willing to do it if it meant I got to stand around with my brothers and feel for a couple minutes like I belonged somewhere.

Didn't take long, and I developed a reputation, too. My classmates were scared of me, the meth heads knew better than to fuck with me, and my teachers stopped caring much whether I turned in my homework or showed up to school at all. I'll be honest: I wasn't much a fan of my reputation, but I thought it was okay if it meant people knocked me around a little less and thought of me as a part of my family.

Pastor Welk cared, though. He didn't say much about it, but I know it bothered him. He kept me busy at the church and did his best to fill up my time with "better activities," but I found time for both. Only thing that ever bothered me was that I liked taking out a guy's knees a little too much, and the only person I wanted to approve of me more than my brothers was Pastor Welk.

I wish I'd have been smarter and made a choice before my time ran out. I wish I'd have realized that you can pick your family, and I was picking the wrong one. I don't know if, in the long run, a different choice would have put me somewhere other than where I am right now, but I still wish I'd chosen different.

FIVE.

In his younger years, Trip liked the autumn. He liked the colors of the leaves and the smell of bonfires and even the noise of the football games he never attended. He likes it in New York, too, at least in theory.

It's the notion of an early winter that takes the joy out of fall for Trip. Winter is the threat of empty sidewalks, frostbitten fingers and an empty coffee can at his feet. Trip can't handle another winter like the last one. He has rent and bills to pay and, though the near-constant emptiness in his stomach is familiar and not as bothersome as it once was, he still has to eat. His roommates tolerate him for now and spot him a few dollars when he needs it, but Trip's not sure how far their kindness will stretch.

For now, he ignores the threat of winter. It's still only September, and this is not such a bad day. It's a Tuesday afternoon and the park is packed with one of the fall crowds, their phones aimed at the trees turned crimson and gold seemingly overnight.

Trip can't find a decent spot to call his own, so he climbs the side of the fountain, drops his bag and shoes a few steps down, and wades into the water with his jeans rolled halfway up his shins. It's a nice way to play in the summer when the sun is unbearably hot, but today, the water raises goose bumps on his skin. Trip doesn't mind. His act draws a decent crowd of people and some of them lean over the edge of the fountain to drop some spare change for him. Most of them, though, watch and move on with their heads ducked when he finishes a song.

The people who don't pay used to make him angry. They stand around for a song or two, shopping bags hanging from one hand, their phone in the other and aimed at him, happy for the few minutes of entertainment he provides them. Trip, in turn, had allowed their cameras despite the creeping fear a photo or video might somehow get him recognized and shipped back to Alabama. He needed the money, so the risk had seemed worth it until his happy photographers moved on without so much as offering the change from the bottoms of their pockets. Shouting after them had done nothing except drive away his remaining crowds, so now Trip applies the same mantra to his potential patrons that he applies to everyone else he knows: Expect nothing and you will never be disappointed.

Trip moves around as much as he can and tries to stay focused on the heat of the sun on his shoulders. It's a bright enough day to require sunglasses, but the air is cold, and after nearly two hours of playing, it's hard to ignore the prickling hurt of his toes beneath the water.

He's singing "Baby, I Don't Care" by Buddy Holly and wondering if certain toes would be worse to lose than others when he spies a familiar face in the crowd. He's only there for a moment, but Trip would know that solemn face anywhere. He finishes his song, gathers his things and climbs back out onto the cement, ignoring compliments and questions from the people he passes.

Nate hasn't made it far from the fountain. He's dressed in a gray suit and is busily fussing with his briefcase. He keeps looking at a cardboard box parked on a bench in front of him as if he's worried it might disappear if he doesn't keep a close enough eye on it.

Trip steps in closer. "You want some help with that?"

Nate nearly jumps out of his skin at the sound of Trip's voice. He looks first at the sunglasses pushed up into his hair and then at the shoes hanging loose in his left hand before looking back at Trip's face. He points at his bag in an attempt at casual recovery from his surprise. "Wanted to tip you for the entertainment."

"Things are good today. Don't worry about it." Trip shifts his bag from his shoulder and onto the open bench space. "Looks like you managed to find me again without that phone number after all."

"Yeah, I guess I did." Nate turns his attention to the trail of wet footprints behind Trip. "Do people tip better when you play in there?"

"Sometimes." Trip peers down into Nate's box. "Crowded today. Had to get creative if I wanted anyone to notice me."

The box holds a plant in a yellow ceramic pot, a few manila envelopes, some picture frames and some more things Trip can't quite see. Everything is packed in tight and neat.

"You're really good," Nate's voice chimes from beside him. He doesn't say anything else.

Trip waves off the compliment. He puts his guitar on top of his bag and pulls Nate's box from the bench. He sits on the cement with it in his lap and rifles through the items inside, destroying the carefully made arrangement. There's more paperwork, another framed photo, a calendar, some pens and a plastic placard with "NATE MACKEY" printed on it in blocky white lettering.

Nate sits down in the vacated space on the bench. "I got fired today."

Trip looks up. "Well, hot damn, Nathaniel, you and Tuesdays just aren't friendly with one another, are you?"

"I guess not." Nate looks caught somewhere between resigned and anxious. "They've been making cuts for a few weeks. We thought they were done, but I guess I was the last to go."

Trip watches him for another moment before turning his attention back to the box. He pulls out the nameplate, most likely from the outside of Nate's former office, and turns it over in his hands. "What'd you do this time?"

"Lacked passion… again."

That gets Trip's attention. "You're lying."

"Afraid not." Nate rests his elbows on his knees and props his chin in his hands.

"Well, can't say I blame them." Trip drops the nameplate back into the box and pulls out a stress ball. He tosses it to Nate. "I've seen pigeons get more excited than you do."

"Thanks." Nate catches the ball and spins it idly in his palm. He looks at the crowd. He pulls at his collar with his free hand, squeezes the ball in the other.

He has clearly come here for a reason, and Trip doesn't mind providing entertainment for Nate for a while. He tugs his shoes over his still-wet feet and pushes himself upright with the box balanced awkwardly between his hip and one arm. He holds out his free hand to Nate. "Be a dear and sling that guitar over my shoulder, would you?"

Nate lifts the guitar by its strap and slides it over Trip's arm. He watches silently while Trip wriggles around, the box still in his arms, until his guitar is slung over his back.

Trip shakes his head until his sunglasses fall onto the bridge of his nose. They're crooked, but he doesn't make a move to fix them. "Lead the way, buddy."

"Where are we going?" Nate reaches out to right Trip's glasses, startling when Trip snaps his teeth at his outstretched fingers.

"Fine, I'll lead." Trip nods toward his bag. "You hold onto that. Lose it and I'll break your goddamn neck, all right?"

Trip doesn't wait for Nate to question him any further before darting into the crowds. Behind him, Nate mumbles apologies to those people whose shoulders he clips, and his shoes click against the pavement as if he's desperate to keep up. Trip makes his way quickly through the crowd and then waits near the entrance of the park for Nate to catch up.

Nate emerges from the crowd only a few seconds later looking flustered. Trip's bag is slung over his left shoulder and his right hand is patting his pocket; no doubt he's worried he's just been robbed based on what he learned about Trip during their last encounter. When he sees Trip, he relaxes.

Trip leans on a cement pillar and raises his eyebrows. "You stop to chat in there or something?"

"We're not all small enough to weasel our way through giant crowds." Nate shifts on his feet as if they're bothering him, and Trip notices that his shoes don't look very comfortable.

Trip hums in acknowledgment, but then he's stepping into the street, one hand raised in the air, the other balancing the box against his thighs. A cab pulls up, so Trip waves Nate over. "Hurry it up, pal. This car's not going to wait all day."

Nate hesitates, but in the end he climbs into the car. Trip's bag is on his lap and his body is pressed close to Trip's so the guitar can take the space behind the driver.

Trip drops his sunglasses into the box on his lap. "Sugar, I know this has been a tough day, but do I really need to remind you how taking a cab works? The driver needs some cross streets."

"You got the damn cab. How the hell am I supposed to know where to tell him we're going?" Nate raises his voice in frustration. Trip can't really blame him. He's making this plan up as he goes and doing it so fast he barely knows what he's doing.

"You're a very angry person, Nathaniel." Trip clicks his tongue. "Your address. We're going to your place."

Nate balks at him. "When did I invite you to my place?"

Trip stares at him. He's found that the best way to get someone to take him home when they're feeling uneasy is to say nothing at all.

Nate holds his gaze for a beat. He looks at the cabdriver and mumbles an address in the east nineties.

Trip turns his attention back to Nate's box of personal items. He pulls out a photograph of a woman and man caught in an embrace with their foreheads pressed close so that they can stare into one another's eyes. "Save the Date" is printed across the bottom in swirly, dramatic script. Trip squints to look more closely at the woman, who is no doubt Nate's sister. She's got his height and his ears. Her hair's been dyed to a magenta shade of red that contrasts nicely with the paleness of her skin. "This Nora?"

Nate shifts closer to look at the picture. "Yeah. And Chris the UPS Guy."

"Is that how he introduces himself?" Trip turns the photo over in search of more information on Nora and Chris the UPS Guy, but he finds none.

"No, I just can't really think of him any other way." Nate leans over Trip to roll the window down.

Trip tips his head into the breeze. "Is Nora a UPS Girl?"

"Hair stylist," Nate replies. "Or a beautician. I don't remember which."

"Good brother." Trip prods Nate in the arm with the invitation.

"She went to school for both, and the salon she works at does hair and makeup." The vinyl of the seat creaks when Nate shifts on Trip's left. "I'm not an angry person."

"What?"

"When we first got in the cab," Nate clarifies. "You said I was an angry person. I'm not."

"Sure you are." Trip waves him off. He drops the wedding invitation back into the box and pulls out a pen with an Ashbury-Whiteman logo printed across the side. He doesn't know much about Nate, but he does know a thing or two about monsters, and Nate has some right behind his eyes, which Trip has seen plenty of times despite their relatively few encounters.

"No, I'm really not." Nate shakes his head. "It's just been a rough couple weeks and I'm under a lot of pressure."

"It's not a criticism." Trip turns to look at him. "I am, too."

Calmer now, Nate looks from Trip's smile to his eyes. "You don't seem all that angry."

Trip works at closing the lid on Nate's box. "Sometimes I think I might be the angriest person alive."

It's not what Trip means to say and it seems to take them both by surprise. He considers taking it back, but he remains silent instead. In the sudden quiet between them, Trip is aware of a peppy television anchor on the monitor behind the passenger seat talking about Madame Tussauds Wax Museum. The speaker crackles loudly with the tinny background music that accompanies her enthusiastic tour around the museum. Nate punches first at the volume control and then the off button, but neither seems to work, so the rest of the cab ride is filled with the sound of unwanted information about tourist hot spots and

Trip's fingers beating out a pattern on the edge of the vinyl seat. Neither of them speaks.

When the cab pulls up to the curb, Nate doesn't wait to see if Trip is going to pay. He swipes his card and shakes his head at the offered receipt. When he slides out of the cab, Trip is already standing on the edge of the sidewalk. Nate pushes his wallet back into his pocket and shifts Trip's bag higher on his shoulder. "You happy?"

"I'm not inside yet." Trip knows this neighborhood, or at least he thinks he does. He's never seen it in daylight and it's been a long time since he made it this far east.

Nate moves toward the doors, his keys in hand and Trip's bag sliding down toward his elbow. "This is it."

Nate nods hello to the doorman at the desk before going to a bank of mailboxes and fussing with another key, leaving Trip to study the lobby. The floor is dark laminate wood and bare, save for a black rug at the entrance with "The Stockton" printed across it in gray lettering. The mailboxes line the wall across from the doorman's desk, and a few worn red chairs and a coffee table with a vase of flowers are tucked across from the elevators. It's not the nicest lobby Trip has seen, but it's an impressive space for someone as young as Nate to afford. Trip spins in a slow circle, whistles. "Hot damn, Nathaniel, I'd pay a pretty penny just to live in this lobby. Is your place this nice?"

Nate looks around, too, but offers no response. He pushes the up button for the elevator with the edge of his hand and flips through his mail during the ride to the ninth floor.

The doors open on a beige carpeted hallway lit with dim sconce lights. The smell of fresh paint and new carpet hangs in the air. Trip glances at himself in the mirror across from the elevators before following Nate to an apartment marked 9C.

Curious to see where Nate calls home, Trip follows Nate into the apartment. The entire space is immaculate. Every blanket is folded, the granite counter tops gleam and the windows are spotless. The whole place is decorated in cool neutrals that seem to only exaggerate the pristineness of the space. "Hot damn, boy, I had you pegged for a neat freak, but you really are something else."

"Yeah, well." Nate points at the box in Trip's arms. "You can set that down somewhere, you know."

Trip hikes the box higher in his arms. "You sure there's not some special space for I-just-got-fired boxes of shit?"

"I'll make one later." Nate toes off his shoes and stoops to lift them. "Just… here, put it in the hall closet for now, I guess."

Trip obediently follows Nate to the closet beside the front door and deposits the box inside along with his bag. He tugs off his shoes to leave beside the door before venturing back into the apartment. He walks along the edge of the breakfast bar and then deeper into the apartment to circle the couch and eye the bookshelves. He drags his fingers along the spines of the books as he keeps up his slow tour. He pauses between the sliding door to the balcony and the black metal of a spiral staircase. He raises his eyebrows. "Nathaniel, there are stairs in your apartment."

Nate is refolding a dishtowel and hanging it from the handle of the oven. He looks over his shoulder at Trip. "My room."

"Multiple floors in one apartment." Trip shakes his head in silent wonder. He moves back into the kitchen and busies himself opening and closing all of the cabinets. Nate's dishes and cooking utensils are as meticulously organized as the rest of the apartment. There is nothing out of place; not a knickknack drawer or so much as a randomly placed box of matches can be found.

Nate sits at the breakfast bar to watch him. "By all means, please go through all of my stuff. Totally acceptable behavior."

"Thanks." Trip winks at him before throwing open the fridge. He prods at a plastic container of spring greens and peers into the egg carton, but then he's tugging a bottle out of the door. "What in the hell is this?"

Nate looks at the bottle. "Green juice. It's, like, vegetables and stuff."

Disgusted at the notion that this green sludge is edible at all, Trip turns the container to squint at the label. "Do you cook with it?"

"Probably could, I guess. Usually you just, like, drink it." Nate scratches at a spot of something on the countertop, but he keeps his gaze on Trip, smiling as though amused with Trip's increasing disgust as he studies the bottle.

"There is kale in this, Nathaniel. Kale and, God help me, collard greens." Trip meets his eyes, and his expression is completely earnest. "Collard greens ain't ever done nothing good for no one, and that is an honest fact. You should not be *drinking* them."

"It's a health thing. I don't know!" Nate loosens his tie. "People swear by it, so I guess I bought in or whatever."

"Do you like it?" Trip lifts the bottle up high to study it from the bottom. "Like none of that 'it's good for me' bullshit. I mean, like do you *like* like it?"

"It's not too bad. You're being dramatic." Nate takes off his suit jacket and drapes it over the back of his seat. "Try it out. See what you think."

"Nuh-uh. No way." Trip points the bottle at Nate. "Like I said, all this dark green shit's bad enough in solid form. I don't want anything to do with it when it's been liquefied."

"Come on and just do it." Nate rests his elbows on the counter. He looks decidedly more comfortable with the weight of his jacket gone. "One sip. It's not going to kill you."

Trip regards the bottle for another minute before twisting the cap off and tipping it to his mouth. He makes a choking sound and pulls it away from his lips fast.

Nate laughs. "Okay, so it's kind of bad."

"That's god-awful." Trip tucks the bottle back in the fridge. He scowls at it before turning a happier expression to Nate. "Know what we should do?"

Nate leans back in his seat and watches while Trip moves on to exploring the contents of the drawers. "What?"

"We should tear up the grass from all the neighborhoods in the city, juice it and then open up one of those stupid juice shops. We'll call it Urban Juice or something tacky like that and market it by the neighborhoods we got the grass from. Like, charge more for Upper East Side."

"Gotta up that price on Tribeca, too," Nate agrees. "Probably Williamsburg, too, if we're being real."

Trip folds his arms on the counter across from Nate, leans his weight into it. It occurs to him that he's never seen Nate out of a full suit before this moment. His shoulders look broader without the jacket; the muscles of his arms are evident through the thin white material of his shirt. His face is closely shaven, his short blond hair is styled and his clothes are carefully tailored and ironed. Nate looks much like his kempt lofted apartment: meticulous and neat. The honey-tinted brown of his eyes, though, hold none of the cool clean of the rest of Nate; they are soft and warm and watch Trip with a content sort of quiet. Trip offers no further comment on the green juice or their budding business plans while they study one another.

When the silence stretches on too long, Nate's ears turn pink and he has to drop his gaze to the counter. "You, um… you want a drink or something?"

Trip nods fast. "Yes, please."

Nate moves to Trip's side of the counter and sets to work pulling bottles from the cabinet beside the fridge. "You have anything in particular you like?"

Trip's lost interest in the kitchen and has moved back to the living room to study the bookshelves some more. He shrugs off his guitar and leans it against the arm of the couch. "I'll have whatever you're having so long as that green juice stays far away from it."

"I can manage that." Nate is quick and sure as he opens cupboards and the fridge. No movement is wasted and not once does he have to check a different place or hesitate as he makes their drinks. "You're kind of young to be drinking, aren't you?"

"You stay sober 'til you were twenty one?" Trip studies the titles on the spines of the books. There are a lot of them—autobiographies, memoirs, novels, science-y sounding things about genetics and running, books about things Trip remembers vaguely from history class and many books about business success. He pulls one from the shelf, points it at Nate. "You read all of these or are they just here to look nice?"

"Probably a couple I haven't done cover to cover." Nate seems to give up on pondering the ethical repercussions of giving a minor a drink because he pours a few fingers of Scotch over ice into each glass and adds a twist of lemon peel. "Most of them, though, I think."

"That's a lot of reading." Trip pushes the book back into place and pulls another. He thumbs through a few pages before closing it and turning it over to look at the cover. "*Ethics of the Millennial Businessman*? You make it all the way through that one?"

"Yeah, I did." Nate offers one of the glasses once Trip has replaced the book on the shelf. "Guess I just can't stand to leave something unfinished."

"Me? I don't think I've ever made it all the way through a book. Started plenty of them, but—" Trip makes a vague motion with his glass toward the ceiling. "S'pose I'm no good at finishing anything at all—except drinks. Which, by the way, I'm gonna do real fast. Give me that glass."

Nate looks disgruntled, but he offers his glass anyway. "That's just how you're supposed to pour Scotch."

"You and 'supposed to,' Nathaniel." Trip shakes his head and moves back to the breakfast bar. He sloshes another few fingers of Scotch into both of their glasses. "You need me to remind you that you got dumped and fired in the same month in the middle of a couple of good for nothin' Tuesday afternoons?"

"Thank you, Trip." Nate looks at him. "Really. That's great. I needed that pick-me-up. So glad you're here."

"You will be. Don't worry." Trip shoves the tumbler into Nate's hand. "Next order of business: Is there furniture on that balcony?"

Nate lifts his tumbler to eye level, clearly displeased with how full it is. "A couple chairs."

"Perfect." Trip goes to the sliding door. The lock is flipped closed and there's a wooden dowel between the door and the wall. "You really that worried about someone scaling the building all the way up here and breaking into your place?"

"Better safe than sorry," Nate states simply.

Trip bites his tongue to keep himself from pointing out Nate has willingly let someone he knows to be a thief into his apartment. He stoops to pull the bar out and flips the lock.

The balcony is small and does not hold much. There are two wooden chairs with earth-toned cushions on them, a small table between them, and a potted plant taking up a large amount of the right corner. Trip chooses the seat closest to the plant and sits crisscross on the cushions while he sips his drink. The smoky burn of it in his throat reminds him of bonfires and winter months. He prefers the sweet heat of honey whiskey, but this is better than vodka and he isn't here to complain about a free drink, no matter what it is. He pulls a crumpled pack of cigarettes from his pocket and lights one. "Is this your favorite thing to drink?"

"Um..." Nate clears his throat. He looks pale, shaken. He clears his throat a second time. "Yeah, I guess." He scratches at his throat hard enough to leave a spot of pink on the skin above his collar and Trip notes the soft glisten of sweat on his neck.

Trip rests his glass on the small table between their chairs and moves to stand in front of Nate's chair. He pulls the glass from his hand, settles it beside his own and shifts his cigarette farther back between his fingers before reaching for Nate's tie.

Nate startles at the contact; his eyes jerk from his knees to Trip's hands as they pull his tie loose and then reach for the cuffs of his sleeves. He doesn't object when Trip rolls one cuff up to his elbow and then the other. He watches in silence; his gaze eventually moves up to Trip's face.

Trip sits back down and waves his cigarette at Nate's looser clothing. "That any better?"

"Thanks," Nate mumbles. He reaches for the top couple buttons of his shirt and undoes those, too. "Sorry, I was—"

"Getting fifteen shades of panicked over being freshly dumped and fired?" Trip takes a drag on his cigarette and blows the smoke out toward the street. "I noticed."

"I can start talking to people tomorrow. Maybe call some old professors to see what they know, maybe get something temporary at least while I keep looking for something bigger. Could probably try for an associate spot since I have the analyst experience." Nate talks to the melting ice in his cup.

"You gonna have to move outta this place if you don't get a new job?" Trip blows smoke into the top of his glass, watches it swirl above the ice before dissipating.

"No. I mean if I never got one, then I guess I would have to." Nate takes another drink, then touches the side of his glass to his cheek before lowering it back to his lap. "I got a good severance package and I have money saved up."

"So what's the rush?" Trip flicks the side of his cigarette and sends ash flying. He takes a last drag before throwing it over the railing.

Nate watches it sail through the air in a high arc, but he loses interest before it hits the street below. "Want to hit the ground running or whatever. Make a plan so I can get going again."

"You put any thought into the fact that you keep getting dumped on account of you're kind of a miserable drone, Nathaniel?" Trip twists to face Nate. He pulls an ice cube from his glass and pops it into his mouth. "You know what I think?"

"I don't think you're exactly withholding with any of your thoughts."

Trip chews his ice cube despite the reproachful look it earns him. "I think it wouldn't kill you to stop planning and just live for a couple minutes."

"Wow, Trip, thanks for the fortune-cookie tidbit of wisdom." Nate glowers at him. "That sounds fantastic. So I should just spend a few months binging on Netflix and booze and maybe that'll get me my life back."

"You really want all that back?" Trip pulls another ice cube from his glass. "I know I met you raw off a breakup, but I don't think I'm wrong in guessing you weren't all that fuckin' happy before the breakup happened."

"What, you reading my mind again?" Nate takes a larger gulp of his drink.

"Maybe." Trip drops the ice cube back into his cup. He's worried Nate might get too angry and kick him out altogether, so he switches tactics. "Listen, I know stubborn and maybe I can't get you to admit that you've been a miserable bastard for a good long while, but I can offer you a deal."

Nate appears to deflate; his shoulders droop and his expression turns weary. He turns his gaze to the buildings on the opposite side of the street. "What kind of deal?"

"You let the whole plan thing go for..." Trip says, screwing up his face while he thinks. "Two months—no, three, three is good—and just live for a bit, and I'll keep you entertained."

"Doesn't sound like much of a deal."

"I beg to differ. You can supply the food and the booze." Trip polishes off his drink before pulling Nate's glass from his hand. He settles both on the table. "And I promise I'll be plenty good to you."

Nate startles when Trip moves out of his chair and kicks a leg over Nate's knees so he's straddling his lap. Nate braces a hand on his waist as if wary of the open space behind them. "You some sort of prostitute now?"

"Just a good friend." Trip reaches for Nate's hand still resting on the arm of his chair, moves it back to settle on his waist with the other.

Nate's hands stay where they are. His gaze shifts from Trip's left eye to his right. "We're not friends."

"No, I guess we're not." Trip's hands shift to Nate's chest. His heart's hammering under Trip's palm through the fabric of his shirt. He pulls one of Scarlett's favorite lines. "Everyone could always use another friend in this city, though, right?"

When Trip kisses him, Nate sighs into it as if it's a relief; his left hand shifts up to Trip's neck to hold him in place. It's oddly intimate, but Trip doesn't mind. Nate's not a bad kisser. His hands are warm and his tongue tastes like Scotch and smoke; it makes Trip slightly dizzy. That might be hunger talking, too.

He shifts his hips so he can get a hand on Nate's belt and undoes it with quick fingers before working his hand down Nate's boxers. He's bigger than Trip expected, but that's not a surprise he minds.

Nate groans when Trip's mouth shifts to his neck; he presses his hips higher into Trip's hand. Trip works him slow, sinks his teeth into the shell of his ear in the place he knows will raise goose bumps on Nate's skin. All men are the same in this sense. Trip knows how to make them comfortable, knows how to make them feel good. Nate is probably not as violent as some, though only time will tell. He's definitely more polite than most, but that does not make Trip any less wary of him. Trip is tough and knows how to fight, but he is small and that has worked against him even with some of the most docile-looking men. Nate could hurt him if he wanted to. It's a risk Trip has always been willing to take, but it is also one he is constantly mindful of. Nate is not an exception.

He slips off of Nate's lap. The pavement is cold on his knees and bare feet and he has a fleeting wish he hadn't thrown away those socks with the hole in the toe. He shakes the thought and reaches for Nate's pants, intent on pulling them down farther to make his work easier.

Trip has his hands halfway up Nate's thighs when Nate catches both of his wrists. "Wait."

Trip tenses, but he looks up at him with a smirk. He works his fingers against the tight muscles of Nate's thighs. "Hmmm?"

Nate looks toward the street, then down at Trip. "It's still light out. People—"

"Might see?" Trip creeps his fingers up a few more inches before Nate can stop him. "Half of the fun, sugar."

Nate's shirt is wrinkled, his hair is mussed and his cheeks are flushed. It's the most unkempt Trip's ever seen him and he has an intense desire to see him entirely undone.

"You're, like, nineteen."

"And you're like twenty-six." Trip settles his weight back onto his heels. He's been with men twice Nate's age when he was much younger; this age difference is not one he's worried about.

Nate releases Trip's wrists. He scrubs at the back of his neck. "We hardly know each other."

Trip stands with a hand on each armrest of Nate's chair and leans close. "We're getting to know each other right now."

Nate opens his mouth, but Trip silences him with another kiss. He waits for Nate to relax before getting a hand on his undone belt. He hauls him to his feet, tugs him toward the door.

"I don't know if—" Nate's looking around his apartment as if he's not quite sure where he is.

"Shhh." Trip quiets him with another kiss. Most men don't require quite so much assurance, but Trip is charmed by Nate's nervous hands and mouth. He keeps pulling him along, and Nate keeps following. He gets him up against the edge of the staircase and kisses him until they're both breathless.

When Trip pulls away again, he stays close enough to taste smoke on Nate's breath, and he wonders if it's from the Scotch or his own mouth. "What do you say you show me that bedroom, Nathaniel?"

Nate is apparently not capable of finding his voice, so he simply nods in response. They trip over one another trying to move up the narrow stairs, but neither cares. When they reach the top of the staircase, Trip doesn't waste time looking over the bedroom. He's aware that it's small, with the bed taking up most of the room. That bed is all he needs to know about in this space. He pushes Nate down onto it with a hand on his chest and settles himself on top of him, one hand already working its way back down Nate's underwear.

Nate makes no protests this time when Trip strips off his pants. He pulls Trip's T-shirt over his head, touches the exposed skin and Trip's hair and wherever else he can reach. He's soft with his hands; he likes pulling Trip close so he can kiss him. This foreplay is strange in its softness, but Trip is not altogether uncomfortable with it.

He's not sure what happens after this: if he will be kicked out while they're still sweating and panting, if he'll be allowed to spend the night, if he'll be asked back. Normally he does not care. He does not have the time to worry about later when he has now to deal with, and right now seems like a pretty damn good thing.

SiX.

Trip has perfected the art of sneaking out after a one-night stand. He usually stays most of the night for the sake of a few hours of sleep in a semi-comfortable bed, but come four or five a.m., his clothes are on, his bag is packed and he is gone. He wonders if some of his more intoxicated conquests think they simply imagined him and chalk up the lightness in their wallets as too much cash spent at the bar.

He wakes, confused, to find himself alone in bed. He reaches for the space Nate had occupied. The sheets are cold and he can hear the muted sound of water running somewhere in the apartment. If he leaves before Nate's out of the shower, he can disappear just as easily as if he'd woken first. He stays where he is, a hand still on the empty pillow beside him.

He's not sure how to handle Nate. He'd made the deal with him yesterday without thinking. It had been like kissing Nate the first time: He hadn't planned on it, but he'd had to do something. Anything.

He pushes himself out of the bed, then moves past his abandoned clothes and down the stairs to the bathroom. He hums "Sympathy for the Devil" by the Stones and makes no effort at keeping quiet when he dances around the running shoes and shorts folded on the floor and slips in past the shower curtain, but Nate startles anyway.

Trip taps his naked wrist. "You know what time it is?"

"Um… five something?" Nate scrubs the water from his eyes, blinks at Trip wildly as though he can't quite figure out what he's doing here.

"Like five something." Trip tilts his head. "You one of them early-bird-gets-the-worm types? I should have known."

"I was going to run, but I changed my mind." Nate looks Trip over and then glances at his own naked body as if them being naked together is something awkward. "I decided to just shower. Sorry if I woke you up."

Trip shakes his head. He hadn't seen much of Nate's body in the dark of the bedroom, but he appraises him slowly now, not at all embarrassed to be caught staring. He has freckles on his shoulders and a scar on the right side of his abdomen, and the whole of him is built solid and strong. Trip meets Nate's eyes again and whistles.

Nate laughs, then scrubs a hand over the back of his neck. "If you want the shower, I can go."

"You were here first." Trip shivers. "Just share some of the hot water and we'll be square."

Nate steps to his left and plasters himself to the wall, but they still end up pressed together while they negotiate the space under the water.

"For such a nice apartment, this shower sure is little." Trip tips his face up to the showerhead. "Not that I'm complaining."

"Trade-off for every place, I guess," Nate mumbles, distracted.

Trip feels the familiar pinprick of eyes on him. He knows this feeling—knows that people are as taken aback by the threading of scars across his back as they are by his eyes. He looks over his shoulder at Nate. "Ugly things, aren't they?"

Nate's gaze jerks up from the exposed skin of Trip's back to his eyes. He raises his hands in innocence. "I, no, they're just, they're—"

Trip considers letting Nate babble on, but instead he reaches around him for a bottle of shampoo. "You don't actually have to answer that."

Nate closes his mouth; his eyes still dart between Trip's face and back.

Trip turns his back to Nate again, scrubs shampoo into his hair and keeps humming to fill the sudden quiet. He's rinsed the suds from his hair and started a new song when soft fingertips touch a scar low on his hip. Nate's voice accompanies the touch, just as soft. "I'm sorry."

Trip shakes off his surprise before looking back over his shoulder at Nate. "For what? Staring? Everyone does. Doesn't bother me no more, promise."

"No, for..." Nate's hand is still on his hip, warm and solid. "For whatever happened. I'm sorry."

Trip licks his lips, not sure what to say to such soft words. He lifts a hand, drops it back to his side. He twists to face Nate more fully. Nate's frowning at him with enough pity to make Trip forget whatever it was he'd wanted to do with his hands. "Bear fight. They're nasty things, them grizzlies."

"Didn't know there were grizzlies down south." Nate's eyes skim Trip's chest before moving back up to his face.

"Never said it happened in the south." Trip's lightheaded, surrounded by so much heat. He prods Nate in the chest with a finger. "For all you know, I could be a worldly guy."

"Hmmm." Nate pushes Trip's hair off of his forehead. "You want some breakfast?"

Trip's stomach growls a loud note before he can respond, and it occurs to him that he's not sure when he last ate. "My stomach says sure."

"Great." Nate's gaze flits between Trip's eyes and his mouth.

Trip gives Nate a quick nip on the shoulder. He twists around fast enough to crank the shower handle all the way to cold before hopping out into the cold air of the bathroom.

To Trip's delight, Nate lets out a startled gasp before stumbling out after him. Nate throws him a towel from the shelf at his side. "Asshole."

Trip catches the towel, snaps it at Nate before wrapping it around his waist.

Nate turns off the water and pulls out a second towel for himself. Outside of the small, shared space of the shower, Nate is awkward and stiff. He steps out of Trip's way whenever he comes too close and dresses in the bathroom despite Trip's teasing.

Trip puts on his underwear and his pants, but he doesn't bother with his shirt. He sits on the edge of the breakfast bar and drinks ice water while Nate busies himself brewing coffee and cracking eggs into a pan.

Rather than drive Nate crazy by stealing bites out of the pan on the stove or fussing with the drawers again, Trip stays in his spot on the counter and watches Nate shift around the kitchen in a routine that is clearly more comfortable for him than having another person in his apartment. Trip wonders about him, about serious, sweet Nate and the boy in his picture who looks more likely to crack an egg over Trip's head for the sheer silliness of it than to monitor them quietly while they fry in a pan. "Why'd you go into business? Number-crunching just really get you going or something?"

Nate pushes eggs out of the pan and onto two plates. "Seemed like it made sense at the time."

"Hmmm, there's that signature deeply-rooted passion everyone loves so much in you, Nathaniel." Trip scoots an inch out of the way when Nate places a set of forks and napkins on the counter beside him.

Nate looks at him sharply before pulling down a couple of coffee mugs. "It's a good career path. There's opportunity for upward mobility and financial security and all that."

Trip waves his glass at Nate's back. "You seem more flat-lined than anything, pal."

Nate holds a plate in each hand. "I don't have to feed you breakfast."

"No, you don't," Trip agrees. He grabs a fork and a napkin before shifting off of his place on the counter and into a seat at the breakfast bar.

Nate stares at him before dropping a plate in front of him with a resigned sigh. "You want coffee?"

Trip nods fast, his fork already in hand. He takes a bite of eggs and moans. "Nathaniel, the sex was good, but Jesus Christ, you're a fucking master when it comes to breakfast."

That earns him a coffee cup beside his plate. "You want cream or anything for your coffee?"

Trip shakes his head, too invested in his plate to care about much else just now. He doesn't remember the last time he ate something this good.

Nate stands on the other side of the breakfast bar and eats standing up. His gaze remains fixed more on Trip than on his plate. "You want anything else to drink? Milk? Green juice?"

Trip meets his eyes. "Look at you, Nathaniel, you can make jokes. This whole single and unemployed thing is doing wonders for you already."

Nate lowers his fork to the counter. "Thanks for the reminder."

"Aw, come on, this isn't so bad. Good shower, good food." Trip points his fork at himself. "And a great fuck. Admit it, this hasn't been a half-bad fifteen hours for you."

"I guess not." Nate lifts his coffee mug, stares into it before taking a drink. "I think I'm gonna sign up for a marathon."

"Yeah?" Trip's nearly cleared his plate. He puts his fork down long enough to take a drink from his coffee cup. He makes a mental note to let Nate know his coffee is almost as good as his food.

Nate's checking something on his cell phone. "Yeah, maybe do some 5Ks along the way. I'll work my way up to it."

"D' you just really need a way to make yourself miserable or what?" Trip sets back to work on what's left of his toast, but he keeps an eye on Nate.

"I like running." Nate glances at Trip's empty plate and drops his piece of toast onto it. "Do you run or do, like, sports or whatever?"

"Are we getting to know each other again?" Trip accepts the offered toast, points it at Nate. "Is this what happens on those dating websites? You just ask each other questions until someone mans up and asks the other guy if he can suck his dick?"

"Kind of." Nate goes back to the stove and pulls the frying pan from the stovetop. He twists on the kitchen faucet. Trip finishes off Nate's toast and offers the plates for washing, but Nate waves him off. "They can go in the dishwasher. It's on your left."

Trip puts the plates and forks in the dishwasher before returning to his spot at the breakfast bar to nurse what's left of his coffee. "I got into fights and slung meth for my dad. Do those count as hobbies?"

Nate twists to look at him, no doubt checking for any sign of a joke. Apparently he doesn't know what to make of Trip's smirk and he doesn't want to ask, so he turns his attention to drying the frying pan with a dishtowel before replacing it in a cabinet beside the stove. "You played guitar, didn't you? That's a thing."

"It's something." Trip turns to check on his guitar. It's tucked safely into a corner beside the couch where he left it the night before.

"You're good." Nate's drying his hands on the dishtowel. He folds it into a neat rectangle before draping it back over the handle of the oven door. "You want to be a musician?"

"I want to stop playing twenty fuckin' questions." Trip drains his coffee mug before sitting back in his chair. He's showered, well fed and well fucked, and it is without a doubt the most comfortable he's felt in a very long time. This deal with Nate, so far, is turning out to be a good one, but he's not interested in getting too intimate, explaining the details of his life. This is business. "I do believe I promised you some entertainment."

Nate throws away the coffee filter and fusses with the empty pot. "I don't know if I want any."

"Nathaniel, we're making your life some semblance of interesting and a deal's a deal. I owe you for breakfast, and I don't like being in the red with people." Trip shoves himself upright and jogs up the steps to Nate's bedroom to hunt for his shirt.

Nate scrubs down the rest of the kitchen; his gaze follows Trip while he moves around the apartment collecting the rest of his things. He offers no commentary other than to offer a toothbrush still in its plastic wrapping. He scowls when Trip asks if he's got a whole drawer full of unused toothbrushes for random fucks.

"It's from the dentist. I was keeping it until I needed to replace mine."

"You sure? Thought I spotted some condoms in that drawer, too."

Nate ignores him and stands in the bathroom doorway while he brushes his teeth. Trip keeps wandering the apartment, curious about records and coffee table books and art prints. When they finish brushing their teeth, Trip doesn't know what to do with the toothbrush. Nate takes it from him and puts it in the drawer beside his. Trip wants to make a joke about it, but he can't find the words, so he ventures toward the front door.

Trip pulls the box of Nate's personal items from the closet. "What do you actually truly want out of this box of shit?"

"What?" Nate is still busy turning off lights and picking at an invisible spot on the countertop. "Why?"

Trip sits down on the floor so fast that it makes his hips and both knees pop. He opts to ignore the ache and the look of concern Nate turns his way. He rifles through the box with quick hands and pulls out a couple of framed pictures, a wedding announcement and a penlight. He is, after all, a professional at choosing which items are worth holding on to. "I have a personal soft spot for these things in particular, but if there's anything else you want, decide now."

"Fine, I'll play along." Nate gives up on the counter and comes to crouch beside the box. He frowns into the mess Trip has made before pulling out a pair of headphones, the plant in a yellow ceramic pot and a pen that looks fairly nice, though Trip doesn't have much knowledge on what constitutes a nice pen. Nate puts the pen back into the box. "There, you happy?"

"Practically a kid at Christmas. You sure that's everything you want?" Trip looks into the box again and then back up at Nate. When Nate nods, Trip springs back to his feet, his chosen items abandoned on the floor beside the closet. He ignores Nate's protests and leaves him behind to lock the door and make sure the lights are off before he joins Trip at the elevator.

Nate holds out a black zip-up sweatshirt as they get into the elevator. There's a logo for Pine View Resort complete with a crop of screen-printed Douglas firs printed on the upper left corner.

Trip shifts the box in his arms. "You can't carry that for yourself? My arms are kind of full over here."

"I just checked the weather." Nate's still holding the sweatshirt out to Trip, looking as if he's slightly embarrassed. "It's cold and you're in short sleeves."

"I'm supposed to wear it?" Trip is still staring at the sweatshirt, suddenly uncomfortable.

"Yeah," Nate replies. "Stick out your arm."

Trip shifts the box to balance between his left arm and hip and does as he's told. He jumps when Nate shifts the jacket over his wrist and up his shoulder. Nate meets his eyes, seeming confused, but Trip just grins back. "I'd think you'd like undressing me more than adding more layers."

"Maybe later." Nate pulls the sweatshirt over Trip's other arm and pulls the sleeve up onto his shoulder before reaching for the zipper. Trip holds the box away from his body to make room for Nate's hand. He nips at Nate's fingers when they reach his chest.

Nate snaps his hand back. He nods at the box in Trip's arms. "What're you doing with that, anyway?"

"You'll see." Trip winks. He steps off the elevator and moves out onto the sidewalk.

Despite the glare of the sun and a nearly cloudless sky, Nate had been right about the weather. The air is cold with the first true bite of fall and it stings Trip's ears and nose. The sweatshirt is too big, and one shoulder keeps falling down to his elbow, but Trip is warm, and the fleece inside the sleeves is soft against his skin.

Nate follows Trip down the sidewalk with the same slightly depressed look he's always got. He reminds Trip of a children's book character, though he can't remember whom. His mother didn't read all that much and he didn't pay attention well in school.

Trip parades them south and then east. They pass coffee shops, bars and apartment buildings and walk beneath scaffolding in a seeming endless expanse of construction. Trip watches as the buildings grow shorter and then taller again as they near the edge of the island, and then they are stepping into Carl Schurz Park. The sun shines brighter here outside of the shadow of the buildings and it lights Trip's shoulders in warm patches through the branches of the trees lining the sidewalk. The park is alive with people, as so much of New York constantly is, although it's a weekday afternoon. Nannies push infants in strollers, nurses in powder-blue scrubs shuffle along slowly beside elderly women hunched over walkers, and teenagers dressed in school-issued gym uniforms sprint down the expanse of cobblestones in front of the river, shouting happily to one another.

Trip passes all of these people and finally pauses beside the guardrail in front of the river. He turns to look at Nate. "You ready?"

"For what?" Nate looks longingly at several joggers in Under Armour and Nike shoes running past them.

Trip drops the box on the sidewalk with a loud thump before turning to peer over the edge of the barricade. The river stretches out long and wide, swirling past Roosevelt Island on the opposite bank. The water below churns in dark eddies; the occasional branch or piece of garbage drifts past in a current that Trip thinks is probably swifter than it appears from so high above. "We are giving this shit a good old-fashioned river burial."

Nate looks back and forth between the box at his feet and Trip, who's leaning over the barricade to get a better look at the water below. "Excuse me?"

Trip pulls himself up so he's sitting on the edge of the barricade, swinging his feet. "You need me to spell it out for you even clearer? Pick up the fuckin' box and toss it in the river."

"Pretty sure that's illegal." Nate points at the pavement. "Get down, would you? I'll hang out with you, but let's go do something different."

"Like what?" Trip rests his palms on the edge of the barricade and gets his feet under himself. When he's sure he's steady enough, he lets go and straightens up to stand on the metal bar. "We gonna go balance checkbooks or brood over bad books all day?"

Nate jolts forward and reaches a hand toward Trip as if intent on grabbing him. He must think better of it because he drops his hands and stares at Trip. "Christ, Trip, could you please just get down?"

Trip pretends to wobble on his perch with his weight shifting from his left foot to his right and his arms outstretched. "Would sure be a good distraction from the whole 'fired and dumped in the same month' thing if I fell in, wouldn't it? I can't swim."

"I'd rather you didn't fall in." Nate holds out his hand, palm up. He peers down at the water and swallows dryly. "Seriously, please get down. I've got a thing about heights and you're about to give me a freaking heart attack."

Trip studies Nate's outstretched hand before taking it and jumping back down onto the sidewalk. "You're no fun at all, you know that?"

"I'll get over it." Nate's shoulders go looser. He turns slightly pale while he peers at the water below. "I may not be fun, but at least I'm not the idiot who was five seconds from falling into the East River."

"Relax, it was a joke. I'm fine." Nate's fun to push, but Trip is uncomfortable and agitated under the sudden concern.

Nate stares at him in silence. He lifts the box before turning to the water. "All of it?"

"You gotta decent arm on you?" Trip raises an eyebrow. He claps his hands together when Nate nods to confirm that, yes, he can throw. "Make that shit fly, Nathaniel."

Nate hesitates before turning the box upside down. His things land with an anticlimactic plop in the water below. Most of it floats.

Trip leans over the rail, but he keeps his feet planted on the ground. "That was not nearly as exciting as I thought it would be. Do you feel better?"

"Not really, no." Nate watches his things get carried away with the current. "You think you can get fined or arrested for doing that?"

"Maybe. Dunno." Trip glances around them, but they haven't attracted any spectators and there isn't a cop in sight. "I really thought that would have been more fun, or at least seemed symbolic or something. You look like a guy who appreciates symbolic gestures."

"I'd rather still have my job and all of my things on my desk." Nate's watching the water and he looks even more put out.

Trip leans back on the rail. "Where's the river go, you s'pose?"

"Flows both ways, so either Long Island Sound or New York Bay, then out to the Atlantic, I guess." Nate's squinting at where his things have disappeared. "Technically not even a river. It's a strait."

"Well, ain't you a regular encyclopedia of knowledge?" Trip turns his gaze back to Nate.

Nate meets his eyes briefly before looking back out toward the water, mumbling, "I read a book about it."

"About the East River?" Trip contemplates sitting on the bars again, but he doesn't want to deal with Nate's fussing, so he stays where he is. "A whole fuckin' book on nothing but a cesspool of a river that's apparently not even a river?"

Nate straightens up. "Taught me something, didn't it?"

"I guess." Trip pushes himself off the barricade and pivots on his heel. "Onward to bigger and better things then."

Nate follows after him, his phone in hand. "Where to?"

"We're gonna get drunk." Trip pulls the sleeve of his borrowed sweatshirt back onto his shoulder. It falls right back down again.

"It's barely eight." Nate's gaze is still on his phone, but he spares Trip a brief look while they're halted at a stoplight. When Trip raises his eyebrows in a sign of "So what?" Nate sighs. "It's a weekday. Nothing's going to even be open."

"We could go back to your apartment and have sex again." Trip eyes the cars farther down the street. He's fairly sure he can make it across the road before they reach the intersection. "By the time we're finished, maybe you'll be less you and relax enough to have some fun with me."

Nate catches a handful of Trip's shirt and tugs him back onto the sidewalk as the blare and fade of a car horn tears past them. "You have some sort of death wish? And I'm still not drinking on a Wednesday morning. I'm unemployed, not an alcoholic."

"They make a decent coupling, though, don't they?" Trip retorts. "I didn't hear you object to the sex either, just saying."

Nate's cheeks flush red. He stuffs his hands in his pockets. "Don't you want to… I don't know, go do something else for a bit? Like, an activity or whatever."

"We have been doing activities. We showered and ate breakfast and dumped your shit in the not-river. Pretty sure sex constitutes an activity, too, by the way."

Nate waits until they're safely across the street to speak again. "What about the Met?"

"What about it?" Trip kicks at an acorn on the sidewalk. It skitters ahead of him, and he kicks it again when they've caught up to it.

"There's, um, there's this Caravaggio exhibit I heard was supposed to be pretty good. Would you maybe want to go for a bit?" Nate focuses on the acorn still making a path ahead of them. "I mean, like, with me. Now. Or the Whitney is a little further down, but—"

Trip kicks the acorn one last time before twisting to walk backward and face Nate. "You know, for a guy who was pretty damn comfortable literally licking my asshole last night, you sure do get tongue-tied asking if I want to go stare at some pictures with you."

Nate jolts to a stop, cheeks scarlet.

"You blush a lot, too." Trip pulls the sleeve of the sweatshirt up again. He zips it up closer to his neck. "Nothin' wrong with that. I like red. It's a good color on you."

"Are you always so crass?" Nate is still frozen in place.

Trip shrugs. He gave up on manners a long time ago unless he really wants something. He feels guilty about it sometimes. Pastor Welk went through plenty of trouble trying to make him decent, but the lessons hadn't stuck much when Trip never had anywhere to use them. Nate's still stuck in his same place, so Trip reaches for his sleeve and tugs him forward a few paces. "Let's go see your pictures, Nathaniel."

• • •

The Metropolitan Museum of Art is one of the only reasons Trip ever comes to the Upper East Side during daylight hours. It's air conditioned to near-freezing levels in the summer months and warm when the snow falls, and, due to its sheer size, no one notices or seems to care if someone wants to spend one hour or a whole day. For the few dollars price of admission, the Met has always been a temporary escape for Trip. He feels safe and grounded surrounded by oil paintings and marble statues the way he used to feel safe and grounded lying on a mahogany church bench with the smell of Pine-Sol in his nose. He says none of this to Nate.

Going to the Met is as nice a way to pass the afternoon as anything else, but when they arrive at the steps, they are greeted by a sign announcing the museum is closed for an event.

"The damn place is as big as a city block and they've gotta close the whole thing for one little dinner?" Trip squints through the window.

"Probably a curator thing or something." Nate studies the sign posted in the door. "We can go some other time."

"Yeah, but we have a whole day to kill now." Trip smiles at Nate. "You got the time?"

Nate raises his wrist and looks momentarily surprised and then angry over his bare wrist. He sticks out his hand to Trip. "Give it back."

Trip pulls the watch from his pocket. "Why do you even wear the thing if you never check it? I've had ahold of that since we got off the elevator."

"Why do you keep taking my things?" Nate struggles for a few moments trying to get the clasp closed on his watch.

"You make it easy." Trip snaps his fingers. "I might have just come up with the perfect activity for us."

Nate has one hand cupped over his watch as if he thinks Trip might take it again. "What?"

"You wanna learn how to do it?"

"Steal from people?" Nate wrinkles his nose.

"Keep it down." Trip steps closer and drops his voice. "We won't take anything important."

"It's *stealing*," Nate hisses back as his gaze darts around the crowd on the steps.

"We'll give it all back." Trip makes an "X" over his chest. "Cross my heart."

"No."

"It's gonna be fun," Trip whines. "Come on, Nathaniel, lighten up. You know you want to know how I do it."

Nate hesitates. He fiddles with his watch. "Fine. Just once."

Trip grabs ahold of the edge of Nate's jacket. He tugs him down so they're sitting on the steps. "All right, listen close."

Trip explains the general rules of how to spot an easy mark, which fingers to use to make the grab, the importance of a distracting environment. It's nothing he's been taught, so he's not sure if there are more refined tricks, but the ones he uses have worked well for him so far.

Nate appears to be a more interested learner than Trip thinks he would care to admit. He leans close and nods along as Trip talks, but when Trip stands and announces it's time they actually put their lessons to use, Nate's eyes go wide.

"I can't." Nate shakes his head hard. "It's interesting and everything, but I just—I can't."

"Sure you can." Trip crouches back down and scans the crowd for someone easy. His gaze lands on a group of women with their cameras aimed up toward the pillars of the museum. "There. Do you see that family? Whole bunch of distracted tourists. Easy."

"I'm not taking stuff from a bunch of people trying to enjoy their vacation." Nate looks reproachful. "That's awful."

"I told you we'd give it all back!" Trip lets out an exasperated sigh. "Fine. Just come with me, and I'll show you."

Nate must be more willing to bear witness to the crime than to participate because he trails after Trip without fuss.

Trip has his person selected before he's even halfway down the stairs. She appears to be in her late thirties and she's built short and sturdy. She's dressed in jeans, an artificially paint-splattered New York City T-shirt and comfortable-looking tennis shoes, no doubt meant for easy walking around the city. She has her hair pulled back into a slightly off-center ponytail and she's directing the camera on an iPad up toward the pillars of the museum.

Trip points her out to Nate. "What do you think?"

"She's distracted and her purse is open and not too close to her body. She's perfect." Nate glances her over. "This is awful. Like, really, really awful, Trip."

"Ya know what?" Trip pauses in their descent. "Let's make this more interesting."

"You gonna steal a painting from the Met, too?"

"That's going to be the final masterpiece of my career. I'm not ready for that yet." Trip rocks up onto his toes. "No, let's play a game."

"Is everything a game to you?"

"Makes life less dull, don't it?" Trip looks at the pack of women to make sure they haven't disappeared. "Here's the deal: You tell me what I ought to pull out of her purse, and that's the thing I'll get."

"How am I supposed to know what's in her purse?"

"Just look at her and you'll get a feel for it." Trip flaps a hand toward their person. "She's got hand sanitizer, a travel bottle of antacid pills, a pen, some cough drops, a granola bar, her wallet, a compact and probably a whole shit-ton of other stuff. Just pick something."

Nate sighs. "Fine. You sure about that granola bar?"

"Might be a fruit snack or some crackers or something, but the lady's got a snack in there." Trip turns to check her again. "I'm positive."

"Fine. That then—the snack thing." Nate sits on the step. "I'm waiting here."

"Suit yourself." Trip moves down the rest of the steps. His group is all fast talking and noisy shouting. No one so much as offers him a second glance as he works his magic. He's gone and back at Nate's side in a minute.

Nate raises his eyebrows. "So?"

"So I should have put money on this bet or something." Trip pulls the granola bar from his pocket and tosses it on Nate's lap.

Nate looks as though he wants to be angry, but then he's laughing, bright and happy. "No fucking way."

"Yes fucking way." Trip points at Nate triumphantly. "I told you!"

Nate turns the granola bar over in his hands as though he needs to check to be sure it's real. "Incredible."

Trip takes a bow. "Could show you how to do it, too, ya know."

"I think I'd rather give things back." Nate glances at the group.

"Putting shit back is harder." Trip shakes his head. "I usually just hand it back to them and tell them they dropped it."

Nate frowns, but it's not all that angry. "Like my wallet?"

Trip winks. "Just like your wallet."

"Fine. Let's give it back then." Nate pushes himself to his feet. "It's cold out here."

They walk down the steps and Trip approaches the women a second time. He taps his mark on the arm. "Excuse me, ma'am?"

The woman pulls her purse closer. She takes a step back.

Trip doesn't mind. He knows her type. He makes her nervous. He holds out the granola bar. "Hate to bother you, ma'am, but I think you dropped this."

She stares at the granola bar and then at Trip. “That’s all right.”

“Not asking for a tip or nothing for returning it.” Trip keeps his smile in place, though it’s starting to hurt. “Just would have felt bad not making sure it didn’t get back to you.”

When it’s clear Trip isn’t backing down, she takes it.

Trip salutes her, loose and lazy. “Enjoy the rest of your visit, ma’am.”

Nate watches the group of women, but turns his gaze to Trip when he returns to his side. “She was kind of a bitch.”

“She’s all right. I make some people nervous.” Trip flaps a hand at his face. “She thought I was gonna steal from her or something. She wasn’t wrong.”

Nate follows Trip down the remaining steps to the sidewalk. He clears his throat awkwardly. “Does that ever make it hard doing the park-musician thing?”

“What? Making people nervous?” Trip looks up at Nate as they make their way east. “Doesn’t happen with everyone, and people usually like me better when I’m playing. I don’t seem like an actual person. I’m just a piece of the park or wherever I’m playing. Cheap entertainment, ya know?”

Nate’s pace slows. “No, I don’t. You are a person.”

Trip holds up a hand, rubs his fingers and thumb together. “People pay me either way, so who cares how they think of me?”

“People need to—” Nate pauses, shakes his head. “I don’t know. It should matter. That’s all I’m saying… you’re a person.”

They’ve reached a subway stop. Trip pauses to the right of the stairs. “That’s sweet, Nathaniel.”

Nate looks toward the steps. He rubs a hand over the back of his neck. “So…”

“So.” Trip shifts his bag down beside his feet so he can free himself of Nate’s sweatshirt. He’s barely got a grip on the zipper when Nate’s hand comes to rest over his.

"Hold onto it. It's cold." Nate's hand stays where it is, warm and solid as it had been on Trip's back in the shower earlier that morning. He meets Trip's eyes and his attention shifts from one to the other. "I'll see you soon?"

"You know where to find me." Trip crouches to pick up his bag. The motion won't allow Nate's hand to stay pressed to his, and its absence leaves a cold spot on the back of Trip's hand and wrist.

"You got a phone number or something?" Nate's brow is knit in a tight frown. He keeps eyeing where the sweatshirt has slipped back off of Trip's shoulder.

"Community phone." Trip pulls the fallen sleeve higher on his shoulder. "I don't carry it much, but if you want the number, you can chat with Scarlett or one of the others whenever you want, I suppose."

"The others?" Nate echoes. He's patting his pockets as though he's lost something.

"Roommates." Trip unzips his bag, rifles through it until he finds a black marker. He holds it out to Nate; his left hand is still buried in his bag trying to dredge up a spare piece of paper. "Got a whole band of 'em."

Nate takes the marker in his left hand, catches Trip's wrist in his right. "How many?"

Trip does his best to hold still. He watches while Nate writes something across his palm. "Um, four and a half."

"Someone not live there all the time?" Nate blows on the ink on Trip's palm. His breath is as warm as his hands.

"Not exactly." Trip lifts his palm to study it after Nate releases his wrist. A phone number is written across it in blocky print with Nate's name above it. Trip points to his name. "Glad you added this. Might have forgotten."

"Sounds like you meet enough guys that you might." Nate clears his throat, reaches for the back of his neck a second time.

"Um, call me if you want. You know where to find me, too, ya know."

"I know." Trip drops his hand, steps closer to Nate. "I'll see you around, Nathaniel."

Nate pulls the zipper on Trip's sweatshirt higher. "See you around, Trip."

Trip could kiss Nate the way you're probably supposed to kiss people goodbye after they've fucked you and washed you and fed you and spent time with you. Trip pushes himself up on his tiptoes, leans close. He licks Nate across the cheek and stays just long enough to see the look of disgusted surprise that crosses Nate's face. He darts down the stairs to the subway.

To his surprise, a peal of laughter sounds behind him, and he doesn't have to turn around to know it was Nate. The sound stays with him for the subway ride to Union Square and only fades as he's closing the door to his apartment.

Devon's shoving him before he can so much as lower his bag to the floor. "Where the hell have you been?"

Trip frees himself of his bag and steps into Devon's space. He doesn't like confrontations that start out this aggressively. They make his skin itch; his hands curl into fists before he can think about it. He's always had a short fuse, and the abruptness of Devon's anger only serves to fuel his temper. He shoves him back, harder. "What the hell do you care?"

"You disappeared Monday and didn't come back, you asshole. It's almost Wednesday night!" Devon growls.

Trip's forgotten he didn't come home Monday. It had been a late night. He'd gone to a club with too-loud music and someone named Amir or Aziz… something like that, who'd ordered over-priced bottles of champagne on ice and held court in a VIP section away from the rest of the club. He hadn't been so bad. All he'd wanted was a blow job and to watch Trip eat maraschino cherries and flirt with other boys. By the time he'd released Trip back into the world, most of the people in suits were already on their way to work, so there'd seemed little point in going home. Trip had gone to the park and stood ankle-deep in the fountain to keep himself more awake and draw a better crowd.

That night and his night with Nathaniel shouldn't matter to Devon, though. He's never been one to get on Trip's back about disappearing for a few days at a time. It's confusing and the confusion only exacerbates Trip's anger. He steps closer with a wicked smile. "What, you jealous or something? If you can pay, you can have a go, too, sugar."

Devon shoves him hard. Moves as though he's planning on doing it again.

"Boys." Scarlett appears from her bedroom with June on her hip. Her hair is in a sloppy ponytail that's not entirely centered at the crown of her head and she's wearing the fake eyelashes and red lipstick meant for nights at the strip club. "That's enough."

It's not like Devon to pick a fight, especially not with Trip. Devon knows where Trip grew up, knows Trip could beat him onto the floor and just keep punching if he wanted to. He knows better than to pick this kind of fight. Trip calms himself enough to remember this, to remember Devon hasn't been Devon lately and it might be best to let this one indiscretion go. Trip takes a step back.

Devon seems to remember, too, because his shoulders go suddenly loose and his eyes drop to the floor. "You missed a lot of shit."

"What kind of shit?" Trip flexes his hands at his sides in a weak attempt at calming himself. "Liam dye his hair again? Ain't much new about that."

Scarlett notes Trip's hands. She steps closer and offers the baby. "Jude's gone."

Trip takes June, but his gaze stays on Scarlett. "Gone how? Missing?"

"Gone like 'followed his method-acting heart all the way to Los Angeles' gone," Liam says as he steps out of his bedroom, wiping a paint-stained rag over his hands. His hair is a muted shade of lavender. "And, yes, I dyed it. Don't say one goddamn word."

"Gone without paying his part of the rent or bills," Devon adds. He crosses the family room to sit on the arm of the couch and pushes at the edge of the window. "Managed to leave a fuckin' note, though. Real good of him."

"We sure this isn't some sort of acting thing? Like for a role or something?" Trip looks around at all of them. When they just stare back at him grimly, Trip sighs. He sits on the floor with June in his lap. "Well, shit."

"Yeah, Morgan, shit." Devon pulls a pack of cigarettes from his pocket with shaky fingers. He lights one and holds it out the window. "I was barely gonna make rent as it was."

"I'm picking up a few extra shifts." Scarlett gives Devon and his cigarette a look, but she doesn't comment on it. Apparently the drama with a sudden lost roommate is enough to shift some of Scarlett's frustrations with Devon to Jude. She looks back to Trip. "I'm sorry that I keep doing this to you, but if you're not working on something, could you take the baby? I'll figure something out if you can't."

"I got her." Trip waves her off. He bounces the baby idly on his knee. This is bad. Going into the winter months when fewer people are milling around the parks and able to drop a few dollars for Trip was going to be hard enough with five of them paying rent; with only four of them now to split the cost of everything, it will be nearly impossible to save up enough each month to pay for all of the bills. He'll have to figure out something else.

Scarlett sits on the floor across from Trip. She reaches for her hair as if she's forgotten that it's already pulled up. Her gaze stays on June. She looks tired, and Trip wonders when she last got more than a couple hours of sleep.

They're all silent for a moment save for June burbling happily while she pulls Trip's shoelaces loose.

Liam drums his fingers on the doorframe. His fingers pause after too many minutes of silence. "I can maybe pay more. I'll look into it."

Liam, unlike the rest of them, has parents he still speaks to regularly. They help him when they can—pay for his bus ticket back to Kentucky at Christmas and offer some cash on his birthday. Trip doesn't know much about them other than that they don't have a whole lot in the way of money and they're supportive of Liam's would-be Bohemian lifestyle. At least for now, that is.

"They need a dishwasher or bus boy or somethin' at the club?" Trip chews a thumbnail, tries to dredge up the memory of anyone he's worked for in the past who might be willing to hire him back.

"They hate you there, and you know it." Scarlett pulls the hair binder from her curls and adjusts her ponytail so that it's more centered. "And, no, I don't have anything for you at the hotel either."

Trip's not a good employee and he knows it. He's no good at keeping to a schedule, he loses track of what he's supposed to be doing and, the second a manager yells at him, he yells back. He's never lasted long busing dishes or unpacking delivery trucks, and there's not much else he can do without a diploma. Still, things are too hard right now to just rely on tips he picks up for playing his guitar.

"Shit," Scarlett murmurs. She reaches for June's chubby ankle, squeezes it gently. "What the hell are we gonna do?"

"Sell June." Trip can't find the energy to put much effort into the joke. He meets Scarlett's gaze when she swats at his foot. "We'll figure something out. We always do."

No one says anything.

"I need to get going. I won't be back until late." Scarlett pushes herself to her feet. She offers Trip a hand. "How mad would you be if I stopped to see Kellan before I came home? It wouldn't be long."

Trip accepts her hand and keeps June balanced on his hip as he pulls himself upright. "Long, short—whatever blows your dress up, honey. We're fine. Nowhere to be tonight."

Scarlett turns Trip's hand over to inspect his inked palm. "You sure about that?"

Trip jerks his wrist out of her hold. "I can find somewhere to be, and you can be out your babysitter if that's what you're angling for."

"Not what I was aiming for, no." Scarlett kisses June on the cheek. She tucks the cell phone into Trip's pocket. "Put his number in the phone."

"And why would I do that?" Trip keeps his tone light. He turns his palm out to Scarlett. "Whether he's into girls or not, pretty sure you're not gonna top my performance, honey, so not entirely worth your time."

"Hmmm, possessive." Scarlett reaches out and tweaks a drawstring on Trip's sweatshirt. "Interesting."

Before Trip can say anything back, Scarlett's gone and he's left trying to calm a suddenly distraught June. Liam soon leaves for a night shift at the diner, leaving Devon, Trip and June alone. Trip passes the time reading a children's board book over and over for June while she works at pulling the drawstring out of the hood of his sweatshirt. He thinks he should tell Nate there is at least one book he's read cover to cover, though he's not sure children's books count.

Devon chain-smokes on the arm of the couch and flips through the pages of one of his newspapers so quickly that Trip is fairly certain he is not actually reading it. He lowers it abruptly to the couch cushions. "I'm headed out."

Trip watches as Devon flicks his cigarette out into the dark and pushes the window closed. He moves to the bedroom he shares with Liam and, formerly, Jude. "Where you headed?"

"None of my business where you go, is it?" Devon reappears with his jacket and shoes on. "I'll mind mine if you mind yours."

"Fair enough." June's teething on the edge of the book, but Trip makes no move to stop her. He keeps his eyes on Devon, who has stopped in his flurry of movement at the door.

Devon speaks down to his hand wrapped around the doorknob. "Sorry about earlier, man." He shakes his head. "It's been a rough couple days."

Trip offers no apology. He's not good with apologies when he's sure that he is the one in the wrong and he's even less interested when someone else started it. Still, Devon is Devon, so he does want to offer some response. He can't stand this constant tension in the apartment. "No harm, no foul, buddy."

The door closes behind Devon with a definitive snap, and Trip has a pang of anxiety that he won't be coming back. He swallows the feeling. He doesn't have the time or the energy to worry over something that hasn't happened.

When June gets fussy, Trip changes her diaper, shoves her toys into the laundry basket beside the couch and sets to work trying to put her to sleep. He walks the apartment and sings to her with one hand patting her back until she goes loose-limbed against him and he can put her down in her Pack 'n Play. He turns off the lights, not interested in paying more than is necessary when the electric bill is due.

In the sudden darkness, Trip is aware of how silent the apartment is, and it sparks another unpleasant wave of anxiety. He isn't good at being alone. He isn't good at silence.

He tucks himself into the corner of the couch and peers in at June before pulling the cell phone from his pocket. By the light of the streetlamp, he copies the numbers written across his palm into the Contacts section of the phone and saves it under "Nathaniel." He stares at the number for a long time, hits Call, waits.

It rings once, twice, three times and then goes to voice mail. Nate's voice solemnly informs Trip that he can't come to the phone right now, but if he leaves his name and number, he'll get back to him as soon as possible.

When the beep of the voice mail cuts off Nate's voice, Trip says the first thing that comes to mind. "If you're not too busy cleaning your kitchen or reading one of your books, give me a call. I have some important questions about the East River that need your attention."

Trip drops the phone beside him, then tucks a hand under the neck of his T-shirt to trace a scar on his shoulder blade. He is good at acting on impulse—it's what's gotten him this far, after all, but he isn't sure how he feels about what he's just done. He wants a cigarette. He jumps when the phone vibrates against his thigh. His anxiety melts as he pulls his hand out from under his collar to press the phone to his ear. "Hello, Nathaniel."

SEVEN.

THINGS ARE GETTING HARDER AND easier all at once. Making rent had been nearly impossible at the beginning of the month, and the full pain of fewer people to split the bills makes Trip and all of his roommates feel the full injury of Jude's disappearance when they can't make electric. Scarlett takes their cash and writes a check for what they have and sends it in, hoping it at least buys them more time.

Trip tries playing in Central Park, the steps at the Met, subway platforms and anywhere else he can think of to draw in a new crowd that might be more willing to pay him for whatever entertainment he provides. The crowds have been steadily thinning in the parks; the weather's turned so cold that most people have brought out their winter jackets and spend little time milling around. Trip throws his shirt at Nate when he informs Trip that he's heard whispers of the possibility of snow before Halloween.

Today there is no snow, but there is freezing rain. The skies are heavy gray, the rain pounds the windows of the apartment, and Liam has a fit when a leak develops above the window near the corner of the living room that holds his sculptures.

Devon puts an empty paint bucket beneath the crack. They take turns emptying the bucket into the bathtub, but no one offers a more long-lasting remedy.

Trip sits on the floor beside the bucket and watches the steady drip, drip, drip of water. He's trying to motivate himself into going out to play for a few sympathy dollars. He'd spent the entire previous day with Nate and he's too aware of how little money he has for their impending rent payment.

Usually spending time with Nate is not a problem. Trip spends his days playing, working his way steadily east until he arrives at Nate's building in the dusky early hours of the evening. The doorman insists on calling Nate the first few times Trip comes over, but he's shifted to only watching Trip with wary eyes as he passes him on the way to the elevators. Nate always answers the door with his near-signature frown, though he steps aside without any coaxing to let Trip into the apartment.

Trip makes a point of getting him to laugh. He sings a lot, strips off his clothes along with his shoes at the door and fusses with the things in the fridge until Nate relaxes enough to put a record on or strip out of some of his clothes, too. Their routine is inconsistent. Sometimes Trip spends the night; other times he sneaks out once Nate's asleep. Occasionally he climbs out of bed, still sticky and catching his breath, puts his clothes back on and leaves with a sing-songed goodbye. Nate never comments on his more abrupt disappearances; he watches Trip as if there's something he wants to say but doesn't know how.

Tuesdays are the one steady part of this thing he and Nate have created together, and Trip has spent the past three Tuesdays with Nate. Nate makes it his rest day from running, and they busy themselves exploring the city. They walk the far reaches of

Central Park, eat lobster at Chelsea Market and walk the Highline one week; explore Chinatown and Little Italy and venture into Brooklyn, where they drink beer and play arcade games another week; and, in a streak of near-manic determination, Trip makes a Tuesday activity out of trying to give Nate a blow job in the bathroom of every museum they visit on the East Side despite Nate's protesting that they'll get in trouble. Trip likes Tuesdays more than he'd care to admit.

Today is a Wednesday, though, and Trip needs to make up for the lost hours. He sticks a hand under the steady drip from the leak above the window frame and shivers at how cold the water is on his palm.

Liam sits beside him with a sketchpad on his knees. "I think I'm going to do a show."

"Yeah?" Trip watches water pool in his palm and drip over the edges of his cupped fingers. "You thinking about figuring out a way to pay rent on time and all our bills in full, too? Maybe running for president or something while you're at it?"

"You're so cynical." Liam squints at his sketchpad. He erases something. "Where there's a will, there's a way."

"Whatever you say." Trip turns his hand over and dumps the water into the bucket. He shakes out his hand and moves to stand. Liam catches a finger in one of Trip's belt loops.

"Sit. I'm not finished." Liam looks at him pointedly; he waves his pencil at the bucket. "Stick your hand back in there."

"No fuckin' way. It's cold." Trip tries to pry Liam's finger from his jeans. Liam begs him constantly to act as a model, but Trip can't stand it. He doesn't know how to hold still long enough for Liam to get what he wants onto paper, and he doesn't like to be inspected with such intensity. Besides that, he gets some small twisted pleasure out of irritating Liam.

"Please?" Liam releases Trip. "I'll feature you in my show."

"How the hell does that seem like a good argument to use with me?" Trip moves again to stand, but Liam pulls him back down.

"You're a total attention whore and you know it." Liam taps his pencil on the handle of the pail. "Stick your hand in the damn bucket, Morgan."

Trip groans but does as he's told. "You've got three minutes."

"That's all I need." Liam immediately sets back to work.

Trip watches the rain on the window and doesn't fuss when Liam adjusts his fingers or twists his wrist into some new angle. The apartment is quiet. Devon's gone missing for nearly three days and Scarlett's at a doctor's appointment with Kellan and the baby.

Trip's not home often, but when he is, he is aware of Kellan's imprint. There are vases of flowers on the card table in the kitchen, containers of date-night leftovers in the refrigerator and, sometimes, his shoes beside the door. Kellan took an immediate liking to June. He accompanies Scarlett to appointments and on walks when he can and takes the baby along to his office on Saturdays when there is free daycare for the office staff. Trip still takes the baby most Fridays and when Scarlett works nights in exchange for help with his bills.

"You're alarmingly docile these days, Trip." His eyes on his paper, Liam chews on the end of his pencil. "Like a nice stray dog looking for a belly rub or something."

"If I dump this bucket on your head, you think maybe you'll change your mind about that?" Trip makes no move to lift the bucket.

Liam waves his pencil at Trip. "It's not all the time. It's Wednesdays. You're practically *nice* on Wednesdays."

"Well fed and well fucked." Trip scratches his nose against his shoulder. "I have a set-up."

"You have a *boyfriend*." Liam speaks down at his sketchpad as he sets back to work drawing.

"I don't do boyfriends." Trip dumps water back into the bucket.

"Not what Kellan says." Liam pokes the point of his pencil into Trip's neck. "He says you and Mr. Mackey are quite the cozy couple. Personally, I can't imagine you doing domestic, but I kind of like the idea of you in an apron making cookies or something."

Occasionally, Kellan shows up at Nate's with a case of beer and cheers noisily when he spies Trip seated at the breakfast bar or emerging from the bathroom. Trip tries to excuse himself on those nights, but Kellan usually insists he stay.

Trip tears the pencil from Liam's hand and tosses it at the side of his head. "I don't have a goddamn boyfriend."

"Ow! Christ, Trip, that temper." Liam rubs his ear and stretches to retrieve his lost pencil. "For someone who can make such a good show of being halfway pleasant, you can be so goddamn mean. One of these days we need to get you in for anger management or something."

"Maybe you can put the money for your fucking gallery space toward the classes." Trip shoves himself to his feet and goes to his room to retrieve his guitar.

"I'm not done with you. Where are you going?" Liam calls after him.

"Unless you want that pencil actually through your neck next time you piss me off, I think it's a good idea for both of us if I get gone." Trip slings his guitar over his back and his bag over his shoulder.

"You're going to freeze to death." Liam puts his sketchpad down on the coffee table and pulls the rapidly filling bucket closer to his side.

"I got a jacket. I'll be fine." Trip pulls up the hood on his jacket—Nate's jacket—and tugs the zipper higher.

"That's a sweatshirt." Liam stands, the bucket hanging from one hand. "If you die, we seriously won't be able to make rent and there'll be no one to watch the baby on Fridays."

"Maybe that show of yours will bring in enough cash to pay the difference." Trip shifts his guitar higher on his shoulder. "And for daycare for the kid."

Liam gives him the finger while he moves toward the bathroom with the bucket, but offers no other smart remarks as Trip makes his way out of the apartment.

GOING OUT TO PLAY TURNS out to be a worse idea than Trip had thought. For the sake of the shelter the arch offers him, he spends some time in Washington Square Park despite its relative quiet. The park is depressing this time of year. Most of the other buskers have moved on to whatever other careers they have; the fortune-tellers, artists and dancers are all gone, too. It should be a good thing—more customers for Trip—but in the three years Trip has been doing this, that has never been the case. After the fountain is drained, it's as if all the magic of the park is drained with it: the colors faded, the people less happy, and the only music in the air coming from Trip and his guitar.

Today is not an exception. He earns some cash, the change out of someone's pocket and a granola bar from a girl whom Trip is fairly sure thinks he's homeless. He's not far from it if he doesn't make rent.

He goes for a walk, willing to brave getting wet if it means some extra cash, but it's no use. The parks and streets are near-empty and there are police stationed in nearly every subway station he checks. They give him sharp looks and, though he's usually up for a fight, Trip doesn't feel like getting himself thrown in jail. It's too lengthy a process, too expensive.

He makes his way to the steps of the Met, where he earns more from a group of tourists after he picks their pockets and offers to read their minds for a few dollars. One of them cries when he mentions her military boyfriend; another offers her number along with a dollar. Trip gets uncomfortable over the crying one, winks at the one who has offered her number. The whole affair earns him ten dollars and he decides he's had enough.

It's slightly earlier in the day than he usually goes to see Nate, but he feels vaguely nauseous and chilled to his core, so he ignores Liam's teasing voice in the back of his mind and makes the short walk to Nate's building.

When he arrives, the doorman calls after him, "Mr. Mackey's not here right now."

Trip does his best to stay on the rug in the entryway so he doesn't drip all over the floors. "You know where he went?"

"For a run or to the gym, judging by his outfit." The doorman looks over Trip's dripping clothes. "I'll let him know you stopped by."

"Mind if I wait?" Trip pulls a hair binder from his wrist and pulls his hair back so it will stop sticking to his neck.

"If you don't mind waiting outside." The doorman looks at him in a way that Trip knows well. He's not welcome here.

He salutes the doorman. "Aye-aye, sir."

He could just go home. He doesn't know when Nate's coming back, and it could be a long time. Nate has himself set on running a marathon and, if Trip's remembering correctly, he's currently doing ten or eleven miles at a time. Trip catches sight of the doorman watching him from the other side of the doors. He sits down on the top step, digs Nate's umbrella out of his bag and waves at the doorman enthusiastically. He doesn't have to wait long before he spies Nate's now-familiar form jogging down the block.

Nate stops in front of him. He rests his hands on his knees while he catches his breath and looks Trip over. "You realize it's pouring and, like, forty degrees out here?"

"I got an umbrella." Trip spins the umbrella. He looks over Nate's soaked running clothes. "Which is more than can be said for you, sugar. Don't go calling me crazy when you're the one running in this shit."

"Can't take the day off." Nate looks unhappy. "How long have you been sitting here?"

"Not long." Trip sniffles, shivers. "Decided to wait around on the off-chance you were gonna get back sooner rather than later. I didn't want to make the walk all the way back down if I didn't have to."

Nate looks at his watch. He's still panting for breath. "Why didn't you wait in the lobby?"

"Got kicked out." Trip pushes himself to his feet. His knees hurt. "Don't think your buddy who mans the door likes me much."

Nate's expression grows dark. "Come on."

Curious about Nate's agitation, Trip follows him back into the lobby. Nate stops at the doorman's station and points at Trip. "You let him in when he comes by."

The doorman's eyebrows go up. He lifts both hands in defense. "You weren't home."

"You've seen him before. You know him." Nate snaps. "You let him in."

Trip has to make a conscious effort to mold his expression into something neutral. Nate usually makes idle chat with the doormen on his way in, asks about their families and offers to make a coffee run for them when it's especially early or late. He is never rude, never angry.

The doorman looks equally alarmed by Nate's sudden anger. He turns his gaze back to Trip. "I'm sorry. My mistake."

"No problem." Trip turns to Nate. "You gonna beat the poor guy up or are we going upstairs?"

Nate's expression goes softer. "I'm sorry… just let him wait in here next time."

The doorman's expression is still a mixture of shock and concern over the sudden outburst. "Of course."

Nate is silent in the elevator; his gaze is trained on the buttons.

Trip nudges Nate's ankle with his toes. "You ever beat someone up?"

Nate casts a short glance his way. "Once. In high school."

"You win?" Trip looks Nate over. He doesn't seem like much of a fighter, but he's strong enough to probably hold his own.

Nate nods. He looks at Trip again. "You?"

"Beat people up?" Trip smiles at his shoes and nods. "Only when people make me real angry, though."

"Thought you were the angriest person in the world," Nate mumbles. He steps off the elevator when the doors slide open. His shoes squeak as he walks down the hall.

"I get into a lot of fights." Trip follows Nate into the apartment.

"What else do you do?" Nate turns to face him. He's dripping all over the wood floor, but he doesn't seem to notice. "When you get angry, what do you do with it all?"

Trip lowers his things to the floor beside the door, steps closer to Nate. "Wanna make a guess?"

Nate lifts a hand to Trip's hip, but makes no other move to touch him.

Trip reaches for Nate's wrist, pushes his hand down below the waistband of his wet jeans. "Could fuck me up against the wall. You think you'd like that?"

Nate's fingers twitch against his ass, but still, he does not move.

"No?" Trip raises his eyebrows. "What about over the kitchen counter? Work out all that aggression with some rough sex; maybe leave a bruise or two."

It has the opposite of the intended effect. Nate pulls his hand out of Trip's pants and puts one hand on his arm to push him back a pace. "I'm gonna shower."

Trip's hands hang useless at his sides as he watches Nate strip out of his wet shirt. "You want me to go?"

Nate goes to the bathroom, pauses in the doorway. He shakes his head. "Go change. I'm cold just looking at you."

Trip stays where he is and listens to the sound of the shower running. He considers going into the bathroom and climbing in along with Nate. He thinks better of it and makes a move for the stairs to seek out dry clothes.

Most of Nate's things are too big, but he finds a white T-shirt that fits and a pair of sweatpants he only has to roll up three or four times. When he goes downstairs, wet clothes in hand, Nate is still in the shower. It occurs to him he has never been left alone quite like this. No doubt wary of Trip's sticky fingers, Nate always keeps a close eye on him as he wanders the apartment.

He drops his things into the dryer tucked into the utility closet in the kitchen before moving to explore. He's inspected nearly every inch of the apartment already. He knows that Nate's books are organized by genre, his records are arranged by the year they were released and his DVDs are alphabetized. Usually Trip likes to put at least one thing out of order, just to see if Nate corrects it before the next time he comes over. He lets everything be for now and pulls a photo from the end table.

He's studied it before. It looks like Nate's family and it can't be more than a couple years old. They're arranged in front of a sign marked "Pine View Resort." Nate has his father's height and his mother's nose. He and Nora have the same ears. There are more people that look like grandparents and aunts and uncles, but Trip is sure at least of Nora and Nate's parents.

The bathroom door clicks open and Nate steps out with a towel wrapped around his waist. "You put your clothes in the dryer?"

"Yeah." Trip settles the picture back on the end table. "You want me to throw yours in there, too?"

"Thanks." Nate pauses at the base of the stairs. "Could you do something else for me?"

"Depends on what it is." Trip leans into the back of the couch; his gaze flits from Nate's naked chest to the towel slipping low on one hip.

"Pull out a bottle of something to drink?"

Trip goes to the kitchen. "I can definitely do that."

He pushes through the bottles in the liquor cabinet until he comes up with an unopened bottle of whiskey. He pours some into two tumblers and goes to the couch with them.

Nate comes down the stairs dressed in a black T-shirt and jeans. He retrieves the bottle of whiskey from the kitchen counter and puts it on the coffee table before taking the open spot beside Trip on the couch.

Trip raises his eyebrows when Nate throws back most of his drink and reaches for the bottle. He refills his glass and pours more in Trip's. "You're gonna get us drunk, Nathaniel."

"That's the plan." Nate takes another long pull from his glass.

Trip takes a smaller sip, wary of this stormy side of Nate. "You have a shitty mile time or something this week? Didn't get your spot in the New York Marathon?"

"Marathon sign-up was a long time ago." Nate mumbles. "I'm trying for next year."

"So it's the mile time that's got you so bent out of shape?"

Nate doesn't answer. "Remember when I got fired?"

"Kinda hard to forget." Trip tucks his too-cold feet under Nate's thigh.

"I worked hard there." Nate shakes his head. "Put in more hours than Kel and half those pricks combined. I was good. Really good."

"But lacked passion." Trip leans back into the arm of the couch. "Much like your failed relationship."

"I am passionate." Nate mutters. "Or at least I thought I was. I don't know what I am anymore. This was the plan, you know? I went to the right school and picked the right major and got the right job. I did it all right. I had a plan."

"We've talked about this before." Trip sips his drink and watches Nate pour more into his glass. "Ain't the whole 'plans not working out' thing why we got our deal going?"

"I need a plan. Plans are how you move forward. It's how things get done." Nate shifts in his seat.

"Relax, you're fine." Trip pushes his toes up into Nate's leg. "You can go get a job whenever you want. Breathe for a bit, huh? Pull that stick out of your ass."

"If I bother you so much, how come you stick around?"

"Who says you bother me? I like you fine." Trip tips his glass from side to side, sloshing the whiskey inside. "And a deal's a deal. I'm holding up my end."

Nate looks at his glass. "It's been over a month and I don't feel any different."

Trip tucks one of the throw pillows behind his back. "You lookin' to bitch or you actually want some advice?"

"I don't know. Both, I think." Nate pinches the bridge of his nose. "You got advice on what to do when you start realizing you're twenty-six and still have no idea what the hell you're doing?"

"Stop letting small people make you feel small, Nathaniel." Trip takes a drink. "So what if Lovett dumped you and your boss is a prick? Say 'fuck you' and just keep going."

"You said it, too." Nate drops his hand to his lap. "You said you could see how they'd think that."

"I'm a dick." Trip lowers his glass to the edge of the coffee table. "And so are you today, by the way. I know you like to feel sorry for yourself, but, Christ, you are in special form this evening, sugar."

"I hate when you call me that." Nate sits back against the couch cushions, his drink on his lap.

Trip isn't sure what to make of this situation. He and Nate talk plenty, but it's rarely so contentious. He wishes he could get Nate undressed. Sex is so much easier.

Nate reaches for the bottle again and Trip catches his wrist. "You looking to puke?"

"Just getting drunk." Nate holds his gaze. "Thought you liked doing that."

"I do, but I don't like doing it alone." Trip pulls the bottle from Nate's grip and settles it on the end table beside the picture frame. "You're well on your way to the bottom of the bag, sugar, trust me. Give it a few minutes or else you'll be passed out and I'll be bored."

Nate doesn't respond, but he doesn't reach for the bottle. He works his jaw for a moment before speaking; his voice is quiet. "I'm sorry. It's a bad day."

"Aren't all your days kind of shitty lately?" Trip raises both eyebrows.

Nate looks somber. "This one's a little worse."

Trip shifts in his seat. "Any particular reason?"

Nate finishes what's left in his glass and puts it on the table. He rests his elbows on his knees and looks terribly tired while he studies the area rug under his feet. "Remember my brother?"

"The dead brother." Trip makes a point of remaining blasé.

"Nick." Nate picks at a hangnail.

"Nicholas, Nathaniel and Nora." Trip hums a happy note. "Your parents Nina and Ned?"

"George and Laurie," Nate mutters. "Nick was two years older than me. He was gonna take over managing the resort when he graduated, go part-time to school—my parents, they own a resort on Big Sand Lake."

Trip stays quiet, afraid to interrupt this story with questions about where Big Sand Lake is and what sort of resort and everything else he wants to know.

Nate turns his gaze back to his hands. "We never got along. Do you have brothers?"

Trip's caught off guard by the question. "Five of them."

"That's a lot of brothers," Nate murmurs.

"Too many brothers," Trip agrees. He's fairly certain Nate won't remember any of this, so he adds, "All older. Real mean."

"Mine, too." Nate speaks to his knees. "We got along sometimes, but mostly we just hated each other. Used to kick the shit out of each other when our mom wasn't around and when we got older we just didn't talk at all except when we had to. Did your brothers get better when they got older?"

Trip shakes his head. "Got meaner. Haven't seen any of them in a long time, but probably not any nicer now."

Nate rests a finger on the lip of his glass, tips it toward himself until it topples to its side. "He tried talking to me once a long time after we'd had our falling out. He came into my room and said something about me having to take over the resort. I never wanted to—run it, I mean. I wanted to move down to the Twin Cities. I didn't think about why he was saying it. I was so pissed with him for even suggesting it, I didn't hear anything else."

Trip doesn't know where the Twin Cities are. He nods anyway, scoots closer to Nate's side.

"He, um, that same night he came to talk to me, he went back in his room and shot himself in the head." Nate flexes his hands and stares at them as though he's not sure what he usually does with them. "We all heard it. It was loud, really loud. He had the room next to mine, so I got in there first. It was... messy."

The silence between them stretches, and Trip can't stand it. He hates the quiet and he hates the way Nate's hands are shaking, so he reaches out and folds them up in his own. "You didn't know. It's not your fault."

"Maybe I should have, though." Nate looks at Trip.

"You didn't." Trip holds onto his hands tighter.

Nate drops his gaze to their hands. "I couldn't stand being in the house after that. I kept seeing it and hearing it."

"So you ran away."

"Yeah. I thought New York would make me better or something, I guess. The whole 'if you make it here, you can make it anywhere' thing, ya know?"

"Yeah, I know." Trip traces the neatly manicured lines of one of Nate's fingernails.

"I'm not making it," Nate mumbles. "And, sometimes, I still get angry at Nick. My brother put a bullet through his head, and sometimes I resent him even more for doing it than I resented him when he was alive."

Trip traces a thumb over Nate's. "Easier than hurting over it, I guess."

"My sister called this morning to say she's pregnant." Nate's fingers shift in his. "Not married yet, but she's all excited, and now I feel angry at both of them. My brother for being dead and my sister for being pregnant and happy."

It occurs to Trip that, for all the things he has done, he's never held someone's hand, not like this. He closes his hands tighter over Nate's. "Told you that you were an angry person."

"I guess you were right." Nate stares at their joined hands with tired, hazy eyes. "I don't think I'm a very good person either."

"I'm not either." Trip smiles at him grimly.

Nate pulls his hands free. He rests his elbows on his knees and presses the heels of his hands into his forehead. He lets out a long breath and something in the sag of his shoulders reminds Trip of a deflated balloon.

"It happened tonight, didn't it?" Trip studies what he can of Nate's profile. "Your brother—it was this night. That's why you're so bent outta shape?"

Nate nods. He sits up straighter, blinks as though he's dizzy.

"You gonna be sick?" Trip watches him closely.

Nate shakes his head. "No."

"Good. Come on." Trip stands. "We'll get you some water and send you to bed. That way we can put the day behind us, yeah? Then it's a whole year before you gotta deal with it again."

It's too early for bed, but Nate doesn't protest the plan. He climbs the stairs with Trip behind him. He stumbles a few times, but he makes it up with no more than a banged shin.

Trip strips him out of his jeans and ushers him under the covers before going back downstairs, where he fills a glass with ice and water and turns off lights, then makes his way back up the stairs.

He nudges Nate's shoulder and offers the glass. "Drink this or you're gonna have a rough morning."

Nate accepts it, and Trip watches while he takes a drink.

"Good," he says. The dryer downstairs is still running, and he's dreading putting on his still-damp clothes. "Finish it and sleep on your side or something. I'll be majorly bummed if you go and choke on your own vomit."

He turns to go, but Nate's hand closes over his wrist. "Are you leaving?"

"Doesn't look like my services are needed here tonight." Trip shrugs.

"Stay."

Trip shakes his head. "It's fine. It's still early. I can walk, maybe jump a train."

"Stay." Nate doesn't release his wrist. "Please."

Trip hesitates before pulling Nate's hand from his wrist. "Okay."

He slips into the right side of the bed, still dressed in his borrowed shirt and sweatpants. He accepts the glass of water when Nate offers it and takes a drink before leaning over Nate to put it back on the nightstand.

They lie facing one another. Trip can feel Nate's eyes on him in the dim light.

Nate breaks the silence. "You ever done something really bad?"

"Sure." Trip yawns.

"What'd you do?"

"How's your memory after you drink?" Trip asks.

"It's okay."

"Then I'm not telling you." Trip snorts.

"You never tell me anything about yourself," Nate mumbles. "Know what I think?"

"Hmmm?" Trip shifts farther beneath the covers.

"I think you won't tell me 'cause you don't want anyone to know you're not that bad of a person." Nate slides closer. "Wanna know something else?"

"I'm gonna have to remember you like to run your mouth when you're drunk." Trip rolls onto his back, then turns his head so he can still see Nate beside him.

"I like you." Nate yawns. "Even though you're kind of insane and you're a nineteen-year-old park musician."

"Thanks." Trip pats his shoulder. "I like you, too."

"Like I like you a lot, though."

Trip runs the fingers of one hand through Nate's hair. "Go to sleep."

Nate is alarmingly obedient. Trip listens to the hum of the dryer downstairs and Nate's breathing, loud and even with alcohol-induced sleep. When the quiet stretches too long, Trip rolls back to his stomach.

"Nathaniel." He whispers and prods his shoulder.

Nate doesn't respond.

"You wanna know a secret?" Trip finds Nate's hand under the covers and brushes his fingers over it.

Nate's fingers twitch under his, but otherwise he is still and silent, fast asleep.

"I've got a picture of you and your brother, and I don't think you always hated each other." Trip closes his fingers over Nate's. "I think you're a good person."

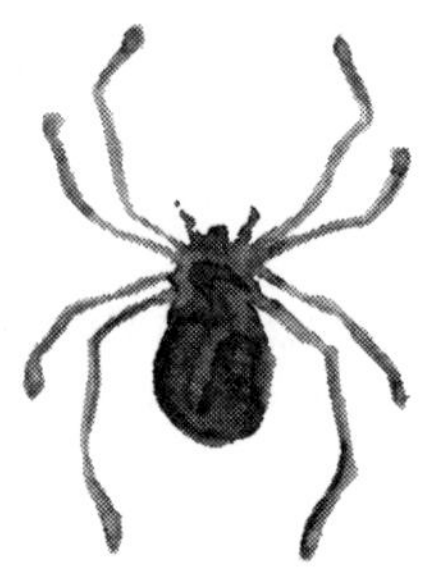

iv.

HERE'S THE THING ABOUT FATHERS where I'm from. Well, parents in general, I guess. Whuppin's are a fact of life when you're young. It's the thing that connects all of the kids around here—whether you're the kid in the house with a garage and your own room or you're living in your grandma's trailer sharing a bed with five of your brothers—if you make your parents good and mad, you're gonna get a whuppin'.

It ain't much for most kids—couple swats on your ass, maybe a smack upside your head from your mama. Still, to see the way some of them kids get to blubbering when the teacher calls their parents, you'd think they were going to receive a flogging worse than the one Jesus Christ himself got. Bunch of fucking babies, if you ask me.

I don't know how teachers know as soon as you get in their class—if we've got a look to us or if they talk about it in meetings or something—but they always know which parents to call when kids are cutting up in class and which parents you can't call because those kids—kids like me and my brothers—we don't get a whuppin'. We get a beating.

I had a substitute once when my second-grade teacher had to leave on account of having a baby, and I guess she didn't get the memo or couldn't read the look or maybe she just didn't like me because she broke that golden teacher rule of "Thou shalt not call the parents of the kids who will beat them senseless for anything and everything." It wasn't all her fault—I was never a good student and was a real fuckin' terror to be reckoned with—so I like to think she thought she was doing the right thing calling my parents.

That was the most scared I'd ever been in my life—sitting there at my table and trying to add seventeen and thirty-seven and praying like hell my daddy would be too drunk or too busy to remember I had a meeting with his belt once I got home from school. Bethy Rikken sat next to me back then and I remember her holding my hand for a bit and that was kind of nice—she lived a few trailers over from us with her aunt, and I think she felt bad about tattling on me for fighting on the playground. I wasn't mad at her. I was too goddamn scared to think about anything else. She held my hand the whole way out to the parking lot after school and even asked if I wanted a ride home with her and her aunt.

I didn't. I wanted to walk and maybe never go home. Putting it off never helped nothing, though, so I walked home behind Gid and his friends and prayed and shook and tried not to throw up my lunch. I didn't cry, though. I made it the whole afternoon in my classroom and all the way up to my daddy's belt coming down on me before I cried. I'm still proud of that.

I wish we only got knocked around when school called, but that belt and I are well acquainted. I'm pretty sure most parents just use their hands to knock around their kids, but my daddy is an old-fashioned kind of guy, I guess. He never seemed to have anything against smacking us with whatever was closest at hand, but he favored the belt. I made up a whole story in my head about that belt. I think it used to belong to my grandpa, and he probably used it to beat my daddy and then passed it on to him when he had his own kids. I wondered sometimes, while my daddy was wrapping it around his hand, if he knew which parts hurt worse, and if he remembered the sick feeling that started in the bottom of your gut when you heard the creak of the leather the same way I did.

I wondered, too, which of my brothers would inherit it. My brothers didn't step in for me that day, and I didn't expect them to. I wouldn't have either if it had been one of them. Being a hero didn't save anyone; it just got both of you an even worse licking than if you'd just let it be. Besides, me and my brothers didn't like each other.

Hell, Gid and I hated each other so bad, we'd try and set one another up for a beating. It was a funny hierarchy we had growing up. The twins were real close and usually did okay taking care of each other, Michael and Jeremiah were that way, too. Probably because they went through it all first before there were more bodies to put between them and our dad. Gid wants our daddy to like him in a bad way, so he didn't have much to say to any of us, and hell, did they all hate me. I've never been sure why—because I was the youngest or I made them have to shove one more body into the already-cramped bed or if there was just something about me that didn't feel like one of them. I really don't know. Not that it matters.

My mama didn't care much for me either. Probably because I embarrassed her. She never did nothing to stop my daddy when he'd come down hard on one of us. I don't blame her either. If she'd have gotten in the way, she'd probably have been smacked around the same as one of my brothers if they'd have tried to do anything.

Even with all of them brothers right under the same roof as me and all those kids who knew exactly what it was to be scared fuckin' silly when you knew you were going to get smacked around by your old man, I didn't have one goddamn friend when I was a kid. My brothers hated me, the kids in the houses hated all of us trailer-park kids, and the trailer-park kids all hated me because they needed someone to look down on, and I was an easy target with my different-colored eyes and being kind of a runt compared to a lot of them.

So that day when Bethy held my hand and walked with me out to the parking lot was something new for me. Having someone there—having someone hold my hand, that made it hurt. When there's no one, you don't know any different, but when someone holds your hand, it makes it so you realize hands are good for more than a beating.

Between Pastor Welk and Bethy Rikken, I think they're the reason I realized I wanted something different, that I was meant for something better. I don't know if I love them or hate them for that.

EIGHT.

"YOU NEED A WINTER JACKET." Nate lifts his hand higher on the doorframe for Trip to slip underneath and into the apartment. "It's thirty degrees out today."

"What do you call this?" Trip pulls at the drawstrings of his sweatshirt as he steps out of his shoes. He's sweating and shivering all at once in the sudden warmth.

"That's a sweatshirt I gave you months ago. It gets colder out, Trip. It doesn't just stay a constant fifty degrees out there." Nate follows Trip to the kitchen. He doesn't comment when Trip immediately throws open the refrigerator door. "It's early in the season, too. Eventually these random cold days are going to turn into a constant thing."

"I'll wear more shirts underneath, how's that?" Trip pulls a can of soda and cracks the tab on it. "Stop hassling me and just say 'hi.'"

Nate sighs, then steps closer to touch a brief kiss to Trip's mouth. "Hi."

Things between them have been good. Really good. There had been an awkward morning after Nate's drunken confessional, but they've moved past it and Nate seems lighter, calmer.

He isn't smiling now, though. He presses the back of his hand to Trip's forehead. "You've got a fever."

Trip steps out of the contact. "I run hot."

"I run hot." Nate touches the inside of his wrist to Trip's cheek. "You run cold."

"So warm me up," Trip purrs. He presses himself close, raises himself up on his tiptoes. He'd planned on kissing Nate, but ends up stepping back to sneeze.

"Sexy." Nate sits at the breakfast bar beside his open laptop.

"What're you working on?" Trip steps around the counter to look at the screen.

"Just research." Nate pulls the open barstool closer, and Trip sits down beside him. "Thinking about working for some place smaller, more personal."

"We had a deal!" Trip shoves the laptop closed. "You still have two weeks left… three? I can't remember anymore."

"Don't touch the screen." Nate shoots him a look before opening his laptop back up. "Deal was I couldn't work for three months. If I want to start at the end of this, I need to start getting interviews now."

"You're no good at this at all." Trip sulks. He doesn't like people breaking their promises.

"You're such a drama queen. It's an interview, that's it." Nate takes a drink from Trip's soda. "I feel good about it. This break's been good for me, I think."

"You develop a soul sometime in the past couple months?" Trip mumbles. He points at the soda can. "You're gonna catch my cold."

"Been talking to my sister more. I'm sleeping more; I'm happier, I'm good. Great, even." Nate frowns at him before looking back to his laptop. "And I'm exposed to a hell of a lot more of your bodily fluids in other scenarios than I am just taking a drink from your can of pop."

"Wanna be exposed to some right now?" Trip closes the laptop again, careful this time to keep his fingers away from the screen.

Nate turns to face him, clearly unimpressed. "Do you practice those lines?"

"In the mirror every single morning," Trip replies solemnly.

"You can practice some more if you want." Nate points at the bathroom. "And shower while you're at it."

"What're you saying?" Trip pouts.

"I'm saying you still look cold and your hair's dirty."

"*Your* hair's dirty." Trip snaps right back.

"I showered this morning. My hair's fine." Nate turns his attention back to his laptop.

Trip lifts the soda can above Nate's head. "You sure about that?"

"Dump that on me and I'll send you right back out into the hall." Nate glances up at the can, but he doesn't look overly perturbed.

"I wouldn't go without a fight." Trip tips the can farther. "We both know I could kick your ass."

Nate stands and moves to one of the cabinets. "Wouldn't need to fight you, could just pick you up and carry you out, shrimp."

"Don't call me that." Trip lowers the can to the counter.

"Don't threaten me with pop in my hair."

"It's soda." Trip folds his arms across his chest, mutters. "Goddamn Minnesotan."

"Nuh-uh. Don't you dare start calling me out on dialect differences." Nate turns to face him. "Not when you say 'lightning bugs' and 'buggy' and 'ain't' and call people 'sugar' and—"

"Enough." Trip sulks. "You won't have to carry me out if I just leave on my own."

"You know where the door is." Nate pulls down a bottle of pills and fills a glass with water from the sink.

"Think I liked you better when you were miserable all the time." It's not an altogether untrue statement. Trip likes this side of Nate that's lighter and happier and funnier, but he makes him anxious. Nate is still uptight and serious and prone to long bouts of melancholy, but those moods have become increasingly rare. At some point, Nate will go back to work. At some point, he'll go looking for a boyfriend, someone with a job that requires a suit and a four-year degree, and that will be the end of his arrangement with Trip.

"If you want me to shower with you, all you have to do is ask." Nate puts the pills and water on the counter beside Trip.

"Never said I wanted that." Trip takes his soda to the other side of the breakfast bar and pulls open the cabinet beneath the sink. He drops the can in the garbage instead of the recycling just to be vindictive.

"If I shower with you anyway, are you going to be nice?" Nate pushes the cup and pills toward Trip again.

Trip takes the pills and chases them with a drink from the glass. "I'm always nice when I'm naked."

Nate watches while Trip takes another sip of his water. "Do you even want to know what you just took?"

"Are they gonna kill me?"

"They shouldn't."

"Then I don't need to know." Trip moves to the bathroom. "Come keep me company and make sure I don't have an allergic reaction."

They shower together and Trip realizes this isn't something they've done since the first time he slept over. Despite it being somewhat unfamiliar territory, being pressed so close in such a small space is more comfortable now than that first time. Trip sings while he rubs a bar of soap over his skin.

"Went and had lunch with Kellan today," Nate ventures. He has his back to Trip, so he has no way to read Nate's expression. "He said he sees you once in a while—like other than when he comes over here."

Trip pauses his singing. "He comes around sometimes. He brought us flowers last week. Well, brought Scarlett flowers."

Nate clears his throat. "He mentioned Scarlett's got a baby."

Trip hums a note of acknowledgement. He hadn't realized he's never mentioned the baby before. "June."

"Cute name. How old?"

"Getting close to one year." Trip can't wrap his head around it. He's not entirely sure where the year has gone, and at the same time he can't imagine a time without June. It seems as though she's been around for as long as he can remember.

"You have other roommates?" Nate speaks again after only a brief pause.

"Yeah, some." Trip pulls a bottle of shampoo from the wall shelf and reads the back. "You know this is for platinum blonds? You trying to color your hair?"

Nate ignores the question. "How many?"

"How many blonds can use this bottle of shampoo?" Trip caps the bottle and puts it back down on the shelf. "None. Just you and your dishwater blond and me and my brown. Unless you got some other guy on the side."

"No other guys, and your hair is auburn." Nate adjusts the showerhead so that the water falls more softly on them. "I meant how many roommates do you have?"

"You've asked that before." Trip picks up the razor and turns it over in his hands.

"Kellan says you guys lost one." Nate cranes his neck farther to keep an eye on Trip and the razor, apparently wary of him potentially trying to carve out a spot of hair on the back of Nate's neck or something equally impulsive.

Trip replaces the razor in the shower rack. "So do the math—and share some hot water. I thought we got in here because you wanted to unthaw me or something."

"'Unthaw' isn't a word. It's just 'thaw.'" Nate shuffles until he's standing behind Trip. "What happened?"

"Skipped out." Trip has the bottle of shampoo again and he's working some of it into his hair.

"What happens to the rent then?"

"Christ, you have a lot of questions." Trip offers Nate the bottle of shampoo. "Don't take a genius to know we're all paying more now and it fuckin' sucks. You got anything else you wanna ask about my roommates?"

"Sorry," Nate takes the bottle and puts it back on the shelf. He falls silent, but then he's speaking in one big rush. "It's just I've never met them. I'm not even sure where you live."

Trip's rinsing shampoo from his hair with his head tipped up to the showerhead. "You've met Scarlett."

Nate's hands come up to fuss with a spot in Trip's hair he apparently deems not well-enough rinsed. "What about the other ones?"

Trip shrugs. "Why's it matter?"

"They're your friends, aren't they?" Nate drops his hands back to his side. "I'm just curious who you hang out with or whatever."

"They're people, Nathaniel. They're who I split the rent with so I don't end up sleeping on a fucking park bench."

"You're not friends?"

Trip squeezes conditioner into his palm. "We get along fine."

"Who are your friends then?" Nate pushes. He tugs a lock of Trip's hair. "I mean other than me."

Trip massages the conditioner into his hair and turns to look at Nate. "Thought we weren't friends."

"That was a long time ago."

"That wasn't even three months ago." Trip faces forward again.

"I told you about holding a grudge against my dead brother." Nate's voice goes softer. "That has to count for something."

Trip doesn't know what to say to that, so he starts singing.

Nate's eyes are on him, prickling like static shock as his gaze drifts from his thighs to his ass to his back. Trip's trained himself to not mind Nate's staring, or anyone else's. People can't help it, they're as drawn by the scars as they are by his mismatched eyes. The scars are too obvious, too strange not to draw attention. He jumps only when Nate's fingers come to rest on a mark low on his back. He twists to face him, irritated and still trying to shake the surprise.

Nate withdraws his hand quickly. "I'm sorry. I didn't mean to—I just… sorry."

Trip flexes his hands at his sides and shifts his expression into something teasing and flashy. "Betcha if you connect a few of them, they'd make an 'N' for Nathaniel."

Nate has a look on his face that says he doesn't think something so violent ought to be joked about. He seems to be learning to play along with Trip's games, though. "Is there a 'T' for Trip?"

Trip faces forward again to finish rinsing the soap from his hair. "Don't know. Go on and check."

Nate hesitates as though he's not sure what permission has just been granted.

Trip glances over his shoulder again. "Go on."

It takes a moment, but eventually Nate touches a finger to a mark on Trip's shoulder blade. The contact is so light it almost tickles, but Trip holds still and keeps washing his hair and singing. Nate's fingers drift to other marks. "Here."

"Yeah?" Trip pauses his song. "How about that—betcha down at St. Mark's they'd charge a hundred bucks to do something like that. That's a thing. D' you know that? People get scars put on their bodies like tattoos."

"Yeah, I've heard of it." Nate traces another scar that curves down from the small of Trip's back to his ass. His fingers linger on it. "Could I ask you something kind of personal?"

"You can ask," Trip replies.

"You seem..." Nate hesitates as though he's not entirely sure how to phrase his question. He shifts his fingers to the mark on Trip's right hip. "Do they ever bother you?"

"Nathaniel, don't know if you've noticed, but I've got two different-colored eyes, and not the sort of 'different in certain kinds of light' variety of different." Trip rolls his eyes, waves a hand vaguely at his back. "Stuck with these just like I'm stuck with the eyes. Just gotta accept it or whatever."

Trip picks up singing again. Nate's hand is still on his hip. He lifts it back to the first mark on Trip's shoulder. "Can I ask you another question?"

"Give it your best shot." Trip tips his head back under the showerhead, closes his eyes against the water.

"Where'd they come from?"

"Grizzly bears, remember?" Trip tips his head down, works his fingers through the hair at his neck. "We've talked about that before."

"There something real they came from?" Nate is feeling out the mark as if it might tell him something more that Trip won't.

"All right, fine." Trip coughs into the crook of his arm. "It was just a regular old black bear—grizzly sounds better, though, right? Big things, grizzly bears."

"You don't like talking about it, so you turn it into a joke," Nate murmurs. "Or maybe you just don't know how to talk about it."

"I put the damn bear down, there's nothing left to talk about." Trip coughs a second time, and Nate rubs his back.

"You okay?"

"Fine—just a cold."

"The Tylenol should kick in soon and help." Nate keeps rubbing his back.

"Here I was hoping you'd given me something interesting." Trip steps farther under the spray of the shower.

He's about to start singing again—Dylan or Prince to sucker Nate into chattering about their Minnesota ties—when he feels Nate's lips, soft and warm, against that mark on his shoulder. He holds perfectly still, his fingers still tangled in his hair.

It must be an unexpected move for both of them, this intimate piece of contact, because there's a pause where neither of them moves. Nate is the braver one in these small spaces with their eyes off one another. He touches another kiss to a mark lower on Trip's back and them moves on to a second and a third nearby.

Trip is paralyzed, frightened and soothed all at once by the softness of this contact. It's boot theory—the other shoe has to drop eventually, and he closes his eyes to wait for whatever shatters this quiet moment. He tries to breathe and keep as still as possible while Nate lowers himself to his knees behind him, still touching and kissing until Trip's sure he's found every mark there is. He ends on the mark he'd first touched on Trip's hip the last time they had shared the shower. His chin is rough on

Trip's skin; his hair is wet and warm. Trip touches his fingertips to Nate's cheek, brushes over it with his eyes still closed.

Nate stands, a hand still on Trip's hip. He presses a kiss to the back of his head but says nothing.

Trip stays as he is. He watches the water ebbing around his toes and disappearing down the drain. "Why'd you do that?"

Nate's voice is warm against his ear. "I just... wanted to."

Trip licks his lips. As he stares at the floor he realizes there's an ache low in his gut and he's hard. "You got condoms down here?"

Nate nods against his neck. He steps out of the shower briefly to retrieve the condom from one of the drawers below the sink. There is no other precursory conversation or flirtation once Nate gets back into the shower. One minute they are both quiet and awkward over a strange intimacy they don't know what to do with, and the next, Trip is pressed up against the tile of the wall, Nate buried inside him. There's not enough space to allow for any position besides this one, but the closeness, for this, at least, is exactly what Trip wants. He keeps one hand on his cock, the other pressed against the tile over his head with Nate's fingers tangled between his. Every time Nate shifts on his toes to press even closer, Trip huffs out a breath like a sigh and murmurs a request for "harder" or "faster." Nate obliges, his arm tightening around Trip's middle and his breath coming fast and warm on Trip's neck. It isn't the best fuck they've had or the worst. It's loud and quick enough that when they're both finished, there's still enough hot water left to finish their shower.

Trip cranks off the water, then turns to face Nate. "You're really goddamn strange; you know that?"

Nate wipes the water from his eyes. "Yeah, I know. Sorry."

Trip doesn't know what else to say to him. He gives Nate a brief once-over before climbing out of the shower. He hums to fill the silence while he rubs himself dry and puts his clothes back on. He keeps his back to the door and Nate in plain sight.

Nate dresses quietly. His gaze drifts to Trip from time to time as if he knows some secret that Trip does not.

The bathroom feels claustrophobic and too hot. Trip leans against the closed door, closes his eyes for a moment.

"You okay?" Nate's hand is back on his forehead. "I didn't hurt you, did I?"

Trip reaches blindly for the door handle. He opens his eyes and shakes his head. "No, you were fine. You were great. Just a little dizzy."

"Have you eaten today?" Nate is still searching his face with concern.

"Does that soda and those pills count?"

"No."

"Then no, I haven't."

"I can fix that." Nate guides Trip out of the bathroom with a hand on the small of his back.

Nate likes cooking. He can make braised lamb and grilled fish and curried chicken and homemade ravioli. His kitchen is always well stocked, but today, like most days, Nate settles for making Trip eggs and toast. Today he adds fried potatoes to the plate before shoving it across the breakfast bar.

"You're trying to make me fat." Trip sighs happily as he takes his first bite. This is a scenario he knows well—Nate standing on one side of the breakfast bar with his plate, Trip sitting on the opposite side with his own—sometimes Nate makes them something more upscale and they sit at the dining room table. Once they sat together on the kitchen floor and drank beer and ate rotisserie chicken straight from the black plastic container with their fingers. This breakfast-bar meal of eggs and toast at any hour of the day, though, is Trip's favorite.

"Preparing you for winter without that jacket." Nate leans his elbows on the edge of the counter and looks at Trip's bag resting on the floor. "What do you keep in there?"

Trip points his fork at Nate. "Severed penises. From previous conquests who asked too many questions."

Nate wrinkles his nose. "I think I'd smell that."

"Duct tape seals it in." Trip mops up egg yolk from his plate with what's left of his toast. "Just gotta open and close it quick."

Nate frowns at him.

Trip rolls his eyes. "If you're so goddamn curious, just go on and look for yourself."

Nate retrieves the bag. He brings it to the family room and puts it down on the coffee table. The zipper sticks near the middle, but eventually it slides open. Nate pulls out a matchbook, turns it over in his hands. "What is all this?"

"Remember how I do the mind-reading bit?" Trip stands, empty plate in hand, and goes to the dishwasher. He tucks the plate inside along with his fork. He fills a glass with ice and water. He sits on the floor beside the coffee table and pushes the glass of water toward Nate.

As if by instinct, Nate's hand drifts to his pocket. It's been a long time since Trip's lifted anything off of him. Mostly he puts new things in his pockets when he can and waits to see if Nate notices. Today, there's an acorn from the park, but Nate doesn't unearth it. "I remember."

"When I lift stuff off of people..." Trip thinks of a way to phrase it lightly. "I don't always give everything back."

"You steal from people." Nate drops the matches back into Trip's bag and pulls out a torn-looking birthday card.

"Nothing anyone will miss." Trip shrugs. He pushes himself up onto his knees to look into his bag. He reaches in and fishes out a blue crayon. "You wanna play a game?"

"Yeah, sure." Nate sifts through a few more items.

Trip pushes the crayon across the table. "Where do you s'pose that came from?"

"Probably a kid. I don't know." Nate doesn't look at the crayon for long before turning his attention back to the bag. "You need a new bag even worse than you need that jacket."

Trip pushes the crayon closer to Nate. "No, come on—it's a game. Tell me a story."

"What kind of story?" Nate takes a drink from the water glass. He picks at a frayed spot of duct tape.

"About the crayon." Trip nudges it another inch closer. He takes the cup of water when Nate puts it down and takes a drink.

"A story?" Nate lifts the crayon to inspect it. "What do you want me to say about a crayon?"

"Anything." Trip puts the glass down and settles back down on the carpet, his legs crossed and his hands in his lap. "You read enough; write a story for a change."

"Once upon a time, some kid had a blue crayon and you took it out of his pocket. The end." Nate lifts the crayon off of the table and rolls his eyes. "Happy?"

Trip frowns at him. "That was pitiful. I was hoping you had at least one creative bone in that perfectly curated body of yours, Nathaniel."

"You're asking me to tell you a story about a crayon. What the hell do you want me to say?" Nate's cheeks flush red with sudden irritation.

"I'm not asking for a goddamn novel, just something small." Trip picks up the crayon. "Like it was some business drone's, a lot like yourself. He likes to get kids' menus when he goes out to eat by himself. Colors them in, and people think he's crazy, but he doesn't mind because it's how he unwinds the same way some people get a drink after a shit day."

"That's not a story." Nate rests his elbows on his knees, peering down into Trip's bag again as though hoping he'll find something in there that actually holds interest.

"Sure it is. It's better than that shit you told me, anyway." Trip gets back up on his knees and rifles through his things. He pulls a receipt with a red lipstick print smudged across the edge. "Try that one."

"It's how girls fix their lipstick. They smudge it on something else." Nate sifts through a few other items, turns his gaze back up to Trip. "Not really sure why they do it."

Trip groans. "Honestly, Nathaniel, would it kill you to indulge me?"

"All I ever do is indulge you." Nate shifts away from the coffee table. "I don't know what you want from me right now. I'm not gonna get it right if I just keep guessing."

"There isn't a goddamn right anything here." Trip rubs a finger over a crease in the receipt. "I s'pose that's why you don't like this game, though."

"What's that supposed to mean?"

"It means you've mellowed out some, but you've still got a five-foot pole up your ass, and you can't stand not having a right answer to things." Trip squeezes Nate's ankle.

"Sorry my personality fucking offends you." Nate pulls his foot from Trip's hold. "If you're such a goddamn perfect novelist, you tell the story."

"Here, look. It's for two beers and two martinis at that bar in Bryant Park and it was back last Christmastime." Trip scoots closer to Nate's knees, flattens the receipt out on the table for Nate to see. "It's a date. Two girls. One of them—the one with the martinis, let's call her Sasha, there's an imprint of an 'S' on the bottom there. She was more into it than the other one. We'll call her Jen. Jen thinks they're just friends; hell, she's going on a real date as soon as this one's over, so they get the receipt, Sasha pays, and Jen fixes her lipsticks on the receipt and leaves for her real date. Sasha gets hurt, stops talking to Jen since enough is just enough, ya know? But she keeps the receipt in the bottom of her purse to remind her why she's not answering any of Jen's calls."

"If that's true, then you just majorly fucked Sasha over by taking this." Nate squints at the imprint of a cursive 'S' on the bottom of the receipt.

"Or maybe she's moved on and forgotten all about Jen already." Trip drops the receipt back in his bag. "Or maybe she'll forget why they're not talking and answer one of her calls now."

Nate pushes aside a few things and comes up with a notebook with a red cover that he immediately moves to open. It's been so long since Trip's written anything in it that he's nearly forgotten it exists down there amongst all of his stolen things. He catches Nate's wrist before he can pull it out fully. He can't prevent a split second of panic crossing his features, but he's grinning when Nate turns a questioning look his way. "Not that."

"Why not?" Nate releases the notebook, but now it's clearly piqued his interest.

"I didn't take that, it's mine." Trip pushes the notebook back down into the bag. He pulls out a plastic spider next. It's black, missing a couple legs, and it immediately falls below the ice when Trip tries to balance it on the lip of their glass of water. "What about this guy? You wanna try again?"

"No, you go. Where'd the spider come from?"

"A guy—around your age—he didn't know it was in his bag. He's real scared of bugs—what's the word for that? When it's of spiders?"

"Arachnophobia." Nate prods an ice cube and it sends the spider tumbling farther down into the glass.

Trip rests an arm on the table, props his chin on it so he can watch the spider. "Jack—that's his name, the guy with the spider thing—he's scared shitless of them and his girlfriend thinks it's real funny, so she hides fake ones in his bag sometimes. He found this one, but he left it in there. Makes him think of her when the day's a bad one."

Nate looks at Trip, surprised. "Didn't take you for a romantic, Trip."

Trip's gaze jerks up to meet Nate's. He sits up straighter. "I'm not."

"You can pretend to be as blasé and tough as you want." Nate shakes his head, laughs. "But you so are—you're a romantic."

"Take it back." Trip stands up, still glaring and all the easy silliness forgotten in his anger.

Nate studies Trip's hands fisted at his sides. He looks at Trip's face. "And you've got a nasty temper."

Trip doesn't say anything. He keeps flexing his hands at his sides.

"Now who's got the stick up their ass?" Nate picks up the water glass and takes it to the kitchen. He drains it in the sink and places it in the dishwasher before pulling down two tumblers and the bottle of Scotch. He fills both the way Trip likes them and returns to the family room where Trip is still busy sulking.

Trip watches with the same stormy expression while Nate places one of the tumblers on the table and offers the second and the plastic spider to Trip. He says the one thing he knows Trip will respond to. "You wanna make a deal?"

Trip is still frowning at the plastic spider. He speaks when he can't help himself any longer. "What kinda deal?"

"I won't tell anyone you're a hopeless romantic if you don't tell anyone I don't know how to tell a decent story." Nate pushes the cup into Trip's hand. He drops the spider into it.

The corner of Trip's mouth twitches in a barely suppressed smile. "That thing's probably really fuckin' dirty."

"Alcohol cleans things." Nate sits on the couch.

Trip takes the spot on the opposite end of the couch. He folds his feet under him. "Fine. Deal."

Nate taps his glass against Trip's. He drags the duffel bag to his end of the coffee table and shifts a few other things aside.

Trip watches while Nate struggles with the zipper pocket on the inside of the bag. He makes no attempt to stop him, just watches and holds his breath. Nate's gaze lands on something else, though, and he abandons the zipper in favor of pulling a business card out from the fray of things. He turns the Ashbury-Whiteman logo toward Trip. "Tell me about this one."

Trip squints at it, grins. "You could probably tell this one."

Nate sips his drink and turns the card back to face him. "Pathetic business schmuck works his ass off for a company he doesn't really like and then gets fired. He doesn't know what to do with all his unused business cards, so he holds onto them like maybe if he waits a bit longer life will go back to what it was. Hopefully he'll have the same office number so he doesn't have to get a whole new set of cards made."

"That was better." Trip tips his glass from side to side so the ice clinks against the glass. "Not great, but not too shabby."

"Thanks." Nate drops the card back into Trip's bag. "I'll keep working on the ending."

"You do that." Trip shifts closer to Nate's side. "I think it might end up being a good one."

NiNE.

"It's a stupid idea."

"It's fun," Scarlet says. She looks at Trip in the mirror over her shoulder. "Why are you making it seem like a chore?"

"Because it feels like one." Trip sits on the edge of the bathtub and rubs a towel through his still damp hair. "Why can't you go do whatever it is you do with Kellan on your own?"

"It's a double date. If there's only one couple, it's just a regular date." Scarlett pauses to brush mascara onto her lashes. "Does Nate not want to?"

"Of course he wants to. It's, like, a temporary big-deal exhibit. He loves that shit." Trip lowers his towel to his lap. He turns to look at the showerhead that's dripping steadily enough to send a fine mist onto the exposed skin of his back. "The only thing that'd make him happier is if there was a lecture, too."

"Hmmm, bookish; that's cute." Scarlett exchanges her mascara for her eyeliner. "Kel says he knows something about basically everything, like, could be on Jeopardy or something."

"Ask him about the Astor Place subway station." Trip twists the shower knob left then right. The dripping gets worse. "On second thought, don't. He'll talk your ear off about beavers and the Astor family, then he'll probably try to loan you a book."

"Maybe I want the book." Scarlett smudges at a misplaced spot of eyeliner with the edge of a red-painted fingernail.

Trip flips the switch to move the water from the showerhead to the tub faucet, but the dripping continues. "You hate reading."

Scarlett rifles through her makeup bag. "Says who?"

"You. All the time." Trip experiments with twisting the shower knob a few more times, but the dripping of the tub does not abate.

"So do you, but I remember someone asleep on the couch last week with a copy of *The Catcher in the Rye* on his chest." Scarlett looks at Trip in the mirror.

Trip grunts and turns away from the leaky faucet. "If I was sleeping, tells you something about how much I liked the book, don't it?"

"You looked like you were pretty far into it." Scarlett prods Trip's knee with the edge of her powder brush. "It was adorable, by the way."

"Not like I had anything better to do. I was stuck watching your fuckin' baby." Trip snaps his towel across the back of Scarlett's calves.

"You volunteered for that job." Scarlett singsongs, "Trip Morgan—volunteer babysitter and avid reader. Who even are you?"

"The man who's about to turn on the shower and ruin your hair with the steam."

"Our water doesn't get that hot." Scarlett turns her head from side to side, inspecting her blush. "Is this even?"

"How should I know?"

Scarlett turns to face Trip full on. "You're being pouty. Do you need to go take a nap with June?"

"Would it get me out of this group field trip?"

Scarlett shoves her makeup bag into the drawer beside the sink. The drawer closes with a loud grating noise. "Oh, my God, seriously, stop being such a baby. Why are you so opposed to this?"

"A double date." Trip makes air quotes around the words, sneers. "That doesn't sound like the fuckin' hokiest thing you've ever heard?"

"We've gone on one before." Scarlett looks disdainfully at Trip's hands. "And please never use air quotes again. I can't take you seriously."

"That was a deal I had with Liam, and you yelled at me for the whole ten minutes I was there."

"Our boyfriends are best friends. *We* are friends. We have to do it."

"Not my boyfriend and we don't have to do nothing." Trip stands and folds his arms across his chest.

"Trip, I say this with complete and total affection: Get the fuck over yourself." Scarlett rests a hand on her hip. "We made the plans, we're meeting the boys in half an hour, and Liam agreed to watch June. This is happening."

"I hate you in mom mode." Trip mumbles.

Scarlett gives him a push toward the door. "Go put a shirt on—a clean one. I washed a couple of yours with June's stuff yesterday."

"Still going to be wet, then."

Scarlett swats him across the back of the head, though there's no force behind it. "Oh, my God, you are such a child. Just go do it!"

"I'm going, I'm going." Trip shuffles past her and out into the family room. "Where are the shirts?"

"I hung them in your room; you're welcome." Scarlett closes the bathroom door in his face but then calls from the other side, "Don't wake up the baby."

The planning of the double date with Scarlett and Kellan was not something Trip was a part of, nor is he entirely sure how it happened. They're going to the Museum of Modern Art to see a visiting exhibit, though Trip doesn't recall the artist or much about her work. He doesn't mind the idea of going to another museum with Nate, but he has no interest in making it a group affair. He likes his time with Nate, likes listening to him prattle on about art and books and a thousand other mundane things. Though Trip won't admit it—to Nate or Scarlett—he's usually interested in what Nate has to say, and he likes the books that Nate loans him, though it takes him a long time to get through most of them. He's not sure, exactly, what he dislikes about the notion of this double date. He just knows he has no interest in participating.

Despite his reservations about the whole thing, Trip puts on one of his clean shirts and a zip-up sweatshirt, and then he tiptoes back out to the family room to wait for Scarlett.

The apartment is quiet. June is napping in her playpen, Liam's painting on the couch and Trip can see Devon asleep in his bed with one arm hanging off the edge of the mattress and his face obscured in the pillow. Trip considers waking him, but he thinks better of it. He goes to the kitchen and drinks water from a chipped glass at the kitchen table. There is a pile of Bekket newspapers, still sealed in their plastic bags, accumulating in a dilapidated pyramid on the far end of the table. Trip pulls one from the bottom and the whole pyramid collapses, but he pays them no mind. He peels back the plastic and shakes the paper out flat. It smells like ink and, Trip thinks, some hint of wet dirt roads and gasoline. He'd only been interested in checking the date to see how long the papers have been accruing here in the kitchen in their plastic bags, but he cannot help but look a little longer.

The paper is from nearly a month ago; the front-page news is about homecoming, complete with a black and white photo of a high school couple wearing plastic crowns, seated on the back of an open-topped convertible and waving at the crowd gathered to watch the parade.

Homecoming seems such a strange tradition to uphold in a town where so few of the alumni ever leave, but there it is all the same, and Trip is surprised to realize he knows the couple in the photo. Her name is Jackie Wilson; his is Mike Ford. They'd been only two or three years behind Trip in school. He stares some more at the picture, tries to make out the grainy faces in the crowd behind them. He thinks he might recognize a couple people, but he can't be sure.

He skims the article, but the words hold less interest for him than the picture had. He flips the page, scans the columns. The paper isn't big. It's only a few pages, and the content of the articles is anything but provocative. There's a piece on Halloween costume ideas, complete with interviews with the women who work at the Yarn Barn; an article about high school honor students going on a field trip to the University of Alabama; another on more details of homecoming.

Trip flips the pages, noting the sports section (they've lost another football game, but the team still looks good), the student section (an article on school start times) and the classifieds (there's a Massey Ferguson utility tractor for sale). He pauses at the police report section. He'd recognized so few of the other names, but this portion of the paper is filled with people and scenarios he remembers well. The first report is about a husband concerned because his wife had left after a fight and hadn't come back yet and she was afraid of the dark. She'd returned safely a few hours later and no further police intervention was required. There are multiple reports from people calling the police station to file noise complaints about a dog barking, and then another slew of calls coming in because someone shot the dog. Trip is about to call out to wake Devon and ask why he wastes money on a paper filled with so little, but the words die on his tongue when he spies the name "Jeremiah Morgan" in the next report. He closes the paper, pushes it away.

"Hey, you ready to go?" Scarlett scrutinizes him. "Are you okay?"

"Peachy." Trip pushes past her toward the door, fishing a cigarette from the pack in his pocket as he goes. "Can we please fuckin' go and get this over with?"

• • •

THEY MEET NATE AND KELLAN in line at the museum. Scarlett walks faster, disappearing from Trip's side to reach Kellan.

Trip watches as she and Kellan embrace. When they finally part, they kiss. Scarlett swats Kellan's arm affectionately when he whispers something in her ear.

Nate watches the proceedings with vague interest, but he turns his attention to Trip when he finally reaches his side. He touches a hand above Trip's elbow and leans in to kiss him. "Hey."

Trip turns his cheek to Nate. "Hey."

Nate's hand stays on his arm, his eyes skimming Trip with mild concern. "You okay? You seem upset."

"Me? Upset?" Trip reaches for Nate's wrist. "Not a chance."

Nate catches Trip's hand. "Nice try."

"Well, shit, Nathaniel, you're starting to get all right at that." Trip masks his surprise at being caught in the act of trying to take something from Nate. "Gonna get you eventually, though."

Nate releases Trip's hand long enough to unfasten his watch. He slips it over Trip's wrist and latches it closed.

The watch isn't on tight enough and slides a few inches down Trip's arm. "You're no fun at all."

Nate steps closer, lowers his voice. "You know, Kellan's watch is nicer than mine."

Trip inspects Kellan's wrist. "Interesting."

Nate rests a hand on Trip's back, shuffles them forward in line. "I might even help you with getting it off him."

"I'll make a criminal out of you yet." Trip steps in closer to Nate's side and they spend the remaining time in line making quiet plans they have no intentions of acting on to steal items from the other people around them.

They don't have to wait long in line and soon they are at the front. Kellan supplies cash for Scarlett and him and Nate flashes a membership card that gets both Trip and him in for free. When they're past the ticketing area, they shuffle as a group from floor to floor, pausing to study sculptures and paintings.

"You know what I hate about museums?" Scarlett walks a slow circle around an abstract piece made of bent reinforcement bars. "I want to touch everything."

"You could touch some of Liam's things at your apartment." Kellan follows in Scarlett's path, pausing to read the descriptive placard. "He makes some stuff similar to all of this."

"Liam doesn't like us touching his work either." Trip shifts his weight from his left foot to his right.

"Not that it ever stops you." Scarlett pauses beside Trip, tilts her head to study the statue. "He could have work in here, don't you think? Someday."

"I saw a pile of garbage a room over, so yeah, why not?" Trip yawns.

Scarlett ignores the comment. "You know what makes me want to touch it? The fact that I'm not supposed to. I'd never think to touch it if I didn't know I wasn't supposed to."

"Children's museums—you can touch things in a children's museum." Kellan looks up from the placard. "We should go sometime and you can touch anything you'd like."

Scarlett drifts closer to him as though pulled by some invisible force. "June would like that."

Kellan turns to face her, closes what space she hasn't yet. "A family date."

They smile at one another, and then Scarlett wraps her arms around one of Kellan's and tips her head against his. They stare at the statue with happy, hazy eyes.

Trip wrinkles his nose and turns away from them. He wanders from the statue and pauses to stare at a large, abstract painting hanging on a wall alone.

As much as he enjoys the Met, he isn't partial to the MoMA. Modern art makes him simultaneously anxious and bored. He doesn't like the chaos or seeming mindlessness of the items. Nate was shocked the first time they wandered into the modern wings of the Met and Trip expressed his disinterest. Nate has tried to explain the pieces to him—offering books and anecdotes and documentary suggestions—but Trip has remained indifferent. He isn't sure where Nate is just now, Trip abandoned him beside a splattered canvas when he could no longer tolerate standing still and he hasn't seen him since.

Trip looks back to where he left Scarlett and Kellan. They've wandered elsewhere as well, but he spies them standing close together not far away in front of another sculpture.

He is bored looking around by himself, but he doesn't feel comfortable interrupting the intimate space they have created together. He turns back to the painting and stares at it listlessly.

"Oh, wow, this one's great." Nate's voice is welcome music in Trip's ear. "Interesting."

He continues staring at the painting. "Interpret it for me, why don't you?"

"Sort of Dada-inspired, I think."

"Nice try, but the placard says abstract expressionism. How's it feel to be wrong for once?" Trip turns to look at Nate.

Nate isn't looking at the painting. He's studying Trip, rubbing his chin in a show of studiousness. He raises his eyebrows as though surprised to hear Trip speaking. "Performance art? Even better."

Trip glances around, momentarily confused. "Are you high?"

Nate circles him. "Incredible details. I really like the shoes. That broken lace and the hole—sort of pulls it all off balance in just the right way."

Trip twists to keep an eye on Nate, but he remains quiet.

Nate is still making a show of scrutinizing him. "Interesting placement, too. You know that's important, just as important as the art itself sometimes, I think—choosing where to place the piece."

A few other people have paused to watch the proceedings, cameras partially raised as though they are unsure whether Trip is truly a piece of the exhibit.

"You gonna blush if I tell you that you're causing a scene?" Trip speaks softly so that only Nate can hear him.

"Reminds me a bit of Marina Abramović, you know?" Nate scratches his head. "A little more nudity in a lot of her work, but still."

Trip remains facing forward, content to keep his voice quiet in the name of maintaining Nate's game. "If I get naked, we're gonna get kicked out of here."

"Great from this angle, too." Nate is still circling him. "I really can't figure this piece out, but I think that's part of the charm."

Trip remains facing forward. "So am I getting naked or..."

Nate jolts to a stop when they're facing one another again. "Christ, those eyes."

Trip's cheeks warm when Nate steps a few inches closer.

"I think this is my favorite thing here." Nate holds his gaze. "Completely unique. Just breathtaking."

Trip forgets the small crowd gathered around them. He is strangely aware of the warm leather of the watch on his wrist, the tickle of his hair on his neck. He feels, not for the first time, an ache beneath his ribs and a tingling in his toes. "What if I told you this is an interactive piece?"

"Really?" Nate looks at him with piqued interest. He steps closer.

"Really." Trip closes the space between them, and, as Nate's hands come to frame his face and the familiar taste of spearmint mixes with the cinnamon of his own tongue, Trip thinks it might not be so bad to kiss Nate Mackey for the rest of his days.

Nate breaks off the kiss after a minute; his hands slip from Trip's face to his waist. "Are you dying of boredom? I know you hate this kind of thing."

"I'm doing okay right now." Trip is surprised to find himself a little breathless.

"We can leave soon, I promise." Nate touches a quick kiss to his lips. "Thanks for being a good sport."

"Thanks for making this at least a little interesting." Trip looks around to see that their crowd has dispersed. "Remember that goal we had when we went to all those museums on the East side?"

"That wasn't going to work on a Tuesday afternoon, so it's definitely not going to work now. It's too crowded." Nate releases Trip's waist and takes his hand so they can walk. "We'll get caught."

"Half the fun, isn't it?"

"I just renewed my membership." Nate squeezes Trip's hand. "Let me get a few more visits in, at least, before you get me banned for life."

Trip moves to walk more closely beside Nate. "Deal."

• • •

THEY WALK THE MUSEUM FOR another couple hours. Kellan and Scarlett sit down on benches to gaze at the paintings with one of his hands tucked around her knee, their ankles bumping and her head on his shoulder. Trip and Nate speak in hushed tones while they create grand art-theft schemes where Nate chooses which pieces to steal and Trip devises the plan. When they all tire of the crowds and the art, they venture out onto the street and hail a cab to take them to Chelsea for dinner.

They can't settle on a place to eat, so Kellan suggests they get drinks beforehand. He leads them to a bar that's lined with small red-leather rounded booths, is dimly lit offers a complicated-looking cocktail menu.

"I'm going to put my finger on a random one and that's what I'm getting," Scarlett declares. She puts one hand over her eyes and drops a finger on the menu atop the little table.

"I don't know what half of the things in these drinks are." Trip scrutinizes the menu.

Nate slips an arm over Trip's shoulders and leans closer so he can look, too. He points at one of the drinks. "You'll like that. It should be strong but a little sweet."

Trip shifts closer to Nate's side and skims the description of ingredients beside his finger.

Nate points to another drink. "You might like that one, too. It's got the same whiskey in it that we used to make Old Fashioneds a couple weeks ago. "

"Dammit, Nathaniel, I had my mind made up." Trip nudges him in the ribs.

"So get what you were going to get."

"You're making me reconsider."

"I'll get this one and you get the other one. We'll share."

"What if I want both?" Trip lowers the menu.

"Then get both."

Trip hands the menu to Nate. "You trying to get me drunk?"

"Since when do two drinks get you drunk?" Nate turns the menu over to read the other side.

"Maybe I'm gonna try the whole menu."

"I'm not paying for you to try the entire menu," Nate replies.

"You won't need to. I'll figure something out."

"One of these has something that sounds a hell of a lot like green juice in it." Nate turns the menu back toward him. "You might want to reconsider your full-menu plan."

Trip snatches the paper, holds it close to his face for easier inspection. "You're lying."

"Right there, look. The drink has the word 'green' right in the name."

"Now I don't trust this place to have even one decent drink." Trip drops the menu on the table.

"Either you pick something or I'm doing it for you."

"So pick it for me then." Trip taps a finger against the face of Nate's watch still on his wrist. "Make it snappy."

Nate looks at the watch and then at Trip's face. "Are you going to pretend to hate whatever I pick?"

Trip crosses a finger over his heart.

"I'm holding you to that." Nate slips out of the booth. "Kel? You going up?"

"Just waiting on you two crazy kids." Kellan touches a kiss to Scarlett's temple. "Be right back."

Trip watches Kellan and Nate make the short walk to the bar. He whistles, hoping to get a rise out of Nate. Nate doesn't turn to respond, but does give Trip the finger.

"Well, well, well."

Trip jumps, surprised by Scarlett's proximity to his left side. "You make a habit of sneaking up on people?"

"I moved maybe three inches closer to you than I was before." Scarlett sips from her water glass. "Not that you would have known. You might as well have been walking on a cloud a million miles above my head."

"Anybody ever told you the clouds ain't that far away?" Trip sees that he has a water glass, too, and he wonders where it came from.

Scarlett kicks his ankle beneath the table. "Has anybody ever told you that you are completely and totally smitten?"

"You're one to talk." Trip makes a face. "My teeth hurt just thinking about you and Kellan Kipley. Christ."

"Fine, I admit it. I'm completely head-over-heels in love." Scarlett looks toward the bar, her expression dreamy.

Trip makes a choking noise before picking up his water glass. "Sorry, I think I just threw up in my mouth a little bit."

"Please grow up." Scarlett tears her gaze from the bar to focus on Trip. "In all seriousness, though, this has been an amazing day, right?"

Trip is ready to fire back with a nasty remark, but he deflates. "It hasn't been awful."

"Coming from you, that's not half-bad." Scarlett tweaks the watch on his wrist. "You and I, Trip Morgan, are doing all right for ourselves."

Trip twists the watch so it's facing the right way. "He's not gonna let me keep it. He just gets pissed when I take it."

"I wasn't talking about the watch." Scarlett nods toward the bar. "I meant them."

Trip toys with the crown at the edge of Nate's watch. "Yeah, I guess."

"I guess," Scarlett echoes in a mock exaggerated Southern accent. "I'm Trip Morgan, and I'm trying to pretend like I'm not a smitten kitten."

"You're telling *me* to grow up?" Trip looks her over, unimpressed. "And I don't talk like that."

"It's close," Scarlett replies in her own voice. "Okay, fine, I'll come down to your comfort level: Kellan is a nice guy. Nate is a nice guy. It's nice to be with nice guys."

Trip doesn't respond. He watches Nate at the bar and twists the leather band of the watch around his wrist.

Scarlett's hand on his knee makes him jump. "He is nice to you, right?"

"Yeah, sure." Trip stops his restless spinning of the watch strap.

Scarlett's hand tightens on his knee. "Would you tell me if he isn't?"

"And what would you do about it if I said he knocks me around or somethin'?" Trip barely manages to suppress his smile.

"I'm being serious, Trip."

Trip is startled by Scarlett's sudden ferocity. "Christ, of course he's nice to me. You're the one accusing me of being all kinds of lovesick over him. What the hell do you think I like in a guy?"

"I don't know. Sometimes we worry about you." Scarlett's hand stays on his leg, looser now. "I think the past couple months is the longest you've gone without coming home with some mystery injury."

"Which should tell you something about Nathaniel. He wouldn't leave a bruise even if I asked him to." Trip eyes her hand, considers asking her to move it. "And who the hell is 'we?'"

"Me. Liam." Scarlett's expression lightens. "Probably June if she could talk."

"Well, all three of you can cut out your worrying, I'm fine." Trip moves to push her hand from his leg. "And what the hell ever made you think I like getting knocked around?"

"I don't think you like it. Sometimes I just think that you're so used to people hurting you that you think it's okay."

"Nathaniel wouldn't lay a finger on me, all right?" Trip pauses, his hand hovering in the air above Scarlett's. "He likes taking care of people—of me. I'm better than okay."

Scarlett hesitates before speaking again. "You know if you weren't—"

"Yeah." Trip rests his hand over hers. "I know."

They're both quiet, but then Scarlett is turning her hand to squeeze Trip's. "You know, you never denied that you're a smitten kitten."

Trip pulls his hand out of hers. "Jesus Christ, woman, do you ever stop?"

Kellan and Nate return with their drinks just as Scarlett lets out a peal of laughter.

"I take it we missed something good," Kellan says as he places a martini glass in front of Scarlett.

"Not particularly. Your girlfriend doesn't have the greatest sense of humor." Trip slides over to allow Nate more space.

"Ignore him." Scarlett flicks a wrist. "It was funny, but one of those you-kind-of-had-to-be-there sort of things."

"I trust your judgment." Kellan kisses her, and they are immediately lost in one another just as they had been at the museum.

Trip turns his attention to Nate and the three glasses on the table in front of them. "You planning on seducing the bar back or something? More drinks than there are people at this table."

"You said you wanted both, you got both." Nate sips his drink. "Deal with it."

"And let me guess, I get both because you couldn't bring yourself to stray from one of your usual." Trip picks up one of the glasses and sniffs the amber liquid inside. It smells vaguely of smoke and oranges.

Nate ducks his head. "Something like that."

"So predictable, Nathaniel." Trip clicks his tongue as he picks up the second glass. It's more red-tinted than the first and there's a spiral of lemon peel at the bottom.

"I'm not that predictable." Nate watches intently while Trip sips from the straw in his glass. "I just know what I like."

"Yeah?" Trip lowers the drink to the table, then hooks his open hand over the edge of Nate's thigh.

Nate leans closer. "Yeah."

Trip closes his eyes when Nate kisses him. With his sight obscured, he's more aware of the slow heat already spreading in his chest from the small sip of his drink.

Nate pulls away, licking his lips. "Though that's not half-bad. Do you like it?"

"Like what?" Trip blinks at him.

"The drink. It's got absinthe in it. You and absinthe seem like a good pair."

"Oh, yeah, it's good." Trip takes another drink, notes the slight bite of licorice. "Absinthe the one that makes people crazy?"

"Shouldn't be much of a personality change for you if it does."

Trip bumps his shoulder against Nate's arm. "Be nice."

Scarlett meows quietly.

Trip kicks her under the table.

The drinks are good, the atmosphere is cozy and intimate, and they decide to remain at the bar in lieu of leaving to find a restaurant for dinner. They share bar food and chatter about the increased subway fare and the sporadic warm and cold bursts the fall has produced so far. Nate and Kellan discuss Ashbury-Whiteman at length, and Nate doesn't seem bothered by the conversation, but Trip tucks a hand over his leg and rubs a thumb against his knee anyway while he talks to Scarlett.

By the end of the night, they are all happy and buzzed as they stumble out into the cold early-November air.

"We should do this more often." Kellan declares. He spins Scarlett. "Maybe go dancing next time."

"We love dancing!" Scarlett agrees.

Trip shivers, chilled after the warm interior of the bar. "Over my dead body."

"I'll second that." Nate pulls off his jacket, drapes it over Trip's shoulders. "We'll drink and watch."

"That's no fun." Kellan and Scarlett are dancing in slow circles, occasionally tripping over one another's feet.

"Scarlett loves an audience." Trip stands content beneath the familiar weight of Nate's arm resting on his shoulders. "And Nathaniel and I like to drink and judge people. It's perfect."

"Fine." Kellan concedes. He stands behind Scarlett with his arms around her waist. "Are we calling it a night?"

Nate looks down at Trip.

Trip shrugs.

Nate looks back at Kellan. "Yeah, I think so. You still good with the gym tomorrow morning?"

"Yeah, yeah, I'll be there." Kellan groans. "You'll never let me forget it if I skip."

Scarlett squeezes Kellan's arm gently. "I'm going back to my place tonight. Do you want to come, or is staying over going to make you too tired to make your gym date with Nate?"

"I can handle both of you." Kellan releases Scarlett's waist. "Trip? You going our way or headed Upper East?"

"I made the mistake of sticking around once when y'all had a sleepover, and I'm still recovering." Trip makes a face. "I'll sleep on a park bench if I have to, but I sure as hell am not sleeping in my room."

"You can sleep in my bed, you know that." Nate chuckles. "You coming now or do you have to go do some mystery skulking someplace else first?"

Trip grins. "I'm coming—"

Nate interrupts. "I'm cutting you off before you can finish whatever terrible joke it is you think you're going to make."

"Speaking of finishing, I—"

Nate closes a hand over his mouth. "Scarlett, Kip, it was fun. Let's do it again soon."

"Very soon." Scarlett takes Kellan's hand, tugs him toward the corner. "Trip, do you have your key?"

Trip licks Nate's palm and speaks when he jerks his hand away. "Yeah, I'm good. See you tomorrow."

After Scarlett and Kellan have gone, Trip and Nate decide to take a cab rather than wait for the train. Trip is overcome with a sudden wave of exhaustion in the back of the cab that only grows worse once they are back at Nate's apartment.

He and Nate brush their teeth together in silence, and the fatigue must be evident on Trip's face because after they've finished, Nate pushes Trip wordlessly to the stairs. Trip doesn't protest. He climbs the steps, strips out of his clothes and leaves Nate's watch on the nightstand before slipping beneath the covers on his side of the mattress.

Nate shakes his shoulder gently when he slips into the right side of the bed. "Hey, sit up for a second and take these."

"I don't need anything." He murmurs but sits up all the same.

Nate hands him the pills. "You were coughing the other night. I don't think you're totally over that cold."

Trip takes the pills and the glass of water Nate hands him. He yawns, rubs an eye.

Nate places the cup back on the nightstand when Trip's finished with it. "You're cute when you're tired, you know that?"

"Mmm, I'll wake up enough to be fun. Just give me a second." Trip blinks hard and stretches.

"You're fine just like this." Nate lifts the covers. "Lie down. Sleep. You're never going to get healthy if you keep running yourself ragged."

Trip stretches out on his stomach. "I'm not opposed to you fucking me while I'm asleep if you aren't."

Nate touches his arm. "I'm good, just come here."

Trip slots himself closer to Nate's side and rests his head on his chest. He inhales the smell of the body wash still clinging to Nate's skin and releases his breath with a sigh.

Nate massages his scalp with soft fingers. "I had fun today."

"Me, too." Trip closes his eyes. "Thanks for the drinks."

"Anytime." Trip recognizes the click of the lamp and he's aware the bedroom is suddenly darker.

He coughs into his shoulder. "If I'm doing that all night, feel free to kick me to the couch."

"The medicine will help." Nate's voice is a low rumble against Trip's cheek. "You're fine right where you are. Do you want a cough drop or something to help?"

"I'm okay." Trip nuzzles closer. "I'm good."

"Okay." Nate presses a kiss into his hair. "Wake me up if that changes."

Trip is soothed by the slow rise and fall of Nate's stomach beneath his arm. He lies for a long time, drifting in the gray space between reality and dreams, wondering exactly when he fell so hard for Nate Mackey.

TEN.

The light in his room doesn't work. It's not a burned-out light bulb; Trip's sure of it. He pushes his door open so he can inspect the cord for a short. It's still dusky out and the lack of light through the open door is a surprise. Trip's been waking up earlier these days, too used to Nate's early-morning hours to make it much later than nine before he's rolling out of bed and starting his day, no matter how late he got in the night before.

He squints at the cord, but there are no signs of mouse-chewing or any other injury. He takes the light bulb out and screws it back in. Nothing. He pulls the cord a few more times, irritated. He gives up and ventures out to the family room where Liam is busy with a canvas and Scarlett's feeding June a bottle.

Scarlett looks tired and she's still dressed in last night's clothes. "Power's out."

"I noticed." Trip pulls his hair back into a ponytail, shivers. It's too cold for the early weeks of November. "We pay the bill?"

She shakes her head. "Not yet. We were short last month, too."

"And the month before that." Trip flips the light switch on the wall as if it might change its mind about not working. "I s'pose that means there's no coffee then either, huh?"

"No coffee to make coffee even if the power was still on." Scarlett tucks June's blanket more securely around her middle. "Trip, what the hell are we gonna do?"

"Get caffeine headaches and have some very long days." Trip leans against the wall. "I don't know what we're gonna do about electric. Is the water heater still broken? I'm freezing."

"You'd stay warmer if you weren't so damn skinny." Liam chimes in. His hair, Trip notes, is a mix of lavender and pink.

"You'd have more to contribute to electric if you didn't spend all your fuckin' money on hair dye." Trip takes the open space on the couch beside Scarlett.

"So would you if you could get a real job." Liam smudges a spot of paint onto Trip's shin. "And stop complaining, this isn't so bad. Struggle is good for the soul."

"My soul's had enough struggling for five lifetimes." Trip tugs at the edge of June's blanket. "Can I hold the baby? She's practically a portable space heater."

"No. I haven't seen her in ages, and I need to leave for work in a few hours." Scarlett gives him a look. "You can stick your toes under my legs, though."

Trip is grateful for any added heat. He wishes he didn't run so cold all the time. Liam's squinting at him—he's been doing it a lot the past few weeks and the added attention is irritating. "You keep looking at me like that, Li, and I might get the wrong idea."

Liam holds his gaze for an uncomfortably long time before looking back at his canvas. "I'm doing a study on roommates. Unfortunately for both of us, I need to stare at you."

"Can we focus?" Scarlett snaps her fingers at both of them. "Seriously, what the hell are we going to do about this?"

Trip scrubs at his eyes. "Fuck, I don't know. How long does it take to get it turned back on once we pay?"

Scarlett shakes her head. "I don't know. I've gotten late notices before, but I've never actually had the lights cut before."

"*Can* we pay?" Trip drags his bag close to his side so he can unearth one of his coffee cans of money. He pries the lid off of it and pours the contents out onto his lap. It isn't much. "What if we pay part of it? Will they give us a few extra days or something?"

"I don't know. I tried calling Kellan, but he's gone on business." Scarlett puts the empty bottle on the floor beside her feet and shifts June until she's sitting more upright. "He's good at figuring these kinds of things out."

Trip drums his fingers on his knee. He knows someone responsible and good enough at math to make sense of this issue. "The phone got any charge?"

Scarlett pulls the phone from her pocket. "Not much—I'll charge it at the restaurant later."

"Give it here." Trip sticks out a hand. "I might know a guy."

Nate picks up on the fourth ring.

"Good morning, Nathaniel." Trip pulls one foot out from under Scarlett's thighs to prod at June. "You got plans today?"

"I'm thinking about scheduling that job interview." Nate clears his throat. He's never very good on the phone, and Trip can't tell if he's in a bad mood or just being Nate.

"What? No, you can't. You still have a couple weeks to go." Trip wiggles his toes when June tries to pull off his sock. "We have a deal."

"Trip, we talked about this." Trip can hear the sound of his closet doors sliding open and closed. He's probably just out of the shower after a run. "I need to move forward, and it's a good office."

"Nuh-uh, no way." Trip tugs his foot out of June's hold when she leans down to suck on his toes. He can feel Scarlett and Liam watching him, but he pays them no mind. "What if I make you a better offer?"

"You have an office with health benefits and opportunities for upward mobility?" Somewhere in the background, Trip can hear the sound of drawers opening and closing.

"No, but I got an apartment with no power that you can come see." Nate has an odd preoccupation with getting to see where Trip lives, and he knows it's too tempting an offer for Nate to let pass by. "Couple of the roommates are home. You can see them live and in-person and everything."

Nate's quiet, then says. "I don't know."

"Pretty please?" Trip is not about to resort to begging, but he's running out of ways to ask without sounding desperate. "This issue might even require research and maybe you can make a spreadsheet or something. You'll love it. And I'm here—math and research and me. What could be better, huh?"

Nate's breath crackles against Trip's ear. "Fine. Okay."

"Okay?" Trip shifts his feet down to the floor, warmer now.

"I said okay," Nate replies. "What's the address?"

Trip resists the urge to give Nate the number for the building across the street and recites the address correctly and then listens while Nate repeats it. "Perfect. If you wanna bring coffee, I wouldn't complain."

Nate sounds less gloomy when he says he'll stop at a Starbucks.

Trip drops the phone onto the coffee table. "We officially have someone with a college degree coming to figure this out for us; you're welcome."

Scarlett and Liam are looking at him with twin smiles.

Scarlett looks at Liam. "Told you so."

"I know you did. Seeing is believing, though." Liam giggles.

Trip narrows his eyes. "What?"

Scarlett and Liam chime in unison, "Nothing."

Trip, unsettled by whatever secret it is they suddenly share, looks from Scarlett to Liam and back again, but he'd never admit to feeling left out, so he lets it go.

Nate arrives barely an hour later, a box of coffee in one hand, two paper bags in the other. Trip eyes the box and steps aside to let Nate through the door.

Liam and Scarlett watch him with the same overlarge grins they'd directed at Trip when he got off the phone.

Nate nods a hello to both of them; his eyes rest for a long time on the baby. "Hi, I'm Nate. I'm Trip's friend."

"Nice to see you again, Nate." Scarlett stands. She waves June's hand for her. "This is June, that's Liam."

Liam stands, offers a hand, still smiling first at Trip and then at Nate. "Nice to meet you. It's always interesting to find someone else who can tolerate Trip for prolonged periods of time."

"Hilarious." Trip watches the way Nate's eyes go wide when he tips his head up to meet Liam's gaze. "Terrifying thing, ain't he?"

Nate frowns at Trip before turning back to Scarlett and Liam. He lifts the cardboard box higher. "I brought coffee and bagels."

"We love you already." Liam applauds and goes to the kitchen for mugs.

Nate puts the coffee and one of the bags on the table. He pulls a book out of the second bag and offers it to Trip.

Trip studies the glossy yellow cover and flips through the pages. "Is this to make a fire for extra light? Cause I'm pretty sure that'll just get us kicked out."

Nate rolls his eyes. "You said you didn't have a laptop for the online course. It's a GED test prep book."

"I can see that." Trip squints at a page in the science section. Taking the test to get his GED had been a conversation held in passing while they were lying naked in bed late one night a week earlier. Trip hadn't put much thought into it beyond mentioning that he was considering taking the test.

"We should get your eyes checked." Nate accepts an empty mug from Liam. "You do that all the time."

"Do what?" Trip inspects a section on test taking skills with distaste.

Scarlett returns from her bedroom with a shoebox of torn-open envelopes that she places on the coffee table. "You squint when you try to read something."

"Like, all the time." Liam fills his mug with coffee. "You need glasses."

"I do not." Trip tosses the book at Liam.

"Don't throw it." Nate lifts the book from the floor. He puts it on the coffee table between them. "It wasn't cheap."

"Didn't ask you to buy the damn thing, did I?" Trip snaps.

"Well, now you're stuck with it." Nate touches a brief kiss to Trip's temple as he takes the seat beside him. "Something for your bag that's actually yours."

Trip stares at the book. "Thanks."

"You're welcome. We can check test dates later." Nate sips his coffee and casts a look around the apartment. "This is where you live."

Trip looks around, too. The wood floors are recently scrubbed, but the sunflowers over June's playpen are chipping and the painted clouds around the window have blurred from the leak in the ceiling. Liam's added a new abstract mural above his corner of projects; it's done in soft earthy shades of green and brown.

"This is where I live." Trip pats a hand against the faded floral cushions of the couch. "Little bit of a roach problem, there's no hot water, and now there's no power. It's not exactly the Ritz."

"I've been trying to figure out why you always smell like clean laundry since we met." Nate looks at the floor where the laundromat hums below. "Makes sense now."

"Mystery solved." Trip crosses his legs on the couch.

"One of a thousand when it comes to you." Nate starts sifting through the box of paperwork. "The hot-water thing should get fixed by your landlords. Have you contacted them?"

Trip and Liam exchange a look. "Not exactly."

"How long's it been out?" Nate peers up from the papers in his hands.

"It comes and goes, so two weeks, maybe?" Scarlett bounces the baby on her knee and feeds her shredded bits of a bagel.

"You need to call; that's not normal." Nate looks up at the crack above the window. "Does that leak? You should mention that, too. They can probably get in and fix all of that—the roaches, too."

"Our living situation is... how should I say this?" Liam takes a bite of a bagel and chews before speaking again. "It's a unique situation."

"What do you mean?" Nate looks around at all of them; his gaze settles on Scarlett. "Kel says you guys have some sort of deal going."

"We do." Trip steals Nate's mug for a drink of coffee. "People across the hall technically have both these places—they're rent-stabilized."

"You pay them rent and they just share the other apartment." Nate pours a new mug of coffee for himself. "And you can't call the landlord to fix stuff because you're not technically supposed to be here."

"See? Told you he was smart." Trip trades his mug with Nate's and casts a wary glance at the GED book still on the table.

"Kel's pretty good with home utility stuff. If you know where the water heater is, he can probably take a look for you." Nate dumps all of the paperwork onto the coffee table and shuffles it into some semblance of order.

"I know how to fix a water heater. I've been keeping the damn thing alive for nearly a year." Scarlett waves him off. "We just need a new one. I'm not sure about the leak above the window, though."

Nate looks at the crack in the plaster. "It probably just needs caulking or something."

"Didn't know you were such a handyman, Nathaniel." Trip watches while Nate scribbles things on envelopes and punches numbers into his phone.

"Used to help do repairs at the resort," Nate murmurs, his attention more on his work than on Trip. "I can't do everything, but I know a few things."

"You got a tool belt?" Trip takes June without question when Scarlett stands abruptly and offers her to him. "I think I might like you in a tool belt."

Nate takes note of the baby and tickles one of her feet. "I'll see what I can do."

Nate writes things down, and when Scarlett comes back into the family room dressed in her hotel uniform, they have a long exchange about interest and missed bills and lawyers. Nate steps out into the hall a few times to make calls.

Trip sits on the couch and eats a bagel while June has a bottle on his lap. Trip watches Nate work and makes a running commentary about how sexy it is to watch Nate punch numbers into a calculator and ponder over old bills that earns him the occasional look or touch from Nate.

There's a scramble for ninety dollars that involves pulling furniture away from the walls and digging through pockets and the bottoms of bags. When Nate offers to spot them some cash, he's answered with a collective no.

Scarlett speaks for all of them. "We can take your help, but not your money. No one here likes being in the red."

Nate looks as though he might argue, but in the end, he doesn't have to. The money is gathered and the conversation is forgotten.

When Nate steps back out into the hall to make another call, Liam smirks at Trip. "If I were going to fall in love with someone, it would definitely be Nate Mackey."

"Turn up the charm and he might be into a quickie before you have to get to work." Trip accepts semi-soggy bites of bagel from June. "He can be a little uptight, but he loosens up eventually."

"Mr. Mackey only has eyes for one person in this apartment. I'm just waiting on my wedding invitation." Liam is busy at work with a canvas and his paint, but he pauses to point his brush at Trip. "I don't know how you do it. I really don't. You've either got a magic penis or you're a better con man than I originally thought."

"Little bit of both." Trip eyes the book on the coffee table. "Don't start planning on hair colors to match the wedding party just yet. As soon as he gets working again, he'll get himself a nice, respectable man, and I'll be slumming it twenty-four seven with your ugly mug again."

Liam clicks his tongue. "I know you're short a few diplomas, Morgan, but I never took you for stupid."

"Nathaniel and I have a good thing going—mutually beneficial." Trip sips his coffee and keeps the mug well out of June's reach. "Gotta end sometime, though. It's just the way of the world."

"Uh-huh. By the way, never go into acting; you're terrible at it." Liam hums "All You Need is Love" by the Beatles while he paints.

Trip's about to threaten Liam's hair or artwork when the apartment door opens and Nate steps back in. He tucks his phone in his pocket. "You should be getting power in a few hours."

"Thank you." Scarlett squeezes Nate's arm with gentle fingers. "Really. You're amazing."

Nate indicates the box on the table where all the envelopes have been smoothed and stacked into a neat pile. "Those are all in order and the calls from today are marked on the most recent bill. If they give you any issues, you've got it documented that all of this happened."

Trip yawns. "Great. Now we just gotta make sure we don't do this every month."

They all exchange a grim look. None of this is getting any easier.

Nate apparently knows it's not his place to say anything. He's looking around the apartment awkwardly, curious and uncomfortable at once.

"We'll figure it out." Liam breaks the quiet. "We always figure it out."

Trip drags his hand through his hair. "Yeah. It's good for now, right? It's taken care of."

They all nod their agreement, though no one says anything.

Liam takes the baby. Scarlett finishes dressing for work and gives them all kisses on their cheeks before disappearing out the front door calling that she's got the night off. Trip gives Nate a brief tour of the rest of the apartment—the bathroom and its cracked tile, the kitchen with the lemon-colored walls, Liam and Devon's cramped bedroom, Scarlett and June's room and, finally, his room.

Nate touches one of the wire hangers near the door. "This is a closet."

"You shut your goddamn mouth. This is a three-bedroom apartment and I've got this room all to myself." Trip nudges his blankets with a toe. "The bed's not too bad; you wanna see for yourself?"

Nate eyes the blankets on the floor. "Maybe later. Your walls are thin and there's a kid in the other room."

The apartment is loud with the rumble of dryers downstairs, and Trip is uneasy under the knowing looks Liam keeps directing his way, so he suggests a move outside.

"No balcony, but we've got a fire escape." He points to the cardboard containers on the table. "We can bring coffee."

"It's the middle of November." Nate looks dubiously at the window. "And I don't know if I trust your fire escape."

"We'll bring blankets." Trip tweaks the edge of Nate's sweater. "And it's not that high up. If it falls, we'll probably only break a couple bones."

Nate reluctantly agrees, so they sit together on the fire escape, their thighs touching and shoulders bumping under the warmth of the blanket. They drink coffee, and Trip lights a cigarette.

"Those things are awful for you." Nate waves his mug at Trip's cigarette. "You're gonna destroy your voice and then you won't be able to sing anymore."

"Can still play." Trip blows smoke out toward the bars of the fire escape. "Besides, I'm cold. It makes me feel warmer."

Nate tucks an arm around Trip's shoulders, pulls him closer. "Better?"

Trip nods. "Still not tossing the cigarette."

"Fine." Nate turns his gaze more fully at Trip. "I have a question."

"You've always got questions." Trip transfers his cigarette to his left hand so he can lift his coffee mug with his right.

"That you never answer." Nate hikes the blanket up higher over his shoulder.

"Maybe you should give up on asking them then." Trip sips his coffee. "Doesn't seem to be working out too well for you so far."

"I helped you get your power turned back on." Nate bumps Trip's ankle with his. "You owe me. Come on."

"You're as much of a fuckin' weasel as I am." Trip sits back against the ledge of the window and kicks his feet in the open space above the stairs. "Go ahead then. Ask your stupid question."

"Do you ever go home?"

"Home right now, aren't I?" Trip waves his mug at the fire escape.

"I mean to wherever you're from?" Nate shakes his head when Trip offers the cigarette. "Have you been back there since you ran away? Does your family know you're here?"

Trip replaces his cup on the ledge outside the window. "Don't go back and don't know if they know. I don't think so."

"They didn't look for you?"

Trip thinks back to the early days in the city. Liam had made it his mission to find a missing child report on Trip and succeeded after a few weeks. He'd printed the page and it had hung proudly on their fridge for nearly a year. "I think so, for a bit. I'm sure there's some sort of law that says you gotta look for your kid when they disappear."

"Do you ever miss them?" Nate's brushing his fingers slow and light over Trip's shoulder. Trip's not sure Nate realizes he's doing it.

"You miss that dead brother you hate?" Trip hooks his free hand over Nate's knee. "Or that pregnant sister you're so bent out of shape over?"

"Yeah, sometimes." Nate's fingers pause. "I've got issues with everything that happened, but he was still my family. I still miss him… and me and my sister are doing better. I called her on the way over here actually."

"Well, ain't you a good brother." Trip blows a smoke ring and watches it stretch and dissipate before blowing another.

Nate snaps his fingers near the circle of smoke and they watch as it forms into a heart before fading. "Do you think your family misses you?"

"No." Trip blows a larger ring and sends a smaller ring tumbling through it.

"Showoff," Nate mutters. "What about your friends? You think they miss you?"

"Didn't have any." Trip waves away the smoke.

"Someone must have cared about you." Nate's hand closes on his shoulder. "Someone loved you. I can tell."

"Thought I was the romantic." Trip points his cigarette at Nate. "And you're outta questions."

"We didn't specify how many I could ask."

"Well, I'm specifying how many answers I'm willing to give right now," Trip snaps.

"You haven't answered anything."

"I've answered everything you've asked."

"I don't know anything new about you."

"Jesus fuckin' Christ, Nathaniel." Trip drags a hand through his hair, exasperated. "You wanna know something? You *really* wanna know something that fucking bad?"

Nate nods. He's not as easily flustered by Trip's irritation as he used to be.

"Alabama. I'm from Southern Alabama." Trip drops his cigarette in Nate's coffee. It goes out with a quiet sizzle and pop. "Now you've officially used up all your questions from now until the end of time."

"Alabama," Nate echoes. He's smiling as if this small piece of information is something treasured. "Small town, right? I can see that."

"You ask me one more fucking question, and I swear I'll—"

"Break my goddamn neck, I know." Nate taps one finger against Trip's shoulder. "This is the last one, I promise."

"I'm gonna throw you off this fire escape."

"If you don't ever go home, and you're not planning on changing that anytime soon..." Nate looks nervous in a way Trip hasn't seen on him in a long time. He clears his throat, meets Trip's gaze. "Would you, um, maybe want to come home with me? For Thanksgiving?"

His anger forgotten in a sudden wave of confusion, Trip blinks at him. "To where?"

"To my parents' place." Nate's cheeks are flushed, but Trip can't tell if they're colored with cold or embarrassment. "I know it's kind of last-second, but I've got a ton of frequent-flyer miles saved up, and it'd only be for a few days."

"To Minnesota." Trip stares at the blanket draped over their laps.

"Yeah. You could meet my sister. See that porch on the house. My family does a huge dinner. We've got canoes and ATVs and my mom's an even better cook than I am. You'd like it."

Trip looks at Nate's face. His expression is a mixture of nerves and something hopeful. "We'd fly?"

"Yeah, too far to drive." Nate's hand drifts from Trip's shoulder to his side. He tickles him. "What? You scared of flying?"

"Never been on a plane." Trip shies away from Nate's fingers. He wishes he hadn't put out his cigarette. "When would we go?"

"I've got a ticket booked for the Tuesday before, so it'll be a quick trip." Nate's talking too fast, stumbling over his words. "Could probably get you different dates if you want, but I think there's still availability on both of my flights if you can—I mean if you want to come. Do you want to go?"

Trip swallows, jigs a foot to rid himself of the sudden adrenaline in his system. "You trying to freak out your parents or something?"

"Freak them out?" Nate echoes.

Trip turns his gaze back to Nate and waves at his face. "Not exactly the best person to bring home to mom and dad."

"Nora's got a worse mouth than yours." Nate looks slightly exasperated with talking about his family, but his tone is fond. "She curses like a sailor, and so does my grandma."

Normally Trip would want to know more about Nora and this cursing grandmother he's never heard about, but right now he's still trying to process what he's supposed to do with all of this. He cannot actually read anyone's mind or see the future, but he's good at knowing how things are going to play out and he hadn't seen this coming.

"I meant my hair and my clothes and my eyes and all that." He tugs at the sleeve of Nate's cream-colored sweater.

"We can get you a couple new shirts if you're that worried about it, but the rest of you is fine." Nate looks from Trip's left eye to his right. "And I love your eyes."

Trip's cheeks heat up and he has to look away. Trip Morgan does not blush. He doesn't know what's happening. "Can I think about it?"

"Sure." Nate pinches his arm. "Don't think too long, though? Tickets get really expensive close to the holiday. I've got a lot of miles, but not that many."

"Okay." Trip shifts under Nate's arm. He wants to take a walk or run or get in a fight. He doesn't know what to do with his body right now.

Nate must notice Trip's sudden discomfort. He shifts his hand to the nape of Trip's neck. He rubs the tight muscles there with his left hand, points with his right toward the street. "If you won't tell me about you, tell me about them, those people down there by the eyebrow-threading place."

Trip looks where Nate's pointing. A group of women are standing in a close circle. "I don't know them."

"You can read minds and make up entire, elaborate novels about a drink receipt, but you can't think of anything to say about a group of people right in front of you?" Nate moves closer to Trip's side. "Come on, tell me."

Trip relaxes. "Lenore, Keisha and Kiley."

"Who's who?" Nate is still massaging Trip's neck. He steals his coffee with his free hand and takes a drink before offering the mug back.

"Dunno. You pick." Trip lights a new cigarette. Nate doesn't comment on it this time.

Nate's better at this game than he had been at making stories for Trip's things, but Trip makes up most of the story. They're all dating each other, but Lenore was recently angry with Keisha for only inviting Kiley to her office party; they've since made up and are all going together to have their eyebrows threaded as a unifying activity before the party.

Trip and Nate keep playing their game with the people they can see through windows across the street and with anyone else who passes below. Trip relaxes; Nate laughs more and more as the stories get increasingly ridiculous. He tips his cheek into Trip's hair and listens while Trip talks.

Trip finishes his cigarette and sips his coffee. It's ice-cold, but he doesn't mind. He's the warmest he's been in a long time.

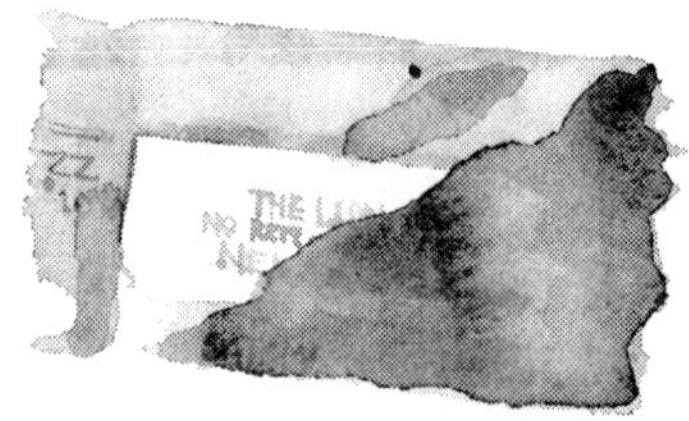

V.

Pastor Welk was the one good thing in Bekket.

I'll never know why he took an interest in me over all the other kids, but if I had to take a guess, I suppose it's because you can get attached to a kid when you help deliver him on the steps of your own church.

From what I've heard, he came by the trailer sometimes with diapers and formula and that sort of thing so he could look in on us, but my mama usually just told him to go to hell. He may have been a man of God, but the only time my mama believed in God was when she was threatening us with eternal fire or citing the commandment about respecting your parents.

Anyway, we didn't really get to know each other until I was five. It happened that I got stupid enough to get in a fight with Gideon, and I was scared out of my mind that he was going to beat me senseless for putting a nail through one of his bike tires. In my defense, he had crushed up all of my cicada shells I'd been saving up for weeks.

I ran out of the trailer park as fast as I could. I kept twisting around to check for Gid, and it made me fall a few times and bloody up my knees. I made it to town but then I didn't know what to do with myself. It was about a hundred degrees out and I knew if I went into anyone's store, they'd just call my parents and I'd be in even bigger trouble. I was thinking about just keeping on running, but then Pastor Welk saw me and invited me into the church.

He fixed up my knees and gave me some water and told me I could stay as long as I wanted, so I did. I laid down in one of the pews in the mezzanine and got goose bumps from the air conditioning and stayed camped out until it was time to close up.

I went back a lot, and Pastor Welk never minded. He let me do my homework on the floor and he mostly left me alone. My favorite part was Wednesdays because it was when they rehearsed whatever music they were going to play that Sunday. The choir sang, Mrs. Foley played piano and Pastor Welk played the guitar. It was nice.

He must have noticed how much I liked it because one day when I was seven, he sat me down and suggested we make a deal: If I wiped down the pews every Monday and Wednesday, he'd give me lessons on the guitar every Tuesday and Thursday.

I started wiping down those damn pews so often that I smelled like Pine-Sol almost all the time.

When I got older, Pastor Welk came up with new things to keep me busy. I tended to squeaky doors, painted siding, vacuumed carpets, washed windows and kept wiping down the pews, and he just kept on going with the guitar lessons.

He didn't like it when I started working with my brothers. Thought I was too good to be getting into that sort of thing and worried I'd get myself killed. Thought I was meant for "better things," but I didn't have a whole lot of choice in the matter and I couldn't think of what better things there were besides maybe getting out of Bekket.

I guess he could have told me I couldn't come around anymore if I was going to get involved in that sort of thing, but he never did. He just said he missed not having me around as much and asked me to leave my bat by the door before I came in, and I respected that.

One day after I got into it bad with a group of guys for trying to short me, Pastor Welk sat me down in his office and pulled out a notebook. He'd been marking down everything I did for him, from thawing out air conditioners to hosing down the front steps. He figured every job was worth some set amount of money outside my music lessons, so we counted it all up and it came to almost four hundred dollars. He made me a new offer: When I hit five hundred, the guitar was all mine.

Hell, I'd never wanted anything so bad in my life. I didn't stop dealing, but he and I made a schedule to figure out how long it would take and what I'd have to do to make the extra cash, and I did my best to behave myself when I could.

It wasn't just on account of the guitar. Pastor Welk was always so proud of me for such stupid shit, like reading a bit of sheet music or passing my science test or memorizing a Bible verse, that it made me feel shitty for all the times I came into the church with a black eye or after I'd been suspended for the day. I probably disappointed him more than I made him proud, but he never let on.

It took me another four months to make the cash and the grades. That was his other rule. I had to pass all my classes if I wanted the damn guitar, but I did it. I made the grades and did the work until one fine Sunday, that guitar was going to be mine as soon as church was over and I helped scrub down the pews.

I didn't ever go to services because I didn't like all the people, but Pastor Welk was okay with me stopping in right after.

"We all seek salvation in our own way," he liked to say. I still don't really know what that means, but if it meant not having to listen to people whisper and see them stare for a whole hour, I was fine letting him say it.

I was supposed to be making a swap out behind the elementary school, but I figured I could make my trip to the church, help out and be on my way fast enough that my guy wouldn't have to wait around for more than a minute or two.

I remember I was humming "Amazing Grace" and dragging my bat on the sidewalk—I can still hear it, the scrape of the wood on the pavement, the plunking sound it'd make going over a crack—and I was feeling good. Real good.

There was a crowd on the steps like there always is after a service, but it seemed funny because I'd waited to go to the church just to avoid the mass exodus onto the sidewalk when everyone likes to stop and shake Pastor Welk's hand and talk to each other about the service and one another.

I got all the way up to the first step before I realized people were screaming and crying and all in a panic. At first, I guessed maybe one of the candles had tipped over and the flame caught on a banner or something, but the crowd was too centered on one thing for it to be a fire. Next I thought maybe Pastor Welk was delivering another baby on the steps, and that got me curious, so I pushed in closer to get a better look.

There wasn't a baby, but there was Pastor Welk.

He was stretched out on the steps, his choir robe was white, the sash green, and it was all billowed out around him like a kite that crashed too hard and snapped the support beams. His eyes were open and focused on the sky and he had one hand balled up over his chest.

I shoved my way in as close as I could get, but then I didn't know what I was supposed to do. I wish I could say I said something nice or he said something important to me, but I was too stupid with shock to speak and I think he was hurting too bad. I held his hand and kept quiet and just kept on staring.

We could hear the ambulance siren a long time before we could see it and people started getting real excited. Pastor Welk looked at the sky for a while and then looked at me, and all of a sudden he looked like he wasn't hurting so much, and I thought—truly, honestly believed—it was a miracle and everything was going to be fine.

It was an ugly thing when his hand went loose and his eyes went empty. I'd had a lot of bad shit happen to me growing up, but that moment between thinking things were going to be okay and realizing that they weren't was the ugliest thing that had ever happened to me. I didn't wait to see the paramedics arrive. I didn't hear any of the screaming anymore.

I went into the church, got that guitar and slung it over my shoulder and I don't think anyone even saw me leave. What happened next was not something I sat down to plan out, but I think it was something that had been a long time coming.

I went back to the trailer, ignored my mama yelling about slamming the screen door and went to find a bag. I'd never left Bekket before, so packing was confusing and I kept on just putting my school things out on the bed and having to shove them out of the way again. My hands were numb and my head hurt and my ears were ringing so bad, I didn't realize my daddy was home until he was clocking me upside the head and dragging me back out the front door.

He got a few good hits in while I was still too numb to think to cover my face, but when his belt came off, I knew I'd had enough. I wasn't clear on what it was that had him so bent out of shape, but I didn't care. I was tired and scared and angry. I was really fuckin' angry, so I grabbed my baseball bat from where it was propped up beside the door and I swung. My daddy's a big man, but I got my bat up good and high and he dropped like a puppet with its strings cut.

I moved fast after that. I went back inside, shoved some things in a duffel bag, dug up the coffee can of cash Gid hid under our bed, slung the guitar over my shoulder and went out the door.

I ran. I ran until I couldn't anymore, caught a ride to Tuscaloosa and traded some of my cash for a bus ticket that got me as far as Virginia. I didn't know what to do once I was there. I'd been cramped up on the bus for a good long time, but I had to sit down again in the bus stop and try to catch my breath and get the spinning in my head under control.

When I stuck my head down between my knees, I found the picture. It wasn't much: just some kids on a porch looking like they'd been shoved together long enough to get the photo. There wasn't anyone around to claim it and I liked the idea of having some other lost kids around, so I put the picture in my bag, pulled myself together and used the last of my cash to buy a ticket to New York.

I met a guy on the bus ride up. He's real fucking tall and says he's an artist. He's not the first person I'd have picked to pair up with, but he's nice enough and doesn't ask a lot of questions, so we're gonna stick together for a bit and see if we can figure out some place to stay that isn't Port Authority or a park bench.

I don't know what happens next. I just hope it's something better than this.

ELEVEN.

Trip doesn't go home with Nate for Thanksgiving. It cuts too much into the playing time he needs to make enough for the next round of bills, and flight prices skyrocket by the time they discuss it again. Nate is disappointed but understanding, and Trip is slightly relieved to not have to find out what could have come of meeting Nate's family. Even without going on the trip, things have changed between them.

Since coming back from his solo visit home for Thanksgiving, Nate has started leaving Trip alone in the apartment. It's never for long—usually it's just an hour or two in the mornings while he goes on his run—but some quiet sense of trust that the action implies makes it matter. Nate usually comes back to bed after with the cold still leeching off his clothes and his skin tasting like salt as he settles in over Trip and smugly mumbles how far he's run while Trip lies in bed.

Sometimes Trip is cognizant enough to catch Nate's wrist as he climbs out of bed and coax him back beneath the sheets so they can have sex before Nate goes for his run. If Trip isn't awake enough, it's no matter; Nate seems to relish waking him with kisses when he's still panting from his workout. Sometimes, when Nate is feeling less rigid than usual, he skips his run entirely and they spend the morning in bed together.

Today, Trip had been so deeply asleep that he didn't hear Nate leave. He doesn't mind, though, when he discovers the cold side of the bed. He shifts to the middle where he can steal the extra pillows and nests himself farther under the covers. If it were possible, he'd be perfectly content to never do anything but remain right here in this place forever. He's fallen hard for this bed. He adores the memory foam mattress topper, he revels in the soft cotton of the sheets and he delights in the down pillows that all smell like Nate's cologne. He would commit to a long-term relationship with this bed if he could.

It occurs to Trip, as he drifts in and out of sleep and basks in the warmth of the covers, that today is December tenth. June will be one year old tomorrow and he will be twenty.

He's never put much thought into his birthdays before. Seventeen had come and gone without much consideration, eighteen had been a relief, nineteen had been forgotten in the drama of the snowstorm and Scarlett's early-morning delivery, and now he is in his twenties. It feels too old and too young to be him at the same time.

Downstairs, the front door slams and Trip can hear the familiar squeak of Nate's running shoes on the wood floor. Nate is happier, funnier and sweeter than he'd been when they first met, but he is no less neurotic nor has he become much more spontaneous. Trip listens to the familiar orchestrations of Nate's shoes going into the closet, his headphones being wrapped and tucked into his jacket pocket. Then comes the sink running, the dishtowel being refolded and Nate's socks being thrown into the washing machine.

The fourth step groans and the one just below the bedroom squeaks and then Trip feels a familiar weight on top of him. He doesn't open his eyes. "How'd you do?"

"Eight miles." Nate's still panting and his skin is damp with sweat. "One hour."

"A seven-thirty mile," Trip mumbles into his pillow. He angles his head up so Nate has more access to his neck. "Impressive."

Nate presses a kiss behind Trip's ear. "That was fast math—you been reading that GED book?"

"No, just been listening to you brag about mile times for a lot of mornings." Trip yawns. "Not your best, by the way. You did a seven twenty-three about a week back."

"Someone's been making me miss runs." Nate rolls off of Trip. "Screwing with my times."

"I'm a good workout." Trip cracks open an eye to look at Nate beside him. "Don't blame me for your plateau or whatever this is."

"You could come running with me." Nate pulls the ponytail holder out of Trip's hair and drags his fingers through the freed locks. "Push me to go a little harder."

"I don't run unless I've got someone chasing me." Trip holds up a wrist toward Nate.

Nate slips the hair binder over Trip's hand. He hooks a finger through it and snaps it against his wrist. "It's good for you."

"Know what else is good for you?" Trip catches hold of Nate's fingers and moves his hand to his waist. "Sex. Sex is very, very good for you."

"Releases endorphins," Nate agrees, but he takes his hand back. "I can't this morning—job interview."

"Cheater!" Trip cries. He pushes himself up on his elbows. "We had a deal."

"We talked about this—it's an interview, not the actual job, so it doesn't count. Besides, pretty sure the deadline or whatever on that deal has come and passed." Nate presses a quick kiss to Trip's mouth as he stands. "You have morning breath."

"You smell like sweat and you've got a shitty mile time." Trip tosses his pillow at Nate's back, but he makes no move to get out of bed.

Nate picks up the pillow and tosses it back at Trip before peeling off his shirt and dropping it in the laundry hamper. "You want to shower?"

"What? So you can fuck me up against the tile?" Trip drops his head back onto Nate's pillow and pulls the other over his face. "No way. If you break your half of the deal, I break mine. No sex. No entertainment. No nothing."

The bed sinks when Nate sits down on the edge of it. He pulls the pillow off of Trip's face. "This deal sounds an awful lot like a relationship, you know that?"

Trip flounders before responding. "If that's the case, then you're cheating on me with this interview."

"Have I told you lately that you're a complete drama queen?"

"No worse than you." Trip folds his arms across his chest.

"Hmmm." Nate drops the pillow back down on his face and stands. Trip can hear the sound of his footsteps going back down the steps.

Trip pushes the pillow to the side and stares up at the ceiling with one hand tucked behind his head. He chews at a hangnail. An interview means Nate is stepping back into his life. All jokes about relationships aside, a job means Trip's time here may be nearly up.

He shakes the thought and pushes himself upright. He can't lie here and think anymore. He joins Nate in the shower, listens to him prattle on and on about the new job. It's a small firm, he says, less money but better hours. He talks a lot about office culture and the places some of the other employees have come from, and Trip nods along as though any of it makes sense to him. He doesn't have it in him to make a joke, so he fusses with the shower knobs and dumps too much shampoo in Nate's hair and harasses him in other ways.

Nate gets ahold of his wrists and keeps Trip's hands away from him while he keeps talking and rinses the shampoo from his hair under the too-cold stream of water. They brush their teeth together in front of the bathroom mirror, and then Trip puts on yesterday's clothes while Nate deliberates over which tie to wear. He holds up two and then two more for Trip. Trip offers no constructive help and Nate chooses one on his own.

"Come here." Nate gets a hand on the sleeve of Trip's Henley. "I wanna see something."

Trip shifts his weight from foot to foot and fidgets while Nate drapes a tie around his neck and knots it with quick fingers. He stands back. "You wouldn't look half-bad if we got you in a suit shirt."

Trip pulls at the knot. "Where the hell would I wear a suit shirt?"

"I don't know." Nate turns Trip so he can see himself in the full-length mirror propped against the wall. He keeps his arms wrapped around Trip's middle, rests his chin in his hair. "I'm just saying you'd look good."

"I ever start playing Carnegie, I'll let you know." Trip looks from his reflection to Nate's behind him. Nate's dressed in a lavender suit shirt, the collar starched and neat. His tie is deep purple and knotted carefully at his neck. The cognac-brown dress shoes peeking out from beneath his gray dress pants appear recently polished. He looks clean-cut and handsome and undeniably happy.

"Bet you could if you wanted to." Nate squeezes him softly. "You'd be the talk of the town."

"Yeah, don't hold your breath." Trip pulls the tie loose and steps out of Nate's embrace. He offers the tie back. "Speaking of playing, I gotta get going. I barely made thirty bucks yesterday."

Nate rehangs the tie and glances at his watch. "I have some time—you want breakfast?"

Trip shakes his head and moves toward the steps. "Gotta go pick up my guitar from the apartment before I head out. No time."

"Right. Wouldn't want your boss to catch you sneaking in late." Nate chuckles as he jogs down the staircase after Trip.

"Time's money, Nathaniel." Trip pulls his shoes from the hall closet. He notices, as he tugs them on, that a new hole has formed at the toe of the left one.

"Now who sounds like a Wall Street drone?" Nate calls from the kitchen. He's fussing with something in the cupboards.

"I don't know if you missed the part where I said I made thirty bucks yesterday or what, but last I checked, I'm wearing a pair of worn-down sneakers to my job and you're the one in the million-dollar suit." Trip calls back. He shrugs his bag over his shoulder. He feels too light and wrong without his guitar. He rarely goes to Nate's without it, and he's already regretting the decision to leave it back in the Village.

"Remind me to give you a crash course on the price of suits." Nate reappears around the corner. He holds out a silver thermos. "Coffee."

"Have I told you that you're a saint?" Trip reaches for the thermos. He closes his hand over Nate's and steps closer.

Nate tugs Trip closer by their joint grip on the thermos. "Not today."

"You're a goddamn saint, Nathaniel Mackey." Trip wraps Nate's tie around his free hand. "You need a reference for that job? I'd be happy to say all kinds of good things about your coffee and breakfast and blow jobs."

Nate laughs, then presses a kiss to Trip's mouth. It's meant to be teasing and quick, but then he's kissing him again, deeper and slower; both hands find their way to Trip's waist.

Trip releases his tie and lifts his hand to Nate's neck as he returns the kiss. Nate tastes like mint and smells like cologne. Trip breaks away to catch his breath when the thermos suddenly clangs to the floor between them.

One of Nate's hands remains on his waist, the other pushes Trip's hair off his forehead and drifts down to cradle the back of his neck. "I love you."

Trip is sure he is not moving, and yet the floor seems to tilt beneath his feet.

Nate kisses him again, more a brush of lips this time than actual kiss. "Is that okay?"

"Yeah." Trip is breathless. "I—I think so."

"Okay." Nate's thumb brushes over the vertebra of Trip's neck softly.

They both jump when Nate's phone chimes a happy note from the kitchen, and the spell they have both been under is suddenly broken.

Nate clears his throat and straightens the already-perfect knot of his tie. He stoops and lifts the thermos.

Trip takes it blindly, his eyes still locked on Nate's face.

Nate is blushing hard. He scrubs a hand over the back of his neck. "I, um—"

Trip steps toward the door. He's sure the heat in his cheeks matches the color of Nate's. "I should maybe—"

Nate nods fast, pulls the door for him. "Yeah, right, I'll see you tonight? Or, I mean if you're—"

"Yeah, cool." Trip stands in the hall, just outside the door. "I'll stop by if I have some time or if you're—"

"I'll be here." Nate stands at the threshold. He's red from his hair to his neck.

Trip rocks back on his heels; he's off-balance and has to stumble another step back. "So, I'll see you around?"

Nate seems to regain composure. "See you around."

Trip takes a step back and then two more, his gaze still on Nate before he's tripping over his own feet trying to turn around and make his way to the elevator. He swallows and keeps his eyes on the glowing down button. "Nathaniel?"

Nate's still in the open doorway. "Yeah?"

"I'll be back later." Trip tears his gaze from the elevator button to look back at Nate. "I wanna show you something, all right?"

Nate smiles. "All right."

Trip returns his smile and steps onto the elevator.

As he makes his way to the subway, Trip feels off-balance. His fingers are tingling and his stomach is fluttery. He blames it on skipping breakfast and drinks his coffee and hums to distract himself despite the looks that garners from the people on either side of him.

When he arrives at the apartment, he is immediately aware of two things: how dark the apartment is and the smell of Raid. He flips the light switch a few times. "Did we lose power again?"

Liam's sitting in his corner wrapping a canvas in brown paper; the can of bug killer is at his side. "Scarlett thinks it's a short or something. It's in here and in the bathroom."

"Great." Trip crouches to get a better look at the canvas. "You two going on a field trip?"

Liam pulls the paper down to allow for a better view. "Finally sold something."

"Good for you, man." Trip drops his bag on the coffee table, rolls his shoulder. "You get a decent price for it?"

"One-fifty." Liam lifts the can of bug killer abruptly with his eyes trained on the corner. After a moment, he puts it back down and resumes wrapping his canvas.

Trip watches the corner. "Not too bad. That can probably buy you a chunk of wall or a pillar or something in terms of gallery space."

"Yeah, or maybe it can buy me a few groceries and take the edge off our next electric bill." Liam looks at the corner again. He nudges the can of bug killer toward Trip. "There's one in the corner—could you deal with it? I need to finish wrapping this."

"What happened to the big art show?" Trip takes the spray and sets to work shoving aside Liam's other projects; his eyes are trained on the ground.

"The show is going to have to be postponed." Liam stretches packing tape down the seam of the paper. "Indefinitely."

Trip spies the roach. He corrals it out into the open space of the family room and sprays it when it's well away from June's toys and Liam's projects. "What? No perfect gallery spaces to fit your art's heart or something?"

"No gallery spaces with a price tag I could ever afford." Liam inspects the wrapped canvas before settling it with his other projects. "That dream's going to have to go on the shelf for a bit. Like a very, very high shelf."

"Weren't any apartments on Manhattan we could afford back when we moved here, but we managed okay, didn't we?" Trip washes his hands and returns to the family room. "Roach crisis averted."

"And what a palace we found." Liam pats the side of the couch where a patch of duct tape is covering a particularly bad tear in the fabric. "Thanks for dealing with that, but he might have friends."

"I'll be on the lookout." Trip goes to his room, calls over his shoulder. "What's with the glass half-empty routine? You're usually all shiny and positive—it's not a bad change, just curious."

"Just tired and really damn cold," Liam calls back. "Whenever the weather gets like this I start wondering why I didn't go to Arizona and join an artist's commune or something."

"Know what you mean, brother." Trip nudges his blankets aside with a foot, but with no real purpose. His guitar isn't here. It's not totally unusual. June's been getting into everything; Scarlett might have just put it up somewhere. He pushes himself up on his toes to check the shelves. Nothing.

Still, he isn't overly perturbed. Things get moved all the time. Trip's come home to find everything from the couch upside down, to Liam's artwork filling his entire room, to the doors all gone off of the kitchen cabinets. He lies down on the floor to hunt under beds and furniture, digs through the other closets, and searches Devon and Liam's room and anywhere else he can think to look.

An hour passes and then another, and Trip has turned over the entire apartment and gone from frustrated to scared. He stands in the doorway of his room and stares at the empty corners. His guitar isn't here.

The front door opens and closes and the apartment is suddenly filled with June's crying and Scarlett's voice. "Who's home right now?"

"I'm here," Trip shouts. He lies down on the floor in Scarlett's room to look under the bed a second time. He spies a few toys, a lost shoe and a couple boxes, but not much else. He pushes himself back to his feet to join the others in the main room.

"Did you see this?" Scarlett slams a piece of paper down on the coffee table. She looks between Trip and Liam, slightly frantic. She doesn't seem to notice how hard the baby's crying.

Trip squints at the paper. It's tinted pink and the font is small, but there is no denying what it says: EVICTION NOTICE. He lifts it for closer inspection. "This on our door?"

Scarlett shakes her head. "Next door. Apparently they're no better at making rent than we are."

"Shit." Liam clutches at his hair as he reads over Trip's shoulder. "If they're out, we're out."

"No shit, Sherlock." Trip sits on the arm of the couch. He feels vaguely sick.

"What are we going to do?" Scarlett holds the baby closer, shushes her. "What the hell are we going to do?"

Liam drops his hands to his sides. "We're going to be homeless. Like 'sitting on the curb with cardboard signs and empty cups' homeless."

"We're not going to be fucking homeless." Scarlett puts a hand over June's ear as though to keep her from hearing. "We'll move. To the Bronx or Brooklyn or something."

"Great. How long do we have to find this magic, affordable apartment willing to rent to an artist, a stripper, a cashier and a professional pickpocket?"

"Could list me under a nicer profession. And we've got three weeks." Trip hands the note over to Liam. He drags his hands through his hair. "Scar? You seen my guitar?"

"No, Trip, I haven't seen your fucking guitar," Scarlett snaps. "Did you miss the 'we're getting evicted' thing?"

"I fucking noticed, but I can't pay no goddamn rent on this apartment or any other place if I don't go make some money!" he shouts.

The baby cries harder.

The door opens a second time and Devon slips in. He stands against the wall near the door; his gaze flits between all of them. He looks dirty and tired.

Liam holds up the note for him to see. "We're getting evicted."

Devon nods as if this isn't much of a surprise. He stays where he is against the far wall and keeps quiet.

"Maybe we can stay." Scarlett pulls a pacifier from her bag and offers it to June. She paces and pats the baby's back. "We can fight it or something—people do that, don't they?"

"We don't legally live here." Liam chews a thumbnail. "Would Nate know, Trip?"

"Why the fuck would he know anything about getting evicted?" Trip turns in a circle, his gaze swiveling around the apartment. "Seriously, has anyone seen my guitar?"

"He knew how to get the power back on. Maybe he knows this, too." Liam pushes his glasses up on his nose and looks at the eviction notice. "Maybe they won't notice if we just stay. Like, do they follow through on this stuff right away or do we maybe actually have a couple months or something?"

"It looks pretty final to me." Scarlett raises her voice over June's wailing. "I'll talk to the girls tonight, see if anyone knows anything about it, or maybe one of them will know about an apartment."

"If we move out of Manhattan, it's going to mean having to buy a MetroCard all the time. I can't afford that and I need to be here to sell my work." Liam flaps a hand at his projects in the corner.

"You think I haven't thought about that?" Scarlett shoots him an icy look before turning her attention back to soothing June.

"Trip." Devon speaks up from his place against the wall.

Trip ignores him. He's tired of Devon right now. Devon who hasn't been contributing enough to bills and picks fights and has become a ghost in the apartment. Trip looks at Scarlett and the baby. “Can you give the kid a bottle or change her diaper or something? That crying is making me insane.”

“She’s a baby, and she’s sick with something, you jackass. She gets to cry if she wants to.” Scarlett throws June’s abandoned pacifier at him. “If it bothers you so much, get the hell out of here for a while.”

“I would if I could find my goddamn guitar!” Trip shouts back. He works his hands at his sides and turns in another circle as if maybe he’s just overlooked something.

“Trip, I need to talk to you.” Devon speaks up, louder.

“Unless you got a solution for the apartment thing or you know something about where the hell a guitar runs off to, it can wait.” Trip sits on the arm of the couch when a dizzy spell grays the corners of his vision.

“It’s about your guitar.” Devon hasn’t moved from when he first entered the apartment. “I fucked up. I fucked up in a big way.”

Trip turns a sharp look his way. “What the hell are you talking about?”

Devon drags a hand through his hair. His gaze stays on his shoes. “I’ve been short on cash lately, I, um...”

“You’re using.” Trip folds his arms across his chest.

Scarlett and Liam go quiet, though the baby keeps crying, and Devon looks up at Trip, surprised.

Trip laughs, dark and angry. “You think I didn’t know? Hoped like hell I was wrong, but I know the look, Dev. You ought to know that.”

Devon’s gaze is back on his shoes. “I guess I should have. I just, shit, I tried to get it back. As soon as I’d done it, I knew it was shitty and—I tried, Trip. I swear, I tried.”

Trip pushes himself to his feet slowly, his hands fisted at his sides. “What the fuck did you do?”

Devon swallows, looks from his shoes to Trip's face. "I sold it."

Trip has his father's temper. Everyone knows it; Trip knows it. He wishes it weren't true. Wishes he didn't see red the second someone looks at him wrong. He does not hit women, he does not lay a finger on children, and he's been getting better—especially the past year—he has tried to reign himself in. Still, he has his father's temper.

He doesn't remember coming at Devon. Doesn't remember getting him on the floor or landing the first punch or if Devon has landed any of his own. When he does come to his senses long enough to process what's happening, Devon's flipped him onto his back and has landed a hard punch to his jaw. Trip fights hard, gets ahold of Devon's shoulder and throws him back to the ground.

"I'll break your fucking neck, you hear me?" Trip throws a hard punch. He's angry, angrier than he's been in a very long time and he can think of nothing else. "I swear to God, I'll break your useless fucking neck."

Devon is angry, too. He throws every hit he can. "Worthless, stupid white trash piece of shit, Morgan. You ain't no different from your goddamn brothers!"

"Boys, you're friends. Cut it out. We can talk this out." Liam circles them, but he makes no attempt to break up the fight. "Trip, you'll kill him. Please, I'm begging you to stop—you don't want this."

Trip is suddenly being pulled up and off of Devon with a hard grip on his forearm. He fights his way free and wheels around, prepared to throw another punch if it's Liam who has decided to intervene.

Scarlett meets his glare with a dark look of her own. Her voice is flat and cold. "That's enough."

When Trip turns back to Devon, Scarlett shoves her way in front of him, the baby still balanced on her hip. "I said enough!"

Liam is kneeling on the floor beside Devon with a hand on his shoulder, but Devon is making no second attempt to come at Trip.

Scarlett holds Trip's gaze, but she speaks to Devon. "Get up and get out, or I will let him kill you."

Devon pushes himself upright. He stumbles on his feet, but he shoves off Liam's attempts to help him. He takes a step backward and then one more, and then he's gone out the door.

Trip keeps watch on the door, but Devon makes no attempt to come back.

"I know you're angry, but you need to settle the fuck down." Scarlett steps back into his line of sight, her expression carefully calm. "You're better than this, Trip."

Trip breathes hard, tries to find his way back to himself. June is crying so hard she's blotchy and sweating in Scarlett's arms, there's blood on the floor, and the apartment smells like bug killer and laundry detergent. He needs out. He needs to run.

He doesn't hear Scarlett's and Liam's pleas to stay put. He shoulders his bag and charges out into the cold air of the street. He considers tracking down Devon and finishing what he's started, but the thought of more violence and blood only further agitates him. He walks and doesn't realize he knows exactly where he's going until he's knocking hard on Nate's door.

"Coming! Christ, settle down. I'm getting there!" Nate's voice is muffled while the locks click open.

Nate is still dressed in his suit, but he's loosened his tie and rolled his sleeves up to his elbows. He looks at Trip with wide eyes. "Jesus, what happened to you?"

Trip pushes past him into the apartment. He drops his bag on the breakfast bar and tears open the zipper. He's aware, as he struggles with the zipper on the inside pocket, that the knuckles of his right hand are bruised and hot, but he ignores them. He pulls the picture out and shoves it at Nate.

Nate stares at Trip for a long moment before looking at the photograph in his hands. He studies it silently, turns it over to look over the back before flipping it again, one thumb rubbing absently at the bent corner. He stares for a long time before his gaze drifts back to Trip, his expression drawn, confused. "What do you want me to do with this?"

"I've had it." Trip fists his hands at his sides, unsure of this suddenly unhinged, shaky version of himself. He doesn't like it. "For years."

Nate looks at the picture again and then back to Trip; his attention clearly split between Trip's bruised face and the photograph. "What do you want me to do with it?" He glances at it again as if he's still trying to piece something together. "I don't understand. Am I supposed to know who they are? Is this one of your games? I'll play, but I think first we should do something about your face."

Trip's hands go slack at his sides and he feels a wash of vertigo that makes the floor tilt and his ears ring too loudly with the suddenness of this realization. Nate doesn't know what to make of the photograph because these children—that seven-year-old bruised-knee little boy, the children who had sparked this whole thing, whatever it is, between them—are strangers to him.

Nate is watching him guardedly. He touches a hand to Trip's shoulder. "Come here and sit down. I'll clean you up."

Trip allows Nate to lead him to one of the barstools. He sits, too numb to think of how to do anything else. The boy is not Nate. The photo means nothing.

Nate's world is apparently not coming apart at the seams. He gives Trip an ice pack with instructions to keep it on his hand, and then he is touching a wet washcloth to Trip's cheek.

"This might need stitches. It looks pretty deep." Nate lifts the cloth to inspect the mark. "I have some butterfly bandages and that sort of thing, but I really think you should get it checked."

"No health insurance." Trip pulls the picture from the counter. He stares at a child version of Nate who is not Nate.

"There are free clinics." Nate's placing two of the aforementioned butterfly bandages on Trip's cheek and then moving on to inspect his lip.

"Don't want to go in." Trip turns the picture over in his hands.

"It's going to scar." Nate inspects him for more injuries.

"One more scar then." Trip turns the picture back over. "You sure you don't know anything about this?"

Nate glances at the photo. He shakes his head. "Where'd you get it?"

"Doesn't matter." Trip stares down at his feet and wonders idly if it's driving Nate slightly insane that he hasn't taken off his shoes.

"Okay." Nate nods, his gaze dancing over Trip's face again. He reaches for his hair again, this time to tuck it behind his ear. "Okay."

Trip rubs a thumb over the bent corner of the picture. "It's June's birthday tomorrow."

Nate is distracted, inspecting Trip's bruised hand. "Yeah?"

Trip nods. "Mine, too."

Nate's gaze jerks up from Trip's fingers to his eyes. "Your birthday's tomorrow?"

"I'm going to be twenty." Trip licks his lips. His tongue tastes coppery. "Twenty years old and I've never been so goddamn lost in my life."

This day has been ridiculous and Trip's fairly certain it should be funny. He means to laugh, but instead he starts crying. He doesn't even realize it's happening until he's pressed up close with his nose in Nate's collar and Nate's arms wrapped too tight around his shaking shoulders. "Hey, hey, it's going to be okay. I promise. Everything's going to be all right."

"Don't make promises you can't keep, Nathaniel." Trip pushes at Nate, but all the strength's gone out of him. He cries harder. "It ain't polite."

"'Ain't' isn't a word." Nate rubs Trip's back and presses his chin to the top of his head.

Trip tries to find his center, but now that he's started, all he can do is cry. "Why's it all coming apart now? Why does everything always have to come apart right when it's getting to be okay?"

"I don't know," Nate murmurs. "Not sure there's ever a good time for everything to go to pieces. Just hush; breathe for a while, okay? Just breathe. You don't have to do anything else right now."

Trip does as he's told. He sniffles and hiccups and breathes until he has a hold on himself again. He inhales the smell of Nate's clothes and wishes he didn't have to start moving again.

Nate lets go of Trip slowly and then moves to pull a glass down from the cabinet. He fills it with ice and water and comes back around the counter to offer it. "Drink that. You'll feel better."

Trip means to only take a small drink, but as soon as the water hits his mouth, he's swallowing down the entire glass.

Nate refills it before speaking again. "You going to tell me what happened?"

Trip sips at his water more conservatively this time. "Devon sold my guitar for drug money, the baby's sick or something, and we're losing the apartment."

"Bad day." It might be meant as a joke, but neither of them smiles.

"Really fucking bad day." Trip passes the back of a wrist over his still-wet cheeks. The touch ignites an ache where Nate has bandaged his face.

"Things fall apart." Nate rests his hands on Trip's knees, squeezes them gently. "It happens. It'll be okay; you'll figure it out and make things even better than they were before. You're good at that. You're good at putting the pieces back together."

It makes Trip irrationally angry. That he's come to this place a bloody mess and fallen apart and Nathaniel—neurotic, nervous Nathaniel—is the picture of calm and comfort. Trip pushes his hands away. "*We* don't have a severance package for when shit goes south. This isn't just going to go away—this is my goddamn life."

"I'm sorry. You're right. I can't imagine how hard this is." Nate sits on the arm of the couch, his expression somber. "And I'm sorry that you're hurting, but this could be your chance, Trip. Isn't that what you told me back in September? These moments—when everything falls apart, they can be an opportunity. Make your life into the one you deserve."

Trip gapes at him. "Jesus, don't be so goddamn arrogant. Don't make it sound like I can have a goddamn white picket fence if I just try hard enough."

Nate lifts both hands in surrender; his gaze flits from Trip's bruised cheek to his eyes. "I'm not saying it's going to be perfect, but it doesn't have to be this hard. Take the GED class, get a job, even if it's just a couple days a week. You've got your roommates and you've got me. It's going to be all right."

"Always moving on and up, right?" Trip sneers. "Sounds like a real dream. I almost forgot how happy you were doing that when we first met."

"You're right. I don't love what I do." Nate shakes his head, talks down to his knees. "I hated Ashbury and it sucked the life out of me—but this new place, this new place is smaller and better and I'll have time for a life. I still don't love what I do, but it's a good environment and it gives me the time and the cash for the life I want outside work."

Trip barks out a laugh. "Wow, you memorize that from the company website?"

Neither of them speaks for a moment, and in the silence, Trip feels the full weight of this day again. Nate isn't wrong—things fall apart. He knew this would happen eventually, but he didn't expect it to feel like getting his heart broken.

Nate breaks the silence, his voice soft. "What do you want, Trip?"

"I want my guitar back and I don't want to get evicted. What the fuck do you think I want?" Trip speaks through gritted teeth. He still doesn't trust himself not to cry. "Don't ask stupid questions."

"What else do you want?" Nate's voice is still quiet. "I've been trying for months to figure it out—I think you want bigger things than you'd ever admit. I just don't know what those things are."

"What the hell do *you* want?" Trip sits up fast enough to jar the ache in his ribs, but he ignores it. "You never know what you fucking want other than to make people think you have your shit together. You're a mess—goddamn neat freak with a temper and a grudge against a dead brother."

It's not fair. It's mean and Trip knows it, but he doesn't take it back. He wants someone else to hurt, too. He doesn't want to hurt alone.

"I want to run that marathon next fall. I want to go home to Minnesota to meet my niece or nephew. I want to be happy enough to stop blaming my dead brother when I feel like I'm falling short." Nate stands, takes a step toward the breakfast bar. "I want you, Trip—I want to actually know you, if you'll let me."

"Jesus Christ, Nate, this was a deal." Trip grits his teeth. "I'm not your boyfriend."

"This stopped being a game between us a long time ago, and you know it." He steps in a closer. "And you call me Nathaniel."

Trip glares at him, defiant.

"I wish you weren't so scared," Nate lifts a hand as though he might touch Trip, but then he must think better of it. "I wish I could help you with a lot of things, but more than anything, I wish I knew how to help you be less afraid."

"Fuck you," Trip bites back. "I'm not scared of anything."

Nate stares at him for a long time; his gaze drifts from one eye to the other. "You know what I think?"

"I think you've got a lot of fucking thoughts today," Trip growls.

"You see people, Trip. I'm kind of convinced one of your eyes maybe does let you see deeper than most people can." Nate smiles, unfettered by Trip's anger. "I'd bet it's the green one, if I had to pick."

Trip stares at Nate, sullen and silent.

"You see people and people don't see you—they look at you, but they don't see you." Nate's eyes flicker over his face. "I see you, Trip."

Trip shifts in his seat, but he can't bring himself to drop Nate's gaze. He wishes he wanted to leave more than he does. "No, you don't."

"You're smart and funny and loyal to the people who are important to you… and you're lost. You're even more lost than I am." Nate shakes his head. "I think that's why you take all those things from people's pockets and make up those stories for them. It's safe and it's consistent, and I don't think much of your life has offered you that."

"You don't know anything about my life." He wants to sound angrier than he does. Instead, his voice shakes.

"So let me." Nate reaches up, tucks Trip's hair behind his ear. His hand lingers against Trip's cheek. "Let me in, Trip."

Nate is steady and consistent and solid. Nate is good. Trip wants to melt into all that warmth and goodness and remain there. He pulls away. "I need to go."

"Your lip's still bleeding." Nate's hand drops to his side.

"It's fine." Trip pushes himself off of the stool, casts a look around the apartment. He knows this space well now. He knows the feel of the stairs under his bare feet and how far to turn the shower knob if you want the water to stay hot. He knows where to find the coffee mugs and tumblers and which book Nate hides his Social Security card in. It feels as familiar as the park and his place in the Village and Bekket. He shoulders his bag, goes to the door and doesn't look back at any of it.

Nate follows him, offers the dirtied washcloth. "Put it on your mouth."

Trip takes the cloth, touches it to his lip. He doesn't have enough fight left in him to argue this one, small thing.

They stand together in the doorway, neither one speaking.

Nate steps closer, wraps Trip up in a hug. "See you around, Trip."

Trip stands in his embrace for a long time before he returns it, his hands clenched hard in Nate's shirt. "See you around, Nathaniel."

Nate presses a kiss into Trip's hair and steps back.

Trip leaves and he makes a point of not looking back as he makes his way to the elevator and then out to the street. He stares at his shoes until something small and white flutters down onto the toe of his left shoe. He pauses to look as another flake and then another joins it before tipping his face up to the sky. It's snowing. It's winter.

Of three things I am certain in regards to my mother.

The first is that she wanted two kids: a boy and a girl. She'd call the boy Michael and the girl Luella. I think she thought Luella would move away to Nashville and be a big country star or something. It sounds like that kind of name, doesn't it? Luella Morgan or maybe Luella Jean to make it jazzier for the stage. Who's to say? Maybe if Luella had ever come around, she would have been a great big star. Or maybe she'd have turned out just like my mama. We'll never know. Or at least I won't. Maybe my mama's got her little girl now. Stranger things have happened.

The second thing I know is that the day my mama and my daddy moved into the trailer in Magnolia Estates, she put lavender-scented liners in all of the drawers and she's been replacing the damn things every year since then. I hated those drawer liners growing up, hated that if you wanted a fork or a knife or a dishtowel, you had to open a drawer and smell that god-awful artificial lavender crawling all over everything. I told her once I could taste lavender on my spoon every time I took a bite of my supper. She solved the problem with a smack upside my head and the immediate removal of my meal for the night. I still think about those liners and wonder why that was the one small thing she kept up in her home.

And the third thing I know about my mama is that she doesn't much care for me. Maybe it's because I embarrassed her silly with the way I insisted on coming into the world. Maybe it's because I was the final straw for her with having all them boys. Maybe it's because I was born just three days after her thirtieth birthday and I don't know anyone particularly thrilled to turn thirty, especially someone like my mama who imagined bigger things for herself than a pack of sons and a trailer in Magnolia Estates. I shouldn't say that. I don't know if my mama imagined a life outside of Bekket, necessarily. Maybe she would have been just fine in the trailer park if she'd of had Mike and Luella and that was that. The way I see it, my mama asked for six boys and a mean drunk for a husband as much as I asked for two different-colored eyes and a mother who doesn't like me.

I'm not making excuses and I'm not saying she did her best by me. Nobody did their best by me, but I'm not sure anybody did their best by her either. She wanted something once; something better than what life handed her. She put the damn liners in the drawers for a reason.

Maybe she'd run out of love by the time I came around. Six boys is a lot and none of us were exactly honor students. Maybe I should have asked her to love me a little more, but I never know how to ask anything right.

TWELVE.

Trip had planned on going out. Maybe getting drunk and finding someone to take him home who would know how to hurt him in the way he wants. He wants to find the side of himself that knows how to forget this kind of disappointment that he thinks he should be used to by now. His back too cold and shoulders too light, he walks the streets of Manhattan for a long time. When the sky grows dark and his feet go too numb, he passes bars and easy marks and goes home. He closes himself in his room to sleep off the remainder of the night.

Liam stops into his room sometime around midnight and pushes a paper-wrapped canvas at him and whispers, "Happy birthday." Trip doesn't open it. He rolls over and goes back to sleep.

When he wakes again, it is to the sound of a quiet whistle from his doorway and an equally soft voice. "Hey, Lark."

Trip shoves himself up and makes a point of not grimacing at the hurt the movement raises under his ribs. "You're awful brave coming around here."

Devon's lip is split; a spot on his cheek is mottled red and swollen. His nose looks wrong and there is a purple half-moon under each of his eyes. He's favoring his left foot over his right. "Liam's out in the family room. He let me in."

Trip looks at the wrapped canvas in the corner of his room where his guitar previously rested. "What do you want?"

Devon sits down in the doorway. He holds out a cellophane-wrapped pack of cigarettes. "Happy birthday."

Trip stares at the pack. He doesn't take it.

Devon drops his hand back into his lap. "Would've liked to have bought your guitar back for you, but it's already gone. I'm sorry—I tried. I really did."

Trip flexes his hands against his thighs. His knuckles are still bruised and sore. "That supposed to make me forgive you?"

"No." Devon swallows audibly. His voice wavers. "I fucked up, Trip. I fucked up big."

"Yeah." Trip gives him a stormy look. "You did."

"I ever tell you why I order those papers all the way from back home?"

"I never asked."

Devon frets with a hole forming in the knee of his jeans. "I like seeing how small everyone seems. Naomi Johnson still running the consignment shop, Jack Reddy won a fucking pie-eating contest and made the front page. Mostly I like the crime reports: lot of drunk and disorderly, bunch of my classmates using. Made me feel like even if I was struggling like crazy out here, at least I was doing better than all of them. Rather be playing my violin on a street corner for pennies than doing it for one of those stuffy church services."

Trip thinks of the papers that have been accumulating in the trash can, most of them still wrapped in the plastic they're delivered in. He hadn't stopped to wonder why they were going unread.

"Made it all the way out here and got into the same shit I got into back in high school—could have just stayed in Bekket. At least I'd be a name there." Devon meets Trip's eyes. "First time I ever bought it was off Mike. You were in the truck with his girlfriend. Do you remember that?"

Trip shakes his head. "We did that a lot."

"Well, I remember." Devon turns the pack of cigarettes over in his hands. "You were just a little shit—maybe six or seven—you were standing up on the bench with your head out the sunroof watching."

Trip still doesn't remember, but he doesn't say anything.

"I remember wondering what kinda shitty white-trash parents let their little kid ride along for drug deals." Devon shakes his head. "I thought I had it rough being stuck somewhere so small, and you—poor fucking kid—you were getting smacked upside the head for saying you were hungry."

"You trying to get yourself out of the hole you already dug?" Trip glares at him, his anger sparked all over again. "Cause from where I'm sitting, all it looks like you're doing is digging deeper."

"I'm trying to say..." Devon sighs, starts again. "I'm trying to say I was wrong, I guess. Wrong about you and home and everything. I fucked up and I'm sorry."

Trip doesn't have it in him to stay this kind of angry. He pulls his hair back and out of his face with the hair binder from his wrist. "You gonna quit?"

"Gonna try, I guess." Devon's briefly quiet before speaking again. "You talked to your family since you came up here?"

"You know the answer to that."

"I talk to mine." Devon picks at a spot where the paint is chipping on the doorframe. "They moved up north of Tuscaloosa a couple years back."

Trip looks at him then. "You're gonna go stay with them."

"Not doing anything here that I couldn't do there." Devon meets Trip's eyes. "I'm tired. I need out of this."

Trip leans back against the wall, the fight gone out of him for now. "Why the fuck did you get back into it in the first place? Things were good, man. We were good."

Devon shakes his head. "I don't know anymore. Not sure it matters."

"Guess not." Trip studies his bruised knuckles. He wants to be angry at Devon—for the drugs, for the guitar, for giving up so easily—mostly he feels adrift knowing there will be no one left who knew him from before New York.

"I, um, I talked to Scar and Liam yesterday a bit." Devon scratches delicately at the bridge of his bruised nose. "If it's cool with you, I'll finish out the week with you guys."

"That's fine." Trip presses the fingers of his left hand against the bruised knuckles of his right. "Whatever, man."

"Thanks. I'll get out of your hair for now. Don't blame you if you're still itching to cave in the rest of my face today." Devon puts the pack of cigarettes down beside Trip's knee. He pushes himself to his feet and he turns to leave,

"I thought things were supposed to get better—isn't that how it's supposed to work? Everything falls apart and then it gets better?" The words tumble out before Trip can stop them. Now that they've been said, though, he looks up at Devon and keeps talking. "We find some magic way to keep the apartment; you clean yourself up and play at Carnegie; June grows up to be one of them, like, genius kids and gets lots of scholarships and shit? Isn't that how this story's supposed to end?"

Devon leans back in his doorway. "You left yourself out of that equation."

Trip leans back against the wall. "Fine. I get my guitar back and make a thousand dollars every day."

"You really think it works that way?"

"No." Trip picks at the cellophane wrapper on the cigarette box. "Would be nice if it did, though, wouldn't it?"

"Yeah, guess it would." Devon drags a hand through his hair, lets out a long breath. "Life's never been all that good to us, though, has it?"

"Keep hoping it'll start." Trip mumbles. He pushes the cigarettes aside.

"It might get better, just not the way we thought it would." The floorboards creak as Devon straightens up again. "Glad I got to see you, Lark."

Trip glances up at him again. "Hey, Dev?"

Devon stops and waits just outside the doorway.

There are so many things Trip thinks he ought to say to Devon before their time together ends, but, in this moment, he can think of only one. He sticks out his hand. "You're not a bad guy, all right?"

Devon's mouth twitches as if he might smile, but the expression dies prematurely. He shakes Trip's hand. "Thank you."

Trip nods, looks away.

Devon hesitates before speaking again. "For what it's worth, if anyone can make it here, Trip, I'd put my money on you over anyone else."

Trip listens to a murmured exchange between Liam and Devon when he steps into the family room, and then the door creaking open. When it clicks shut, Trip is immediately lonely.

He pulls his bag close and trades the cigarettes for the photograph. He stares at it for a long time, but he still cannot make sense of this particular disappointment.

He's considering going back to sleep when there's another knock on the edge of his door.

Scarlett settles beside him and puts June down in the blankets. She offers a red paper cup to Trip. "Coffee for the birthday boy."

"She already have hers?" Trip nods at June. "One year old—she could probably start in on the coffee, especially if you mix it in with some formula."

"She had a doctor's appointment this morning and got a booster shot." Scarlett indicates a purple bandage on June's arm. "She's got an ear infection and I'm sure that shot hurt like a bitch. One hell of a first birthday, huh?"

"I'm sorry I yelled yesterday." Trip squeezes June's hand. "Both of you—I'm sorry."

"Yesterday was a hard day for all of us." Scarlett inspects the butterfly bandages on Trip's cheek. "You especially. Your face looks pretty good, by the way. Better than I thought it would."

"Thanks." Trip looks Scarlett over. Her hair is pulled up into a sloppy bun and she's wearing her interview outfit. "You seem less bent out of shape today,"

"It's her first birthday. All this stress can wait one day." Scarlett tucks Trip's pillow between her back and the wall. "If things are about to get messy, I at least want today to be nice."

"You're a good mom," Trip mumbles.

Scarlett tugs his hair. "You're a good fake uncle."

"Don't think anyone's going to buy that you, me and Junie are blood." Trip presses his arm to Scarlett's to highlight the contrast.

"None of my family's alive." Scarlett studies their arms. "I'll take what I can get."

"Lost two people in under four months," Trip murmurs. "Some family."

"I know." Scarlett's smile slips. "It happens. Shit comes undone."

"Been hearing that a lot lately." Trip looks again at the photo.

Scarlett squeezes his arm. "I'm your family, aren't I? I'm not going anywhere."

"You're my best friend," Trip glances at Scarlett, his cheeks warm. "Don't tell anyone I said that."

Scarlett scoots in closer to his side. "Our secret."

They both fall silent and watch as June navigates the small space of Trip's room on shaky feet.

Scarlett finally breaks the silence. "Nate texted while June and I were at the clinic. He asked me to tell you to check your pockets."

Trip angles his hip up to dig in his pockets. The left one is empty, but his fingers hit cold metal in the right. He pulls out a key with a black rabbit foot hanging from it.

Scarlett smiles at the key. "Guess you got somewhere to stay if we can't get a new place right away."

"You think this is to his place?" Trip turns it over in his hands, wonders when Nate managed to sneak it into his pocket.

"Honestly, sometimes I think you're the oldest soul in the world, and then you go and say something that makes me remember you're still practically a baby." Scarlett flicks the rabbit foot hanging from the keychain. "Of course it's to his place, dummy."

"Kellan give you one to his?" Trip closes his hand around the key and opens it again, mildly surprised to find it still there.

Scarlett pulls a silver key from her pocket. "A long time ago."

"None of this feels too fast for you?" Trip turns his key toward Scarlett.

She returns Kellan's key to her pocket. "When it's right, it's right."

Trip puts the key down and lifts his coffee cup. He takes a sip and stares down at the lid. June fills the quiet with her happy babbling as she tears at the paper on the canvas in the corner.

"I think maybe Liam's thinking about going back to Kentucky." Trip turns the coffee cup between his hands. "He hasn't said it, but I can see it. He wants to go home."

"This is his home." Scarlett turns to look at him in surprise. "He loves New York. It feeds his creative energy or whatever. Why would he leave?"

Trip shrugs. "I always kinda figured he'd go eventually. All the way back when I first met him."

"You think everyone's going to leave you." Scarlett bumps her knee against his. "Stop being so paranoid."

"Jude left, Dev's leaving. I don't have a whole lot of people left." Trip wiggles the fingers of his left hand at her. "Keep waiting for you to come home with a ring and tell me you and Kellan are getting a place in Scarsdale or some shit."

"I'm not going anywhere, I told you." Scarlett pushes his fingers down. "Liam's not either, and even if he does, you've got me and you've got Nate, don't you?"

"We—me and Nathaniel—we had a deal." Trip stares at the too-barren corner of his room. "I was entertainment, he was a meal ticket. It was good, but that's all it was ever supposed to be."

"You wanted more from him than that." Scarlett picks up the key to Nate's apartment. "Clearly he wants more than that, too."

Trip raises his eyebrows at her. "You the mind-reader now?"

"You picked him, Trip. Eight million people in this city, and you picked *him* off of the sidewalk." She prods Trip's neck with the edge of the key. "And he picked you back."

"And Nathaniel accuses me of being a romantic. Jesus."

"You are." Scarlett puts the key back down between them.

"Thought you had to be nice to me today." Trip shoots her an icy look.

"I am being nice." She nudges his shoulder with hers. "It's not a bad thing."

"I'm not some pansy-ass romantic." Trip folds his arms across his chest. "Liam's a romantic, but not me."

"He is, but so are you." Scarlett draws her knees up under her chin. "It doesn't make you weak. It's brave. It's the bravest thing you can be, especially right now when everything's falling apart. It means believing things can still be okay."

Trip sticks a foot out to balance June when she teeters precariously. She keeps upright and turns a sunny smile his way. "When'd she start walking?"

"Couple days ago." Scarlett offers June a finger to hold onto. "She said 'mama' and 'more,' too. All in one day."

Trip watches June take a few more wobbling steps. "She was barely crawling at the end of summer."

"Funny what just a few months can do, huh?" Scarlett elbows him lightly in his ribs.

Trip goes quiet, then says, "He told me he loved me."

Scarlett kisses June's fingers wrapped around the edge of her hand. She doesn't seem surprised. "He's good for you. You talk more; you're sweeter."

Trip doesn't know what to say to that.

Scarlett studies his profile. "Would it be so bad to admit you love him back?"

Trip cradles his cup of coffee. "Maybe some people just aren't built to do it—fall in love, I mean."

"Maybe not, but I don't think you're one of those people." Scarlett sits back against the wall. "You went to him when you fought with Devon."

Trip sips his coffee. It's cold. "Yeah, so?"

"There's something to be said about the people we go to when we get our worst news." Scarlett tips her head onto Trip's shoulder. "Especially when that person is the same one you want to go to with your best news."

"I don't know if I believe that I've got any good news in me." Trip watches as June navigates her way over his blankets with careful steps. "I want things to get better, but I don't know if they're going to."

"You're twenty years old, Trip. There's plenty of time for things to change. You're just getting started."

Trip's heart sinks. "I'm tired, Scarlett. I'm really fucking tired. Aren't you?"

"Sometimes." Scarlett nods. "Especially last year right after June was born. There were days and nights when you went missing and we were living off saltines and I felt like I hadn't slept in a week and I thought I wouldn't mind just dropping dead... but not so much now. Even with everything that's happening right now, I feel okay these days."

She loops her hand under his elbow and runs her fingernails over the inside of his wrist. "You got started doing this a lot sooner than most, though."

"You think that means I can throw the towel in sooner, too?" Trip pinches the bridge of his nose.

Her fingers pause. "As your secret best friend, can I give you some advice?"

"You can try." Trip pulls June onto his lap, kisses her sticky palm when she presses it to his mouth.

"Don't throw out your heart so you don't have to feel it when things hurt." Scarlett tucks his hair behind his ear. "Being a romantic is what's kept you alive this long; don't stop being brave now and throw that away."

Trip fiddles with the cuff of June's sleeve. "I don't know what he wants."

"He wants to know you." Scarlett pulls June off of his lap and into her arms. "Why don't you start with that?"

Trip nods, but he doesn't respond.

"We need to get going—we're meeting Kellan for lunch." Scarlett stands. "You should come. Liam's meeting us there, too. Did you know he sold another piece today?"

"No. That's great, though." Trip draws his knees in close to his chest. "I'm good here, but thanks."

"Gonna spend your birthday holed up in your room?" Scarlett raises her eyebrows.

Trip smiles at her. "Better than spending it in a delivery room."

Scarlett stoops back down to press a kiss to Trip's cheek. "We love you, Trip Morgan."

"You're not too bad yourself." Trip waves. "Get gone. Have fun."

"We'll bring you home something good." Scarlett waltzes out of the room, calls over her shoulder, "Happy birthday!"

Trip listens to Scarlett packing up June's things and then to the slam of the door. He lifts the key in one hand, the picture in the other. The boy has ears that stick out and he has blue eyes. He doesn't actually look all that much like Nate, and Trip's not sure how he ever thought he did. He sets the picture aside and reaches for his bag again to pull the red notebook from the bottom.

It's been nearly a year since he wrote in it, almost just as long since he's opened it to look back on anything. He opens to the first page, rubs a thumb over the words.

He remembers writing that first entry. He'd been on the bus to Tuscaloosa, his hands shaking and his heart still hammering in his chest with a mixture of panic and elation as he scribbled the words down so they couldn't be forgotten.

The urge had come off and on since that day when he's had no choice but to drop what he's doing and write something down before it's forgotten. He's stooped over benches in the park, sneaked from stranger's beds, and awoken in the middle of the night, all in the name of scribbling down a memory on any blank page he can find.

Trip puts the key back in his pocket and the photo and notebook in the bag. He shoulders the bag and leaves the apartment, sure of where he's going.

THIRTEEN.

THE SNOW IS STILL FALLING and it works its way under Trip's collar as he stands with his hands on the barricade overlooking the East River. The water looks cold and dark and it's moving faster than the last time he was here. Trip has been standing here for hours deliberating what to do. He'd been so sure of this plan, but, like so many other things, he's second-guessing himself.

He'd come here to dump his bag in the river much as they'd done with Nate's personal items what seems like years ago. Now that he's here, he's not so sure it's what he wants. He steps away from the barricade and sits on a bench with his things. He's taken years collecting them, and the idea of parting with them after he's already lost so much this week pulls at something in his heart. It makes him a little angry to realize that on top of being a reluctant romantic, he is sentimental.

He pulls open the zipper and touches his collection of treasures with gentle fingers. He no longer needs them, but they deserve something better than being tossed into a river and getting lost with all the other garbage. These things are not garbage.

Trip glances over when a woman sits down in the space of the bench he is not occupying. She settles her bag at her side and stares out toward the water.

Trip studies her bag. It's one of the easy ones—big, slouchy leather with only a snap at the top to keep it closed. He rummages through his own bag until he comes across the plastic spider. With quick, quiet fingers, he slips it in the opening of his mystery companion's purse. He stands and knows what he has to do.

The park is surprisingly busy given the cold. There are runners decked in fleece and leggings—they are harder to catch, but every once in a while, Trip slips something into an open vest pocket. Old women bundled in two and three jackets and walking dogs dressed in a similar number of layers are the easiest targets; he pets their dogs and listens to their near-endless queries about his eyes while he slips two or three things into any one of their numerous pockets. There are families taking photos of babies seeing their first snow and couples walking close with their hands stuck out to catch the snowflakes on their gloved fingers—Trip gives them the more interesting things and hopes they discover them together. The wind off the water makes this place colder than the streets closer to the park, but no one seems to notice the cold or the occasional tug on their pocket or purse. This snow globe day of laughter and joy does not fit with the winters Trip remembers from past years, but he chalks it up to it still being early in the season. Despite his easy marks, his project takes him until nearly dusk. It's so much easier to take things than to give them, but when he's finished, Trip feels lighter.

The walk to Nathaniel's apartment isn't far, but he hesitates for a long time outside the door, debating whether he should knock. There's music playing on the other side of the door and it smells as though Nate's been cooking. Trip lifts a hand, drops it back to his side.

He pulls the key from his pocket, fits it into the lock and swallows down his heart that is suddenly in his throat as he pushes his way into the apartment. He's quiet closing the door and equally quiet pulling off his shoes. When he steps through the entry, Nate is in the kitchen.

He's standing barefoot beside the stove over a large pot of something. He's dressed in jeans and a gray Henley and he's wearing a pair of reading glasses that he takes off every time he goes to look at something pulled up on his laptop screen.

"Think you're supposed to wear them when you're trying to read." Trip speaks quietly from his place beside the fridge. "Could be wrong, though. Never worn glasses."

Nate jumps and his cheeks flush with momentary surprise, but then he's smiling. "They keep steaming up."

Trip shifts his weight from his left foot to his right, suddenly shy.

"You used the key." Nate breaks the quiet.

Trip lifts the key to show off. "Guess I did."

"It's your birthday." Nate takes off his glasses and steps away from the stove.

"It's my birthday." Trip agrees.

Nate closes the distance between them. He hooks a thumb under Trip's chin and tips his head up to press a light kiss to his mouth. "Happy birthday."

"Thank you." Trip's cheeks warm a little.

Nate holds his gaze for a moment, but then he's touching a quick kiss to Trip's forehead and going back to his pot. "Twenty years old—you feel grown up?"

Trip hoists himself up onto the breakfast bar. He fiddles with his bag on his lap. "Does being grown up feel like you just know less and less what the hell you're doing?"

"That's been my experience with it so far." Nate turns down the burner before facing Trip again.

"Then I've never felt so grown up." Trip notes an empty water bottle beside him. He opens the cabinet below his feet and drops it into the recycling bin.

"Speaking of having no idea what you're doing, I have no idea what the hell I'm doing." Nate points at his pot. "Trying to make soup to freeze, and it's way more complicated than I thought it would be."

"Open the can and stick it in the microwave," Trip suggests.

"Hilarious." Nate points a wooden spoon at Trip. "Don't go sticking cans in my microwave, by the way—metal doesn't go in microwaves."

"Don't be so patronizing," Trip retorts.

"Big word." Nate abandons the pot with a grunt and turns his attention to the fridge.

"Took a look at that GED book." Trip picks at a loose spot of duct tape on his bag. "Thinking about taking one of those classes."

Nate turns to look at him. "Yeah?"

Trip pushes the tape back into place when it starts to pull away from a hole in the canvas. "Might need some help studying."

"I can do that." Nate pulls a bottle from the fridge before leaning to kiss Trip a second time. "I'm a good flashcard-maker."

"Not surprised." Trip eyes the bottle. "Champagne?"

"It's your birthday, isn't it?" Nate offers him the bottle. "Hold onto that."

Trip cradles the bottle and watches as Nate pulls out a cake. It's small, undecorated save for white icing piped along its edges. "Y'all really know how to overwhelm a guy, you know that?"

"Call it payback for every time you overwhelm me." Nate sets the cake aside. "It's strawberry, so it sort of goes with champagne, I think."

"Think anything can go with champagne if you really want it to." The cellophane wrapped around the champagne bottle crackles in his arms.

They go quiet. Nate glances around the apartment before looking back at Trip. "You, um, notice anything new around here?"

Trip looks around. He knows the orange Le Creuset stockpot on the stove, the coffeemaker on the counter and the paint on the walls is unaltered. "You forgot to fold a dish towel."

Nate looks at the towel on the counter. "It's bigger than that."

Trip twists in his spot on the counter to inspect the rest of the apartment. His gaze drifts over the counter, the partially-open bathroom door, the couch, the bookshelves and the record player. He does a double take and stares for a long time at the record stand. There, leaned against the wall, is an item he knows well. He pushes himself down off of the counter, stumbling over his own feet as he goes to pick up the guitar.

He runs a hand over the neck and down to the body, checking and admiring every nick and chip in the varnish. He sits on the rug and pulls the guitar into his lap just to feel the familiar weight in his hands.

"I was going to try and get you a new one, but I didn't think it would be the same." Nate's watching him from the kitchen. "I know how much you love that damn thing, so I went on a hunt at all the pawn shops I could think of."

Trip opens his mouth to respond, but there's a lump in his throat and he doesn't know what to say.

The floor creaks and then Nate is sitting on the floor in front of him. "I know that you get pissed when I go too far trying to be helpful. I just... that guitar is as much a part of you as your eyes are. I didn't want you to be without it and I'm sorry if it seems—"

Trip studies Nate while he babbles on. Nate's cheeks are flushed from the heat of the kitchen and his sudden embarrassment; his hair is slightly unkempt, no doubt from running his fingers through it while he fretted over trying to make his soup. He looks more Nate right now than he ever does with his freshly-shaven face and crisp suits—silly, flustered, earnest Nathaniel.

"I love you."

The words take them both by surprise, and Nate finally stops babbling. "You..."

"I love you." Trip's voice wavers. He feels the hot slide of tears on his cheeks. He brushes them away with the edge of his sleeve. "Is that okay?"

"Yeah... yeah, that's okay." Nate pulls the guitar from his lap with a gentle hand and kisses Trip long and deep with a hand on either side of his face.

They make their way backward up the stairs in a familiar dance of fumbled steps and stubbed toes until they're in bed. Nate strips Trip out of his clothes and kisses every new spot of skin he exposes.

The sex is slow and quiet. Trip's head rests on the pillow and Nate's eyes stay on his. Nate is warm and heavy and solid on top of him; he sets their pace and presses in deep and close in a way that makes a pleasant shiver work its way up Trip's spine. Nate keeps his left hand wrapped around Trip's cock and the fingers of his right tangled between Trip's in the sheets. He kisses Trip's neck and his mouth and wherever else he can reach and murmurs sweet words in Trip's ear until they're both sweating and panting and loose-limbed against one another.

Trip and Nate shower together afterward. They bicker over sharing the hot water, use too much soap and agree that Trip needs a haircut. When they're washed clean, Nate coaxes Trip into sitting on the edge of the bathroom counter so he can replace the butterfly bandages on Trip's cheek and kiss his bruised ribs. Nate leaves the ruined soup pan in the kitchen sink for later cleaning after they've finished in the bathroom, and he takes the champagne and cake back up to the bed. Trip follows with his bag over his arm.

They both cry out in surprise when the champagne cork ricochets off the wall and cracks the edge of the full-length mirror and then laugh until they can barely speak, debating whether a crack will bring them bad luck. They decide they don't care and drink the champagne straight from the bottle and share a fork for the cake. They end up celebrating more than Trip's birthday when Nate announces he got the job.

"They're taking me on right after the new year, thought I'd want the holiday off before I got into it." Nate swipes his thumb through the icing on the cake and smudges it on Trip's nose.

Trip catches Nate's wrist and licks the rest of his finger clean before wiping the frosting off of his nose. "Still get to go home and see the family. I guess you really can have your cake and eat it, too."

"Guess so," Nate replies.

"Things been good with them?" Trip tips the champagne bottle up to his mouth.

Nate takes another bite of cake before responding. "It's been okay… I'm better with them, I think. Trying to be, anyway."

"Good. That's good." Trip trades the bottle for Nate's fork.

"I, um, I didn't want to bring it up since it's your birthday, but what's happening with everything?" Nate squeezes Trip's ankle. "We don't have to talk about it today, but you were so upset yesterday and—"

Trip sucks the prongs of the fork clean. "It's fine. Dev and I are okay. He's moving back south. We're getting the boot from the apartment in three weeks."

"Shit." Nate's hand shifts down to Trip's foot. He massages it absently. "I'm sorry, Trip."

"Nothing to be done for it." Trip abandons the fork on the plate. "Some of Scarlett's friends at the club know about some places up in Harlem that might work out. If it takes some extra time, Li's gonna go stay with his family a couple weeks and Scarlett and the baby are going to crash with Kellan."

"Don't think I need to say it, but I will anyway: You can stay here as long as you need." Nate squeezes Trip's foot one last time before releasing it. "Whenever you need."

Trip nods his thanks, but he's bashful again, so he lifts the fork to pick at what's left of the cake.

They go quiet, but then Nate breathes out a laugh. "I think you just gave me more straight answers about your personal life in three and half minutes than you've given me in three and a half months."

Trip's stomach swoops because he knows this is the perfect moment for what he's been planning to do since he left the apartment. He clears his throat, reaches for his bag. "I, um, I have something for you."

Nate puts the cake down on the floor beside the bed to make space. "Aren't people supposed to give you stuff on your birthday?"

"Not giving it to you forever, it's on loan." Trip's fingers shake as he pulls open the zipper on his bag. There's not much left inside. A spare T-shirt, his umbrella, Nate's old business card, the GED book, the picture and the red notebook are all he's kept, all that feels truly his. He pulls the picture and offers it first.

Nate looks at it before glancing up at Trip. "You showed this to me yesterday. You were upset about it."

"Look at the kids." Trip leans closer to look over the top of the picture. He points. "Two boys, one girl."

"Right." Nate frowns.

"And a white porch." Trip points at the railing and then at a few trees in the background. "Couple of jack pine back there."

Nate looks over the picture for a long time. "It reminds you of me? Is that why you're showing it to me again?"

"Remember the first time we had coffee—I read your mind and told you about your brother and sister and the porch?" Trip sits back on his legs folded beneath him.

Nate nods. "Yeah, of course."

"I've had that picture since I was sixteen. When we ran into each other in the park—well, you ran into me—that kid in the middle there—I thought you were him. I convinced myself you were him."

Nate squints at the picture. "His eyes are the wrong color."

"Ears and smile are wrong, too."

"You're not one to not notice details." Nate puts the picture between them. "Still—the porch and the siblings. Damn lucky coincidence."

"If I'd have been wrong, I think I still would have come up with something to make myself believe it was you." Trip shakes his head. "Probably would have just decided it was from a vacation and they were your cousins or something. I just wanted it to be you."

"We'll pretend it's me, then." Nate holds up the picture. "Get the damn thing framed and hang it. If my parents ever get out here for a visit, we'll convince them, too, unless you want it back."

"No, you can keep that here. This is what's on loan." Trip pulls the notebook out. He picks at the metal spiral. "You said you, um... you said you wanted to know me."

Nate scoots closer and accepts the notebook when Trip pushes it toward him. "What is it?"

"They're stories." Trip shifts. He feels anxious and exposed. "My stories."

Nate opens to the first page, passes his fingers gently over the words. "You're letting me read them? This one of your deals where there's going to be some big catch?"

"No deal." Trip resists the urge to start chewing his fingernails. "No catch."

Nate looks down at the page to read and then looks back up again. "People called you a miracle."

"Only some people," Trip corrects, then adds, "I'm not the best at spelling, nothing's in the right order, and I wrote some of it a long time ago, but it's all me."

Nate looks back down at the journal.

When the silence stretches, Trip gives in to temptation and chews at the jagged edge of a hangnail. "Remember yesterday when you asked me what I want?"

Nate's attention is immediately back on Trip. "Yeah, sure."

Trip fidgets with the edge of one of the pillowcases. "All I wanted for a long time was just to get out of where I was from, and I did that. I got here, but then I didn't know what I wanted. It wasn't something I thought about much."

"And now?" Nate's voice is soft.

"I still don't really know. I'm trying to figure that part out." Trip licks his lips, swallows. "I want..."

When the silence stretches, Nate pulls Trip's hand gently away from his mouth. "You want..."

"You." Trip speaks to Nate's hand on his wrist. "Us. I think."

"You've got me." Nate lifts Trip's hand, touches a kiss to his palm.

Trip closes his fingers around the kiss as though to hold onto it a little longer. "I think I want other things, too. I just don't know what they are yet."

"You've got time to figure it out. Lots of it." Nate looks down at the page again. He skims it before flipping through a few more pages. He tucks the photograph in under the cover and closes the notebook. He puts it down on the nightstand and reaches for Trip's jeans on the floor. He fishes out the key and holds it up. "You want me to tell you a story?"

Trip raises his eyebrows in surprise; his previous unease is replaced by curiosity. "It gonna be better than the ones you told me about the crayon and the receipt?"

Nate hands him the champagne bottle. "Cross my heart."

"Yeah, all right." Trip takes a drink. "Let's hear it."

"I had this thing made after we went on that first blind date with Kellan and Scarlett." Nate's cheeks flush red, and he stares at the key with a sort of awe. "And I couldn't figure out what the hell I was thinking doing that."

Trip's ready to make a joke, but then Nate's tangling his fingers in his hair and kissing him. He tastes like champagne. Trip pulls away after a moment, smiling. "Thought you were going to tell me a story about getting a key made for a stranger."

"Shhh, I am telling you one." Nate pulls Trip close and touches a softer kiss to his lips. "Just listen."

THE END

Acknowledgments

A MASSIVE THANK YOU TO my parents, Kim and Jeff, for constantly pushing me toward being my greatest self and for feeding (and often funding) so many of my dreams and beautiful opportunities. Thank you to my siblings, Ben and Molly, for being a constant source of artistry and creative brilliance; you are both such amazing lights and you inspire me constantly.

To Alison Sutter and Kyler Zee for being both amazing friends and incredible cheerleaders through the creation of this story.

A very special thank you to Gina Milne who was kind enough to read some of my truly awful original fiction when we were children and insist that it was good; where would I be without you?

To Becca Burton who has been a constant source of love and support. I would never have found my way out of those waiting rooms upon waiting rooms of writer's block without you.

Long before there was *Small Wonders*, there was Trip Morgan, a character I adore deeply, but who would never have come to the place he is now in this book if it were not for the people who loved him and supported me so kindly. Thank you to anyone and everyone who ever took the time to read about Trip and love him in even the smallest of ways.

I cannot possibly express enough gratitude to the Interlude Press team, especially Annie, Candy and Lex. Thank you so much to all of you for helping to make this story what it is, and for making it such a fantastic learning experience. I am at a loss for words to express how much I love all of you for truly making one of my lifelong dreams into a reality.

Lastly, to one of my favorite cities on earth, thank you for being so beautiful and difficult and such a constant source of inspiration. New York, I love you. •

I SINCERELY HOPE YOU ENJOYED *Small Wonders.* Trip Morgan is someone I hold near and dear to my heart and whose story has taken several years to get right, so I am so appreciative that you took the time to read his story and know him, too.

Now that you're done, I hope you'll consider taking a moment to share your thoughts about Small Wonders on Goodreads, Amazon, and other web sites. And if you'd like to know more about the book, or what I'm working on next, please join me on one of my social media sites. You can find me on tumblr at Courtney-lux.tumblr.com; on Twitter @courtney_lux; and on Facebook at facebook.com/CourtneyLLux.

Thanks again for reading!

About the Author

Courtney Lux is a Minnesotan-turned-New Yorker whose love for the city is rivaled only by her love for wide, open spaces. She is a graduate of the University of Wisconsin-Madison and a soon-to-be graduate of New York University. When not playing writer, Courtney is an avid reader, constant dreamer and lover of dogs, wine and being barefoot. *Small Wonders* is her first novel.

Questions for Discussion

1. Trip had a difficult relationship with his mother from birth. How did his lack of connection with his mother continue to affect him, even in his relationship with Nate?

2. Trip had two major life events on the steps of his home town church, both involving Pastor Welk. Discuss the commonality and differences between the two events.

3. What did Nate and Trip each expect to get out of their arrangement? What did they each get instead?

4. What meaning does the collecting of broken and lost things have for Trip? Why would stealing someone else's junk be his favorite task?

5. Trip says in part II "Maybe some ladies are just meant to be mamas and others aren't, or maybe some babies are just easier to love; something in their chemistry makes them something a mama wants to hold onto." Which one does Trip think about his own life, that he was unlovable or that his Mama wasn't meant to be a mother?

6. Trip's sensory memory of the church where he hung out as a child is very strong. He felt safe there. How is that related to the way he feels at the Metropolitan Museum of Art? Is there any place in your life that triggers that same kind of sensorial connection?

7. Pastor Welk had a profound influence on Trip's life despite Trip not believing in God in the same way. How

did the pastor's influence show up in Trip's life throughout the story?

8. How does Pastor Welk's dying affect Trip? How might Trip's life have been different if the pastor had lived to support him?

9. In part III, Trip says "I wish I'd have been smarter and made a choice before my time ran out. I wish I'd have realized that you can pick your family, and I was picking the wrong one. I don't know if, in the long run, a different choice would have put me somewhere different than where I am right now, but I still wish I'd chosen a little different." How many people in the world have these same types of feelings? What is one choice in your life you would have done differently and why?

10. Nate tells Trip "These moments—when everything falls apart, they can be an opportunity." Is this true? Are blessings disguised as turmoil more often than not? How did that philosophy show itself in Nate's life?

11. What was the key moment when Trip decided Nate was what he really wanted? Why did he give away all his treasures before he knew Nate had returned his guitar?

12. Imagine the future for Trip and Nate. What do you think happens next for them?

—AC Holloway